# Artists

## On The Galactic Tunnel Network

Also by the author in reading order:

Destiny: Union Station

Date Night on Union Station

Alien Night on Union Station

High Priest on Union Station

Spy Night on Union Station

Carnival on Union Station

Wanderers on Union Station

Vacation on Union Station

Guest Night on Union Station

Word Night on Union Station

Party Night on Union Station

Review Night on Union Station

Family Night on Union Station

Book Night on Union Station

LARP Night on Union Station

Career Night on Union Station

Last Night on Union Station

Independent Living

Soup Night on Union Station

Assisted Living

Freelance on the Galactic Tunnel Network

Con Living

Empire Night on Union Station

Space Living

Traders on the Galactic Tunnel Network

Orphans on the Galactic Tunnel Network

Swap Night on Union Station

# Artists

## On The Galactic Tunnel Network

Book Four of EarthCent Auxiliaries

Foner Books

978-1-948691-35-2



Northampton, Massachusetts

# One

The thirteen-year-old boy carefully filed the edges of the shape he'd just cut from a strip of brass, and then checked it against the beach ball printed with a map of Earth Two.

"Which continent is that?" Fiona asked him. "The one we're on?"

Marco shook his head and pointed at one of the larger continents where the terraforming process hadn't progressed much past the soil-creation stage. Then he stood up and test-fitted the shape on the spherical framework of steel wires that he had been adding to since morning. He nudged Semmi with his foot, and the drowsy gryphon, whose eyes could spot a fish under the surface of a lake from the height of a skyscraper, glanced at the nearly completed sculpture and clicked her beak in approval.

Fiona scanned the immediate area to make sure that there weren't any potential customers approaching the blanket where their trade goods were displayed, and then asked, "Do you want me to hold the globe steady while you crimp the tabs?"

Marco nodded enthusiastically, and Fiona went around to the other side of the post with the lashed cross arm from which the metal globe was suspended by a steel wire. She placed a hand on each side and was again impressed with the rigidity of the construction, which measured about two-thirds the size of the beach ball the boy was using as a model. Marco held the final continent in place with one hand while using a pair of needle-nose pliers he'd modified for working in tight places to carefully crimp the thin tabs around the wires he'd previously tack-welded at their intersections.

"Every one of these you've made this week was better than the last, and this one looks perfect," Fiona said, stepping back and picking up the beach ball to compare it to the finished sculpture. The wires of the spherical mesh, where not covered by brass continents, perfectly coincided with the lines of latitude and longitude. "I don't understand how you can eyeball it so accurately. I worked one winter in an art reproduction sweatshop and I was useless at doing freehand stuff."

Marco shot her a questioning look, and then continued with the finishing touches, adding a drop from a tube of Frunge liquid solder to each of the crimped tabs from the rear so they wouldn't loosen up and rattle. Semmi, who had been half-napping all afternoon, sat up on her haunches and turned her attention to Fiona.

"That was around three years ago in New York, when I was fourteen, and I only took the job because the office building where they were set up was warm in the winter," the girl answered the unspoken question. "You guys know I can't draw to save my life, but I have steady hands and I'm good at mixing paint, so they made me a colorist. The food was okay, and they let us sleep under our workbenches, but the pay was barely enough to buy time for my smartphone, so I quit as soon as it got warm."

"Excuse me," a voice came from behind her. "Is this your last day?"

Fiona turned and recognized Gloria, one of the Old Way peddlers who had visited earlier in the week and been very informative about the local market conditions.

"We're leaving tonight," Fiona confirmed. "If you wanted to see John or Ellen, they both spent the last two days at the meeting house watching the debates. I guess the Alts aren't happy about some of the proposed infrastructure projects on the human half of the continent."

"Our people are anxious to build a coastal road and the Alts want us to take it slow," Gloria acknowledged. "Today I'm here to buy. I thought we might come to a deal on any stock that you don't want to pack up again."

"What you see on the blanket is everything we have left of the hand tools," Fiona said. "John unloaded all of the big stuff, like the treadle-powered letter presses and the pianos, the first two days we were here. I think he and Ellen have had their fill of tech-ban worlds because we didn't restock last time we went to Earth. And before they left this morning they told me not to accept any more fresh produce in barter, because we already have too much."

"I'm a cash buyer today, Stryx creds," the peddler said. "One good thing about dealing in hand tools is that shelf life is never an issue, but they take up a lot of space and they're heavy, so I don't carry duplicates on my route. Maybe someday I'll get a donkey or a pony, but for now it's just the handcart, so I have to be careful about weight."

Fiona quickly surveyed the remaining collection of hammers, chisels, drills, and bit-braces on the blanket. "How about fifty?"

"Stryx creds?" Gloria responded incredulously. "I doubt they cost that much new three hundred years ago, and I'm adjusting for inflation. I was thinking five."

"We're planning to eat supper at the food tent the local community set up for visitors from Flower to raise hard currency. Five creds won't go far."

"You can get two chickens with three side dishes and drinks for five creds," Gloria protested. "Maybe your parents could eat a whole chicken between them, but I can't see you or your brother managing more than two pieces."

"John and Ellen aren't our parents, we're all business partners, and two whole chickens is barely a snack for Semmi," Fiona said, indicating the gryphon. "I'd love to save packing this stuff up and carrying it back to the ship, but I've got to get at least forty."

"Well, I wouldn't want a hungry gryphon angry at me, so I could go ten," the peddler said. "But you have to understand that all of my customers deal in barter and I haven't seen many creds, Stryx or otherwise, since Flower brought us here three months ago."

"You were with the first group?"

Gloria nodded. "It's been the experience of a lifetime. If it weren't for the wild fruits and berries, we'd all have vitamin deficiencies, but the Dollnicks did a good job stocking this continent with flora and fauna from Earth. It's amazing how much progress they made in less than a century. I was surprised how knowledgeable Ellen and John were about Earth Two's history."

"Ellen is the reporter for the Galactic Free Press who broke the news last year about the Container Prince terraforming Earth Two," Fiona said. "I'm kind of studying to be a journalist myself, and she made me read all of her recent articles. John is with EarthCent Intelligence, and he was in charge of investigating all the nature stuff that went missing from Earth and ended up here."

"He mentioned something about his work in passing," Gloria said. "So, how about we close at ten?"

"Where was I? Forty?" Fiona again surveyed the tools that she really didn't want to pack up and noted that several of the wooden handles needed replacing. "Twenty sounds fair."

Gloria produced two coins, a ten and a five. "My absolute limit is fifteen because that's all I have. It's what John paid me as an advance on keeping my eyes open for alien visitors. I guess I sort of work for EarthCent Intelligence now myself."

"I didn't realize that spies worked so cheap. Will you be able to carry everything?"

"I'll fetch my cart."

The peddler handed the coins to the girl who deposited them in the tin can with their takings. They hadn't bothered bringing out the mini-register because John didn't expect any of the Old Way colonists to pay using programmable creds, an assumption that proved to be correct.

"What are you looking at?" Fiona demanded of the gryphon. "Do you think you could have gotten more than fifteen?"

Semmi didn't deign to answer, instead picking up the can in one paw and pouring the coins out on the blanket. Marco immediately came over and began sorting them into little stacks.

"That's not all earnings," Fiona reminded him. "We started with eighteen creds for change."

The boy finished counting and held up both hands with just one pinkie folded over.

"Fifty-four?" the girl asked hopefully, but Marco shook his head. "Forty-five, then. Sometimes I think I should have taken my share of the prize money and bought a restaurant back on Earth, including the building. What we're making as traders doesn't even cover the ship's expenses."

Semmi stared intently at the girl, who winced at the strength of the Tyrellian gryphon's telepathic projection.

"I know you and John saved me from becoming collateral damage in an alien medical experiment," Fiona grumbled. "You don't have to keep on reminding me. And, yes, Ellen has been teaching me about journalism," she allowed when a new mental image appeared. "I'm just saying that if we're going to pose as traders everywhere we go, the least we can do is show a decent profit. It's embarrassing."

A neighboring trader who had just folded up his own blanket came over and tossed Semmi a treat. "The three of you are naturals at this," he said. "You had those Old Way colonists lined up to barter for hand tools all week."

"Hey, Larry," Fiona greeted him. "That's because we were trading for provisions. We were selling for cash today, and that seems to be in short supply on Earth Two. I tried throwing in a free chisel with every hammer and free drills with every bit brace, but if that peddler hadn't just come along and taken it all, we'd be carrying it back to the ship."

"That's always the trick with doing business on tech-ban worlds," Larry told her. "Everybody is happy to barter for produce and handcrafts, but coin is hard to come by and they save it for luxuries."

"Not necessities?"

"They take care of their own necessities. How long do you think colonists would survive if they had to depend on independent traders just to live?"

"Okay, I guess I can understand that," Fiona said. "And I suppose those old printing presses and upright pianos John sold earlier are luxuries in a sense, even though I bet they all find use in businesses."

Marco tugged on Larry's sleeve and pointed at the large trader's pack on the man's back. It was hanging limp because it was all but empty.

"Children go through shoes pretty fast, and there aren't many shoemakers up and running yet on Earth Two," Larry explained. "I mainly traded for jars of wild honey and preserves today, and then I hired a kid to deliver it all to my ship around twenty minutes ago. You were working so hard on your sculpture that you didn't notice."

Marco tapped Fiona's arm, pointed at Semmi, and then pretended to be holding something in front of his body and rocking it back and forth.

"Semmi wants to know how the baby is doing," Fiona said to Larry.

"Still sleeping most of the time," he told her. "Georgia stayed on board Flower to rest up before the jump tonight. Do you know where you're going next?"

"We'll have a meeting when we're back on Flower and take a vote, but what we want," she gestured with an arm to encompass Semmi and Marco, "doesn't count."

"Don't you and Semmi own as much of the ship as John and Ellen?" Larry asked, glancing toward the parking area where a Grenouthian four-decker towered over his own Sharf two-man trader.

"We invested our shares of the prize money," Fiona said. "Semmi split her share with Marco, but John also traded in his old ship, and Ellen put in some money too. But it wouldn't make a difference even if the three of us owned more than half of the ship. John's assignments from

EarthCent Intelligence and Ellen's monthly meetings on Earth with the syndicated journalists are what drive our travel itinerary. We're just along for the ride."

"Alright, I suppose I knew that," Larry said. "I mainly stopped to see if you needed a hand carrying anything back, but it sounds like you liquidated your blanket stock. I'm going to head up to Flower and have dinner with Georgia. If I don't see you again before we jump back to the tunnel network, take care of each other."

"Give Georgia and the baby our best, and thank her again for the latest games, even though they are educational," the girl replied for all three of them. As Larry moved off, he was replaced by a tall man wearing a white linen robe of sorts. "I'm sorry," Fiona said, "but I just sold the rest of our stock to a peddler and she's returning to pick it up."

"I'm not shopping for tools, thank you," the man said in oddly accented English. "That's a very impressive representation of Earth Three."

"Don't you mean Earth Two?" Then Fiona put two and two together and realized that he was an Alt. "Do your people call this world Earth Three because your homeworld is Earth Two? I always thought it was Alt."

"That's your name for it," the Alt said. "For our people, after being transplanted from Earth by the Stryx more than thirty thousand years ago, our new home was always Earth Two. May I take a closer look?"

Fiona glanced back at Marco, who nodded proudly. He unhooked the wire that suspended the metal globe from the cross arm and brought it to the Alt.

"Excellent craftsmanship," the Alt said. "And these are all recycled materials?"

"Upcycled," Fiona said as the boy nodded again. "It's like he gives a new life to scraps."

"An interesting philosophy. I've studied some of the religions practiced by your people and reincarnation is a fascinating concept. Allow me to introduce myself," the Alt continued. "I'm Rethan, a certified debate master, and I've taken on the challenge of training Humans willing to apprentice in the ancient art of moderating public discourse. I've been looking for a symbol of unity to hang in the meeting house that the local Old Way community constructed, but I'm afraid that your colonists have had other priorities than creating new works of art, whether representational or otherwise. May I request the pleasure of your acquaintance?"

Fiona puzzled over this request for a moment before figuring out he was asking for their names. "Oh. I'm Fiona, he's Marco, and she's Semmi. Marco doesn't talk, and Semmi only does telepathy with people she knows. We're visiting from Flower, but we'll be leaving tonight."

The Alt's face fell. "That's a shame. I was hoping to commission a similar work for the meeting house."

Marco shot Semmi a look, and the gryphon let out a soft "Scraw" of agreement before turning her gaze on Fiona.

"Marco wants you to have it," Fiona told the Alt after receiving a mental picture of the boy handing over the globe. "It was just for practice, a copy of the beach ball. He says the real artists of this world are the Dollnicks who made it into another Earth."

"That's a tremendous insight for such a young man," Rethan said. "I am honored to accept your gift, and I hope it will bring our people similar insight into the issues that divide us. If you could hold this a minute," he continued, and passed the globe to Fiona. Then he reached inside his robe and drew out an exquisitely crafted wooden flute. "I hope you will accept this gift, not as an exchange, but freely given in the spirit with which your own work is received."

Marco's face split into a toothy smile and his eyes sought Semmi as he took the flute.

"He wants to know if you made it yourself," Fiona relayed the question.

"Yes," Rethan said. "I work as an instrument maker when I'm not occupied with debates. The truth is, if I—" he was interrupted by the ringing of the meeting-house bell. "That's me, I'm afraid," the Alt said with a wry smile as Fiona returned the globe. "It was very nice meeting you all and I hope to see you again in the future."

"Goodbye. And thank you," the girl called after him as he hurried off towards the meeting house. Then Fiona turned to Marco, who was examining the flute like he knew what he was doing. "You really cleaned up," she told him. "Ellen took me to a musical instruments store on Union Station just to get an idea of the prices. Anything made by the Alts is valuable."

"Was that the debate master?" Gloria asked, wheeling her hand cart to a halt at the edge of the blanket. "He usually doesn't speak to—did you barter something for that flute?"

"Marco gave him the Earth Two globe he just finished to hang in the meeting house and then Rethan gave him the flute," Fiona explained. "It was an exchange of gifts, not a trade."

Gloria's eyes widened. "I'm such an idiot. I've seen Rethan working on instruments in his spare time. I tried talking trade, but I could tell that I was just making him uncomfortable. So the way it works is you offer a gift and you get one back?"

"I don't know if it's a system or anything," Fiona said. She began picking up tools from the blanket and placing them in the peddler's cart. "Marco wasn't expecting anything in return. It came as a surprise."

"Still, I'm sure that's the key," Gloria said, her attention obviously elsewhere as she gathered up long drill bits. "They don't use money in their own society, you know, but somehow they maintain an exchange of goods and services. I'll have to try giving a gift if I ever make it to an Alt settlement. I get around more than the farmers and craftsmen, so I've encountered a few Alts, but I've never had any luck trading with them."

"It doesn't seem like a very logical way to run an economy," Fiona said. "I mean, Marco's globe really is art, whatever he thinks of it himself, so I get why another artist, like an instrument maker, sees it as a fair trade. But what if you offered Rethan an apple? He's supposed to give you a flute?"

"Maybe they turn down gifts if they don't have something of equal value to give in return," Gloria said, but then she shook off that idea. "No, there must be something more to it, and I wouldn't want to get a reputation as an ugly human who takes advantage."

"Maybe that's the point," Fiona said, as in the background, Marco experimented with fingering and blew different notes with sufficient expertise to make it plain it wasn't his first time playing a wind instrument. She gathered up four hammers and passed them over. "Maybe for the Alts, reputation is more important than coming out ahead on a trade."

# Two

"Welcome back to Union Station," the director of EarthCent Intelligence greeted John. "You couldn't convince your wife to come to our meeting?"

"No, because Ellen's boss wanted me to come to her meeting, which started five minutes ago," John replied as he shook Clive's hand. "I know that the publisher of the Galactic Free Press is your sister-in-law and that you have some sort of information sharing agreement, but if you want to share people as well, you're going to have to stop scheduling meetings at the same time."

"For your next visit, we'll do this in our joint conference room," Clive said with a grin. "I have to be careful because Chastity is always trying to swipe employees from us. Information analysts and field agents are good fits for a news organization."

"The way Ellen tells it, journalists are a good fit for a spy agency, and you're happy to let the Galactic Free Press pay their salaries while they report to EarthCent Intelligence on the sly."

"That's only because the paper has a better business model than we do, charging their subscribers not to see ads," Clive said as he cleared off the chair next to his desk for John. "Everything we talk about today you're welcome to share with your wife, and I suspect that Chastity is saying something similar to Ellen as we speak."

"It'll be a nice change not having to compartmentalize," John said. "I was never that good at it anyway. What's the assignment?"

"Have you watched the Grenouthian documentary about all of the cultural artifacts smuggled off of Earth since the Stryx opened the tunnel network connection?"

"We caught it on Flower during the jump back to the tunnel network from Earth Two. Even though I took part in the investigation, I'm still a little confused over whether some of those famous works of art were stolen or not."

"That's because there's no clear answer in many cases," Clive said. "If you go back to the generation immediately after the Stryx opened Earth, funding for government services collapsed as large chunks of the population left on alien labor contracts. As your wife learned from the governor-general of New York, some elected officials allowed smugglers to plunder the collections of public institutions in exchange for cash. Most alien buyers would make the argument that they were acting in good faith, and in some cases, the originals were replaced with reproductions so flawless that it required laboratory analysis to discover they were gone."

"I take it the aliens aren't in a hurry to return their purchases."

"You take it correctly, but that's not what your assignment is about. The Grenouthian documentary was only released to the public two months ago and it's already having an unanticipated effect."

"I thought all of Earth's governments had been warned to alert the museums and historical societies about a possible gold rush," John said. "It would be a real shame if publicizing our past problems leads to humanity's remaining cultural treasures going missing."

"We think that the documentary is having a positive effect on that front," Clive said. "Collectors can no longer play innocent about Earth's registration system for important works, and according to our contacts with alien intelligence agencies, the black market for stolen art on the tunnel network is actually quite small. The unanticipated problem that I'm referring to is imitation—alien artists cashing in on Earth's brand."

"You mean counterfeiting?"

"More like stylistic theft and cross-species appropriation. EarthCent has retained intellectual property attorneys from one of the top interspecies law firms on Union Station to research the issue, but so far it looks like we don't have a tentacle to hang from."

"You've been spending too much time around Drazens."

"They are our main allies in the intelligence world," Clive reminded his agent. "Thanks to President Beyer attracting major alien-owned businesses to open their doors on Earth, the other species now have a financial interest in respecting our intellectual property because they have skin or scales in the game. But the possibility of imitation in the arts is new to us and we don't really have a handle on how much it will hurt."

"Let me see if I have this straight," John said. "Aliens who never would have given human culture a second look before the documentary now think there must be something to it because shady collectors were willing to buy our famous artworks under questionable circumstances?"

"That's pretty much it in a nutshell. It's a mystery to me what drives art markets, but my wife keeps up, and she went to a Horten exhibition on the station last week that featured works from their new Humanist school. She even bought a painting of dogs playing poker for our Cayl hound."

"But the documentary was only released a couple of months ago!"

"Van Gogh completed a painting a day the last two months of his life," Clive said, watching closely for the other man's response.

"The artist who cut off his ear?" John asked.

"I knew you were the right choice for this mission. You're the first agent I've had in here who recognized the name."

"They probably pretended they didn't know because they could see where the conversation was headed. You're sending me back to Earth?"

"Just until the Aarden Arts Festival next month," Clive said. "I want you to visit the major boutiques and studios selling to aliens. Try to get us a number for how important alien purchases are to Earth's arts economy, and ask people on the business end whether they're seeing alien works targeted for our markets."

"One month won't be enough to scratch the surface of the art world," John protested. "And I'll be surprised if the people involved will give me the time of day, especially if they think I'm there to snoop into their sales."

"It's not just paintings and sculptures we're interested in, it's all of Earth's culture, including performing arts." Clive laughed outright at the look on John's face. "That's why I advise getting Ellen and her syndicated journalists involved. And I'm not expecting you to produce a comprehensive report. Just get a feel for the potential impact and buy some art that you can display for sale at Aarden. It will be great cover for you to talk with alien buyers, and we'll see if they sound you out about making black-market purchases."

"Like a gallery? You're choosing me to buy paintings and set up a booth at an alien art fair because I knew that poor Vincent cut off part of his ear?"

"See? You even know his first name. And you won't be there for the entire festival. Each of the major species attending is featured for the Vergallian equivalent of a week during which there's a juried show with prizes and such. You'll arrive before the start of Human Week and have a chance to look around. Flower's schedule won't get her there in time so we needed an independent like you." He paused for a moment, as if something had just occurred to him, and asked, "Are you okay with spending a couple of weeks on Aarden?"

"Why wouldn't I be?" John asked.

"Well, you were fatally poisoned the last time you were there."

"I was only dead for a little while, as M793qK keeps reminding me, and I don't have a problem with going back. The Fleet Vergallians did a good job hosting Rendezvous."

"I've been meaning to talk to you about the Farling doctor," Clive said, lowering his voice despite the fact that his office was as secure as EarthCent Intelligence could make it. "I don't know quite how to say this so I'll just put it out there. Herl showed me the file that Drazen Intelligence keeps on you. Their analysts have you marked as a possible triple agent, and I imagine the other intelligence services have reached the same conclusion."

"But I report to you every time Myort drags me into one of his deals, and everybody and his uncle owes M793qK a favor," John said. "And why are the Drazens even keeping a file on me? We're supposed to be allies."

"We keep files on their agents, the ones we know about. And I don't have any concerns about your dealings with Myort or M793qK, but it could affect how some of the alien agencies treat you when you're seeking cooperation on criminal matters in their jurisdictions."

"You're talking about my work with the Interspecies Police Operations Agency." John frowned. "I'm supposed to give a presentation about our progress at the next ISPOA conference."

"You'll work it out," Clive said. "And here's my lovely wife to fill you in on your cover story for Earth."

John shot to his feet to greet Clive's wife, Blythe, who had grown up on Union Station and co-founded InstaSitter with her younger sister, Chastity. The business was spectacularly successful, employing tens of millions of part-time babysitters from all species on Stryx stations, and Blythe had donated part of her fortune to fund the startup of EarthCent Intelligence. Still in her early forties, she was several years younger than her husband, and the mischievous look on her face alerted John that he was in for a surprise. As soon as the handshake was released, she reached in her purse and produced a programmable cred.

"Expenses for your assignment," she told him. "I've had some dealings in the art world and the best way to get information is to be accepted as a buyer or a buyer's agent. The top galleries and studios on Earth maintain a blacklist for window shoppers, so the only way we can make your cover solid on such short notice is for you to splash out."

"Clive told me I'll be buying stock to sell at the Aarden Arts Festival," John said. "I don't know the first thing about it so I'll stick with unknown artists who sell cheap."

"He knew Van Gogh's first name," Clive told his wife smugly.

"Everybody knows who—is this real?" John interrupted himself when he saw the figure displayed on the programmable cred that Blythe handed him.

"We need to find out what's going on at the high end of the market because our analysts say that's where most of the economic activity is, at least in terms of sales amounts," Blythe explained. "I'm not suggesting that you blow all ten million creds on a famous painting at auction, but flash it around as you shop and the gallery owners will take you seriously. Say you're buying for the headquarters of my publishing company, and if anybody bothers looking farther than that, they'll stop when they get to my ownership stake in InstaSitter. If somebody is diligent enough to run a background check on you and finds out you work for EarthCent Intelligence, explain that my husband is your boss and I asked you to shop for me because you're a trusted family friend."

John remained frozen in place, holding the programmable cred at arms-length from his body like it was radioactive.

"Do you need her to repeat that?" Clive asked. "You look like you're in shock."

"I've never seen so many zeros on a programmable cred," John croaked. "Doesn't the value decay if I don't start spending it?"

"Not in four weeks," Blythe told him, trying not to laugh at the agent's obvious discomfort. "When you get to Earth, check in with the president's office. As EarthCent's director of public relations, Hildy Grueun is always hosting galas and events for well-heeled aliens visiting Earth, and she knows all of the movers and shakers in the art business. I've already been in touch with her and she can provide you with a list of both reputable and disreputable galleries and studios. As long as you spend money at reputable outlets, whatever you buy will probably turn out to be a good investment in the long run."

"Then you really do want me to spend all ten million?"

"As much as you feel is necessary to get the information we need," Blythe said. "If I've learned one thing in the publishing business, it's that when it comes to culture, the first-mover advantage can be insurmountable. New genres in literature are often associated with a single author or group of authors who end up with eighty percent of the readership. Earth needs all of the capital inflow it can get, and we're more than a little worried that the aliens will outcompete us in our cultural exports if we don't move quickly."

"In our cultural exports to them?"

"To ourselves," Clive said. "Ultimately, EarthCent's greatest worry remains the rate at which our people who leave home as contract workers are going native. Given that the aliens are more advanced than us in every way imaginable, it's easy to understand why our expatriates look up to them. But if the contract workers and their children completely reject their Earth identity, humanity will fragment into isolated populations. Our analysts predict the day will come when people emulating different species won't even intermarry with each other."

"Okay, I can see that being a problem, but I still don't get the art connection," John said. "Counterfeiting makes sense to me, but who would buy a painting by a Frunge that only reminds them of a Van Gogh, or go to see a Horten band playing Apologist music?"

"You know about Apologist music?" Blythe asked. "I'm impressed."

"Fiona listens to it. She even has a poster of a lead singer named Cringe. Ellen says it's not bad once you get used to it, but I'm not that ambitious."

"Speaking of Ellen, you couldn't convince her to come?"

"I already asked and she's in a meeting at the Galactic Free Press," Clive informed his wife. "Tell your sister that next time John and Ellen are on the station we should plan a joint meeting."

Blythe pointed at her ear and said, "Speak of the devil."

"Did you give him the ten million?" Chastity's voice asked in her sister's ear.

"I think it scared him," Blythe subvoced in reply.

"Alright, we'll talk later," Chastity said. She lowered her own hand and turned back to Ellen with a smile. "I guess I'm off the hook for funding this outing. Do you have any questions?"

"A zillion," Ellen said. She smiled politely at Chastity, as one might to a crazy person, and then turned to her immediate superior, the editor of the freelance desk for the Galactic Free Press. "Do you understand what she's talking about, Roland?"

"It's a little vague," he admitted. "I guess the problem is that we're not really sure there's a problem, we just want to make sure that one doesn't arise."

"This reminds me of why I went to M793qK to quit drinking," Ellen said. "I was having too many conversations like this in bars."

"You quit drinking to get John to take you back," Roland contradicted her.

"My point is still valid. You just told me to give the syndicated journalists I work with on Earth carte blanche to investigate stories about alien interpretations of human culture echoing back on the source. Are you really worried that the Vergallians or Hortens are suddenly so smitten with our art and music that they'll do a better job at it than we do and squeeze us out of the market?"

"It's not as crazy as you think," Chastity told her. "Imagine if alien journalists got it in their heads to start covering humanity in depth. Do you think you'd still have a job, or that I'd be running this paper? I know a lot of us have fallen into the habit of thinking that the half-million-year head start that the Hortens and Drazens have on us explains their success, and all the more so for the other species that have had interstellar travel even longer, but don't forget that they're also smarter and better educated than we are."

"I'd be pretty smart if I graduated from a Verlock university," Ellen countered.

"You'd be pretty dead if you graduated from a Verlock university—humans don't live long enough," Roland told her. "I had the same reaction as you when Chastity first explained it to me, but after I slept on it, her fears seem plausible. If the aliens start doing our culture better than we do, market forces will put all of our creative people out of work."

"Because of one new Grenouthian documentary?" Ellen asked skeptically. "They've been producing documentaries about Earth for at least fifty years, mainly to make fun of us."

"And that's the change," Chastity said, leaning forward earnestly. "If you were an alien who saw a documentary about human actors poisoning themselves with lead in their makeup or starving artists who committed suicide in obscurity only for society to recognize their genius after their deaths, it would hardly tempt you to try the human oeuvre. But this new documentary focused on the masterpieces that collectors across the galaxy thought well enough of to acquire under questionable circumstances."

"But what about all of the package tours to Earth the last decade, and the Grenouthian theme parks?" Ellen asked. "There must be tens of millions of aliens who have been exposed to human culture in positive ways."

"Retirees and family vacations," Chastity said, waving her hand dismissively. "Sure, there are alien wedding bands on Union Station that will play our music, and some Open University theatre programs perform Shakespeare, but this latest documentary has woken up the tunnel network art world. In the last week alone, I've fielded requests from Dollnick, Frunge, and Chert news organizations interested in running our weekend Arts section in translation."

"They like our creative arts that much?"

"The opposite," the publisher of the Galactic Free Press said with a laugh. "But any artist will tell you that hate is better than like—at least it's a stronger emotion. The important thing is to evoke a reaction, and human culture has just gone from largely unnoticed to worth criticizing."

"And worth writing about," Roland said significantly. "So on your next Earth trip—when are you leaving?"

"Later today, unless EarthCent Intelligence needs John to stick around," Ellen said. "Fiona has been using Marco's teacher bot to read the student newspapers from Earth, and a band she likes is performing in New York this weekend. She never had the money to go before."

"That's perfect," Chastity said. "Didn't Roland tell me you're teaching her journalism?"

"We're still working at the writing part, but she's got street smarts that put me to shame."

"Send her to as many concerts as her ears can take and save the receipts," Roland said. "We could use a teenager's perspective."

"Fiona finally let M793qK give her an implant, so she can always block out the sound if it gets too loud," Ellen said. She turned back to the publisher. "I think I'm beginning to see what you want here, but what was that you said earlier about funding?"

"My sister gave John a programmable cred to shop for art that he can take to show at the Aarden Arts Festival," Chastity said. "That's the second part of your assignment, and ten million creds worth of paintings will give your husband cover as a dealer."

"But he doesn't know the first thing about paintings!" Ellen exploded. "John thinks holograms of alien warships are high art. If I let him decorate our cabin we'd be living in a barracks."

"From what I saw of Earth's art galleries on my honeymoon, they push nonrepresentational art, so his lack of aesthetic sense may be a plus," Chastity said. "Anyway, it's my sister's money."

"If John concentrates on paintings and Fiona covers popular music, you can cover sculptures and stand-up when you get to Aarden," Roland said.

"Comedy?" Ellen asked in surprise. "Does that even count as culture?"

"Stand-up comedy often leads society, at least in terms of breaking taboos," Chastity said. "And unlike abstract art, you can figure out what stand-up comics are talking about without having to be told. Nobody thinks that modern art will cause humanity to join hands and march off a cliff."

"Wait a second. Is that really what this is all about? You're afraid that if one of the other species masters our arts, they'll be in a position to influence humanity in ways that are awfully hard to detect or prove."

"If the people who say that art imitates life are right, there's no problem. But if life imitates art, the last thing we need is to have Earth's art replaced by something calculated to manipulate humans. It's bad enough that so many of our contract workers wish they were aliens."

"And don't forget to take in an opera if you get a chance," Roland added.

"Do you think opera has an especially strong effect on people?" Ellen asked.

"I just thought you'd enjoy it. My wife dragged me to an opera about a mine disaster put on by a touring Drazen company. I couldn't understand a word, but I cried all the way through."

"And that's good?"

"I'm not sure," Roland admitted, "but the next day I saw somebody in the Little Apple collecting for some mine-related charity and I gave them five creds, so it was effective."

# Three

"M793qK says that it's safer than a bath," Larry told his wife. "Flower Shipyards has already sold hundreds of these baby centrifuges, and nobody has reported even a minor mishap."

"I can't believe I let you talk me into buying it in the first place," Georgia said. "If babies were meant to sleep in centrifuges, they'd be born with—oh, I don't know."

"You're the one who put us on the waiting list to buy a nursery upgrade for our ship, and you couldn't stop talking about how you were looking forward to having a healthy way for the baby to travel in Zero-G," Larry protested. Then he saw her anxious expression hardening into something more stubborn and began to backpedal. "I mean, it was a decision we made together because we knew the only other option would be to stop traveling until Jimmy is old enough for the exercise equipment."

"My son's name is James." Georgia turned slightly away as if to shield the baby in her arms from both the centrifuge and the nickname. "And I'm not being irrational. I get that the Cayl developed a breathable gel that acts like a semiconductor for oxygen and carbon dioxide all while providing internal cushioning for high acceleration maneuvers, but does it really make sense that it would be safe for human babies? I want to see more data."

"I'm sure it's hard for every mother the first time. Just pass Ji—James to me and I'll put him in. We both went through the training course."

Georgia took a backward step towards the ladder that connected the bridge of the Sharf two-man trader to the cargo deck. "What's the rush anyway?" she asked. "Flower is going to stop at Earth in a few weeks, and I promised my parents we'd visit so they could get to know James. We'll get a spot in long-term parking at the elevator authority and rent a floater to go up and visit them on the weekend. My parents still work full time on the commune, and I just heard from Ellen and she's got research work for me on Earth."

"Whatever happened to maternity leave?" Larry asked. "I thought the Galactic Free Press based their benefits package on tunnel network standards."

"I'm not an employee, I'm a freelancer. If I was still back on Union Station writing the food column, I'd get six months with full pay, plus free InstaSitter babysitting. But then I never would have met you."

Larry sighed. "I guess we don't have to start getting him accustomed to the centrifuge today. But if we aren't going to be able to travel for the next two years, I'm going to have to find somebody to replace me as the head of the Traders Guild."

"I just need a little more time," Georgia pleaded. "Maybe if I could see somebody else's baby try it first."

"I suppose I could ask Samuel and Vivian to loan us Rose, but she's probably never been in a centrifuge."

"I've got one," Flower announced over their implants. "Is now a good time?"

"What do you mean you've got one?" Larry asked. "Have you started adopting orphans or something?"

"Laura is still on maternity leave from managing the shipyard but she seizes every excuse to come in to visit. Her behavior is quite the opposite of what I was told to expect from Humans, and little Iris enjoys a good spin in a centrifuge."

"She enjoys it?" Georgia looked doubtfully at the newly installed device which reminded her of the giant industrial clothes driers from her university days, except the drum was double-walled, with an empty interior cylinder and a gel-filled crawlspace around the outer section. "I still don't get why the gel doesn't fall out when the door is opened."

"Because the gel preferentially sticks to itself and it's no heavier than the ambient air. You can think of it as a room-temperature solid-state. When the gel is exhaled into the air, it reverts to the gaseous state, which is no different from what you're breathing as we speak."

"But how is that possible?"

"If I understood the chemistry, I could earn a fortune manufacturing the stuff, but the Cayl are the only species who know how to make it," Flower replied. "My shipyard is one of the few facilities outside of Cayl space authorized to resell breathable gel, and that's only thanks to the emperor's granddaughter living on board to mentor the Human Empire."

"What do you say, Georgia?" Larry asked. "If Laura wants to come in and let Iris demonstrate, we can get this out of the way and take her and Don out to dinner."

"You're just in a hurry to get back to trading," Georgia said, but it was obvious that her sudden bout of anxiety was fading. "If it really won't be any trouble for Laura…"

"I already pinged her," Flower said. "Iris just got up from her morning nap so your timing is perfect. They'll be around five minutes."

"Maybe she'd like a Frunge Fascination." Georgia thrust the baby into Larry's arms and stepped over to the hatch that led to the cargo deck. "I'm going to pick something out for Laura from my stock. I never gave her a baby gift."

"We weren't on board when she had the baby," Larry called after his wife as she disappeared down the ladder.

"So, are you planning to stop at the Aarden Arts Festival?" Flower asked him. "I have a consignment going there."

"I thought you were stopping at Aarden immediately after Earth this circuit."

"I am, but if Georgia lets you put James in the centrifuge and you take the tunnel to Earth yourselves rather than remaining on board, you could get to Aarden before me."

"I'm not crazy about making deliveries," Larry said. "I'm a trader, not a teamster."

"But I happen to know that your cargo deck is largely empty," Flower said. "I'll pay double the standard freight rates."

"Why?"

"The consignment is artwork and the owners don't trust just anybody to handle it."

"I don't want to be tip-toeing around my own ship for fear of damaging some fragile shipment," Larry said. "And you never know, I might come across a great deal on Earth for something in bulk form."

"The works are all packaged in Dollnick road-show cases and ready to go," Flower said. "You could use them as the base for a load of iron ore and they'd be fine. The only complication is that the Aarden Arts Festival runs a tight schedule, and if the consignment is late, the works won't be accepted for display."

"Is there a penalty clause for me?" Larry asked suspiciously.

"Nothing like that. It's just that the artists wanted somebody especially trustworthy."

"How much of the cargo deck are we talking about?"

"Barely a quarter if you stack the cases efficiently, and I can send a bot to help since you got rid of Genie," Flower said.

"Georgia was afraid to have a bot without artificial intelligence on board with the baby," Larry explained. "I gave Genie to my parents for their ship since they're getting too old for pushing around cargo. Alright, you have a deal. Ping me with the delivery instructions and I'll make sure we get to Aarden with time to spare."

"In time for what?" Georgia asked as her head reappeared through the hatch.

"After we leave Earth we're taking a consignment cargo of artwork to Aarden for Flower's delivery service. Double rate," he added smugly as if he had negotiated the premium price.

"Did she know that we were already scheduled to go there?" Georgia asked. "I'm looking forward to it myself. Two weeks of covering the festival food scene, sunshine, and fresh air, with all of it paid by the word. It's a freelancer's dream job."

"A deal is a deal," Larry said to head off any renegotiation efforts by the Dollnick AI. "Is there a Frunge Fascination in that box?"

"I decided to go with a Verlock Sky. It's what I plan to start James on as soon as his vision is better developed, probably around three months. Right now I don't think he can focus on anything much farther than my face."

"Anybody home?" a woman's voice called up the ladder.

"Is that you, Laura?" Georgia shouted back. "We're up here."

Thirty seconds later, the manager of the shipyard climbed through the hatch, a baby in a hands-free carrier strapped across her front. "Thanks for giving me an excuse to come in to work," Laura said, her face colored from the quick climb up the ladder. "I bring Don his lunch every day, but when I pushed too hard with snacks for coffee breaks, Flower banned me outright for a week. Three more months to go," she added wistfully.

"You want to return to work that badly?" Georgia asked. "I'm enjoying being on vacation."

"You sent the Galactic Free Press an article about foods for nursing mothers five days after giving birth," Larry reminded her. "And how many afternoons did you spend at Flower's bazaar selling your educational games this week?"

"Thanks for reminding me," Georgia said, crouching to open the box she had set on the deck just a minute before. "This is for Iris," she told Laura. "It's a Verlock Sky, and I think she's old enough for it now."

"I've heard of those but I've never seen one," Laura said. "Isn't it a holographic projector that does something like a planetarium show right over the crib?"

"Better," Georgia declared, removing the device which resembled nothing more than a melted blob of volcanic glass. "It has settings for every tunnel network species, and it starts with a static display of the night sky from the appropriate homeworld and surface location. As soon as the baby can identify the planets and the primary constellations, it—"

"Wait a minute," Larry interrupted. "How are babies supposed to identify planets and constellations when they can't even talk?"

"They can point, can't they? And did you expect James to teach himself to read as well? There's such a thing as parental participation."

"You have to let me pay you something for it," Laura said. "I can't imagine what the Verlocks charge."

"A lot less than you'd think, and I stocked up on them wholesale the last time we stopped at a Verlock academy world," Georgia said, waving off the offer. "They only charge for the holographic projector and the interface. The content is all free from their open-source educational network."

"Enough about the Verlocks," Flower put in. "I said fifteen minutes, Laura, and I meant it. I won't have you hanging around the shipyard and word getting out that I don't respect tunnel network labor laws."

Laura rolled her eyes, but rather than arguing, she headed for the custom nursery upgrade that the shipyard had just finished installing and opened the door of the centrifuge. When she lifted Iris out of the carrier, the baby reached for the Cayl gel with two pudgy hands, gurgling with glee. Laura gently placed Iris on her back in the gel at the bottom of the drum and closed the door.

"Now, if you were doing this in Zero-G, the centrifuge would spin faster," Laura said, tapping on the control pad. "But since we're already at around eighty percent of Earth normal on this deck, it will be spinning fairly slowly." Then she pressed the green start button and the centrifuge began to turn.

"Why isn't Iris sliding down the space between the cylinders?" Georgia asked, clenching her fists from nerves. "Isn't it going too slow for the centrifugal force to hold her in place?"

"You're forgetting about the gel," Laura said. "See how she's reaching for her toes? It doesn't restrict her from moving because of her body temperature, but where the gel is only in contact with itself or metal, it stiffens to the point that it's practically a solid. The centrifuges are designed for Zero-G operation. When you run them on a ship like Flower, essentially a centrifuge inside a centrifuge, it's more like riding a roller coaster, but the babies enjoy it for short spins."

"It makes my brain hurt just thinking about it," Georgia said, watching through the glass as the baby played in the gel. "Doesn't she know that she's in a centrifuge? What if she looks out and sees the world going around?"

Laura laughed. "I wouldn't be surprised if 'centrifuge' is her first word, though she'll probably shorten it to 'fugey'. It's just normal to her, like being in a playpen. She's becoming our official show-baby for nervous centrifuge owners. I don't know what we're going to do when she's too big."

"Have another one," Flower contributed. "Children do better with siblings."

"Is she waving to us?" Georgia asked, her eyes following the baby through its circular path. She began waving back with both hands like an excited adolescent girl. "She *is* waving. Hello, Iris."

"I think she's just trying to grab her toes," Larry said. "Are you ready to give James a turn?"

"Check his diaper first."

"Just take it off," Laura said, pressing the red 'stop' button. "Have you forgotten that the drum is lined with the same permeable material that the Hortens manufacture for reusable diapers? It wicks away the moisture and any solids pass directly into the recycling system." The drum stopped with the baby at the bottom and the door unlocked. When she lifted Iris out of the gel, the baby squirmed around and reached back for the centrifuge.

"I guess she really does like it," Georgia said, accepting her now-naked infant son from her husband. She carefully supported his head as she laid him on his back in the bottom of the drum. "But what about the gel that's lost every time the baby comes out and exhales it?"

"There's a reservoir good for making up at least two hundred uses, and the centrifuge won't operate if the level gets too low," Laura told her. "The caution light comes on when the reserve is eighty percent depleted."

Georgia grimaced as she closed the door, and immediately crouched down to look at James through the glass.

"He's fine," Larry reassured her. "I bet you when we run the centrifuge in Zero-G he'll fall asleep within a minute."

"I forgot to enable the monitor when Iris was in," Laura said and touched the screen over the 'start' and 'stop' buttons. "Some of our customers have told me they'll put their baby in the centrifuge just to check if he has a temperature because it's super accurate."

"I remember that part from the training course." Georgia steeled herself and then pressed the green start button. The centrifuge began to spin and the lines tracking the baby's vital signs barely changed. For the next two minutes, Georgia's head pivoted back and forth from the monitor to the baby as if she were watching a tennis match. "I can't believe it," she muttered.

"Believe what?" Laura asked.

"He's asleep. It must feel like one of those bouncy seats with his weight changing all the time. I wonder if it will work when he's crying?"

"It's a centrifuge, not a surrogate parent," Flower cautioned. "If you remember the rest of your training, it's best to let the baby nap for at least five minutes the first time he's spun up. If you take him out too quickly you can transfer your anxiety to him."

"Just what I need, childrearing advice from an alien artificial intelligence," Georgia groused.

"The centrifuge isn't making any sound at all," Larry said, stepping up close and putting his hand on the glass door to check for vibrations. "You'd think his weight would unbalance it enough to make some kind of periodic sound."

"Like 'waah, thump, waah, thump'?" Laura asked facetiously. "Don't forget it was designed by M793qK, and he showed Flower how to manufacture some kind of magnetic bearings that the Farlings use for heavy equipment. If you could squeeze yourself into the space between the inner and outer cylinders it would run just as smoothly with an adult weight."

"Then why don't you make them for adults who hate exercise equipment?"

"For one thing, it would have to be six times as deep, and whether we shrank the inner cylinder or expanded the outer, it would end up requiring ten times as much gel. So even if you wanted to spend eight or twelve hours a day lying on your back and spinning around, it would cost a fortune. The extra depth would make the centrifuge take up three or four times as much space, and we barely fit the baby-sized one on the bridge of two-man traders as is."

"Since when do you have a problem with exercise or Zero-G?" Georgia asked her husband.

"I don't," Larry said. "I was thinking about the Tunnel Trips rental fleet. Flower is planning on building Sharf two-man traders for commercial rentals, and some of those customers might pay extra to spend the trip in a centrifuge."

"It would add a lot to the cost and the ships we're building are bare-bones fleet rentals," Laura said. "I suppose it wouldn't hurt to look into it, but—"

"Fifteen minutes," Flower interrupted. "And I thought we had an agreement that you wouldn't talk about work issues while you're here."

"Sorry," Laura said, and shot Georgia and Larry a wink. "I'm glad that Iris could be of help, and I thank you again for the Verlock Sky. I won't be able to carry it down the ladder while I have the baby, but if you leave it with Don, he'll bring it home after work."

"Thank you so much for coming," Larry said. "I was beginning to worry I'd have to give up trading until Ji—James was old enough for the exercise equipment. Now we'll be able to leave for Earth as soon as Flower lets us off at a tunnel entrance."

"I'll give the Verlock Sky to Don, and if you have any problems setting it up, ping me before we leave," Georgia said. "Thank you again for your help. You wouldn't believe how nervous I was about this."

"Another happy customer," Laura quipped, and she disappeared through the hatch.

"Just look at the monitor," Larry said, pointing at the uniform waveforms. "He's sleeping like—really well. Heart rate, respiration, REM?"

"Rapid Eye Movement," Flower said before Georgia could open her mouth. "Human infants spend much more time dreaming than adults. It helps with brain development."

"How can the monitor follow all of that without any wires?"

"M793qK incorporated a few pieces of Farling medical scanner technology in the design. If you bring up the next screen, you'll get some digestive tract information, though it probably won't mean anything to you."

"Does the information get logged?" Georgia asked.

"Logged and transmitted back to me whenever the centrifuge can connect to a free network," Flower told her. "M793qK insisted on receiving the data as part of his licensing fee."

"I don't remember agreeing to that. Do you, Larry?"

"I know we had to sign something before the training session, but I didn't read all of the small print." He looked towards his ship's command console as if Flower was resident within it and demanded. "What else did we miss?"

"You agreed to receive reminders about preventive health checkups for your baby via the ship's Stryx controller, plus helpful tips about nutrition for the whole family," the Dollnick AI replied. "There's also something about participating in a beta trial for a new line of organic baby food that I won't bore you with until James is weaned, but you can opt-out after four weeks if you aren't satisfied with the results."

# Four

"I want to thank you all for making time for this unscheduled meeting," Ellen began, speaking directly at her smartphone in its desktop holder. "Our regular monthly meeting is still on for next Tuesday, but we got here ahead of schedule, so I thought I'd give you all the long weekend to think about stories you can pitch."

The teleconferencing software shifted to a distraught-looking woman who asked, "Did I just miss 'Bring your daughter to work day' again?"

"The camera is on the wide-angle setting," Fiona said, reaching for Ellen's phone and quickly making the change. "Everybody can see me on your feed."

"You could have just moved your chair over," Ellen said, and then looked back at her smartphone. "Sorry for the technical problem. Allow me to introduce Fiona, my new intern. Fiona, say something to your smartphone and the feed will change automatically."

"I know how it works," the teenager said. "Are any of you overseas?"

"Most of us," a man replied immediately. "I'm in Australia, but our syndicate covers the whole world. Why do you ask?"

"I just got an implant and I want to see if it works on Earth languages. Everybody I know speaks English."

The video feed switched to a Japanese woman. "We conduct our meetings in English," she said. "We all speak it, and it's the language of record for the Galactic Free Press."

"They can't translate articles if you submit them in your native language?" Fiona asked.

"They could, but word choice has significant meaning for journalists, and submitting in the publication language is the best way to avoid translation errors."

"A hundred years ago, you could have heard dozens of different languages just walking around the streets of Manhattan for an afternoon," the local journalist sitting across the table from Ellen and Fiona ventured. "These days, everybody speaks English."

"Then why did you want to know about buying an implant the next time Flower is in orbit?" Ellen asked him.

"Aliens," Gerald replied. "With the Wall Street Preserve and the other tourist attractions in Manhattan, you can't go out at night without tripping over a tail or a tentacle. Most extraterrestrial tourists wear those external translation pendants that allow them to speak the local language, but I've heard that the implants shrink the delay to the minimum possible."

"It's true," a woman with a French accent said, and the video feed shifted to show her sitting in front of a large poster of the Eiffel tower. "We get a lot of tourists here for the museums and the Paris Commune theme park. I can always sell a good alien interview to the local rag, and since I got my implant, it's much easier to sustain a friendly conversation. It's not just about getting rid of the delay from the external translation pendants. The implants do a much better job on idioms and emotional coloring."

"Does the Galactic Free Press buy implants for all of their regular employees?" a reporter from South America asked.

"Yes, and they spring for the high-end ones with image capture," Ellen said. "Most of the pictures you see in the paper are literally taken through the eyes of the reporters."

"You can pick up cheap ear-cuff translators as a compromise," a journalist from Egypt put in. "The downside is that they can't cancel out the sound of the language that they're translating, but I've picked up a few words of the pronounceable alien languages that way, just from hanging around the pyramids to do reaction stories."

"How do the aliens react when they see the pyramids for the first time?"

"Usually it's something like, 'They looked bigger in the holographic travel brochure.' But I earned enough to buy a new floater by being on the spot when that Verlock mage opened a secret passage into a tomb that nobody had ever discovered."

"That was your scoop?" Gerald asked. "The video was awesome."

"Took it on my phone," the Egyptian reporter said proudly. "I have the hands of a robotic surgeon."

The conferencing app swapped to video of an older woman clearing her throat. "This is all very interesting," she said, "but I have an editorial meeting in ten minutes I can't skip and I was hoping to hear what the Galactic Free Press will be buying this month before I have to drop off."

"Thank you for reminding me," Ellen said. "I've gotten so comfortable with this conferencing technology that I sometimes forget I'm supposed to be working, plus I only paid for a fifteen-minute slot today. Did everybody see the Grenouthian documentary based on the stories we were reporting a year ago about the theft or sale of important cultural artifacts from Earth's history?"

There was a chorus of assents, and a man from the African continent added, "A satellite channel here has been playing it on a continuous loop for the last month. There must be a dozen different versions, though I haven't sat through enough of them to work out how much of the content is repeating."

"The Grenouthians are masters at getting the most out of their footage, and almost every documentary they produce has a much longer companion piece with all of the raw content detailing how the documentary was made," Ellen explained. "All of you know that the publisher of the Galactic Free Press has close ties with EarthCent. They're very concerned that the unexpected popularity of Earth culture created by the documentary is giving rise to copycat artistic movements across the tunnel network."

"Isn't that a good thing?" one of the syndicated journalists asked.

"Nobody wants to see humanity's creative community losing their export market when it was just showing signs of life. The paper is interested in any stories about the possible impact of the documentary on cultural events and art shows here on Earth."

"That's a bit vague," Gerald observed. "Are you worried about aliens showing up at live concerts and pirating recordings, or should we be watching for works of art in exhibitions where the origins of the artist are unclear?"

"I'm in the L.A. city-state and I've been covering the attempts to revive the old movie industry as retro entertainment," the older woman who had another meeting said. "I have a friend at a small production company that was hired by the Grenouthians to capture 3-D video of the

Hollywood reboot efforts for a potential documentary. But that's an example where the alien interest is helping us."

"It would still make an interesting story," Ellen said. "Write up what you have and I'll send it along."

The conferencing app swapped to the feed of a girl who didn't look much older than Fiona. "Have you published anything about the proxy shoppers?" she asked.

"You must be Lena, I recognize you from your Swiss bond interview for the Children's News Network," Ellen said. "I heard you were doing some freelance work for us but I didn't know you had joined the syndicate. What are proxy shoppers?"

"I only know about them myself because I have friends who have taken leaves from university in the last couple weeks to do it," Lena said. "It seemed a bit fishy so I started looking into it, but with two-thirds of humanity living somewhere other than Earth, I didn't expect the trail to lead to aliens. Now I'm wondering if it's related to what you're talking about with the documentary sparking demand for Earth culture."

"You have friends getting paid to shop?" Fiona asked incredulously. "Where do I sign up? What kind of stuff are they getting paid to buy?"

"That's just it," Lena said. "If they were filling shopping lists with local delicacies or native-language books, the kind of things you could imagine an expatriate wanting, I wouldn't have given it a second thought. But my friends are getting paid to go to festivals and street fairs to buy works from a particular category of artists or artisans based on their own taste. That's why the job is so popular."

"And now you think the money may be coming from aliens?" Ellen asked.

"I just started looking into the agency that's been hiring proxy shoppers on university campuses. It's not a publicly listed corporation, and the recruiters either don't know or won't say who's behind it all."

"Where do they send the stuff they buy?"

"That was my next thought, and it all gets shipped to the closer of the two elevator stalks for repackaging. I'm coming into New York for a concert tonight, so I'll head out to the Elevator Transit Authority tomorrow and see what I can find out."

"That's where we are, so let me know if you need local support," Ellen said. She tapped the screen of her phone to regain priority when somebody else began to speak. "Sorry to interrupt, but I want to make sure I cover the other issues involved before we get carried away with specifics. Along with the economic impact, my publisher is also concerned about the possibility of backwash."

"You mean EarthCent is worried about human-derivative alien art returning to Earth and diluting our culture?" a journalist from the Sao Paulo city-state asked.

"You can add that to the list, but EarthCent's intelligence people are a little more paranoid than that. What scares them is that aliens will crack the code of how art influences people and then use it to manipulate our public opinion."

"If they're going to start worrying about that, I've been working on a story about the Ladies in Waiting," a reporter from India said. "The group started here a few years ago, and there are already over ten million members, plus they're opening new chapters abroad every day."

"I'm afraid I'm not familiar with—what are they?" Ellen asked.

"It began as a sort of fan club for dramas, but it's turned into a movement to adapt the Vergallian form of government for Earth."

"Has anybody else heard of the Ladies in Waiting?" The smartphone screen split into quarters, then eighths, then sixteenths, as that many journalists all tried to talk at the same time. Eventually, Ellen gave up waiting for the software to resolve on a single speaker and tapped the screen again to regain focus. "So it sounds like a popular movement and something definitely worth reporting on, uh, I'm afraid I don't recognize you."

"Aanya," the woman replied.

"With two A's?" Ellen asked suspiciously.

"I know what you're thinking, but it's a Hindi name meaning 'different' or 'unique,'" Aanya said. "I'm not a Vergallian wannabe, though my name didn't hurt any when I signed up with the local Ladies in Waiting chapter to get access to their chat group. I haven't worked out all of the major players yet, but they seem to be moving towards a schism."

"Over which drama is the best?"

Aanya laughed. "Between the women who want to elect queens from Earth and the women who want to invite Vergallian princesses to come rule us."

"Then it's already serious," Ellen said. "Have you published any reporting on this?"

"I wrote a piece for the Bollywood Observer, but it's one of those things that everybody already knows about so it's not really news."

"Send me what you have. Even though it's not directly related to the Grenouthian documentary, it's a good example of the sort of thing that worries the higher-ups."

"When you said backwash before, I immediately thought of something unpleasant flowing the wrong direction, like if alien versions of our art and music started polluting the creative scene here on Earth," Lena said, and the video feed swapped back to the young journalist. "I've been covering bands ever since my student newspaper days on the teacher bot network, and all of the musicians I've ever interviewed talk about their influences."

"I watched your interview with Cringe like a hundred times," Fiona blurted out, and then reddened when she realized she was being a fan girl on a professional conference call. "Sorry."

"Cringe is great," the older girl said. "I have backstage passes for tonight if you want to meet up at the concert."

"I'm texting you my number right now."

"So let's take a moment to review," Ellen said, and tapped her screen twice to lock the video feed on herself. "Aliens may master human-style art and use it to influence our development," she ticked off on her thumb, "or they might simply outcompete us," she continued and folded down her forefinger. "There may be deep-pocketed tunnel network art investors buying Earth's best works," the middle finger went down, "or aliens hiring young humans to shop for the latest hot thing so they can spot our trends before we do," she folded in her ring finger and then reached with her other hand to tap the smartphone screen. "Anything else?"

"I have an artist cousin who works for Drazen Foods designing packaging," Gerald said from across the table, where his own smartphone fed him into the video conference call. "I saw him last weekend, and he mentioned that he's started getting offers from headhunters trying to lure him away to work for other alien businesses exporting from Earth. It turns out that some of his hand-colored labels are becoming collectible."

"Drazen foods exports jars with handmade labels?"

"Not everything, just some of the high-end products, like certain types of honey and maple syrup. My cousin said that the glass blowers he works with on the gift items have been contacted by headhunters as well. So far everybody has stayed put because Drazen Foods takes care of their people."

"They also paid for the meeting hall I'm sitting in now," Ellen said. "The Drazens have a tradition of building facilities for independent traders at their elevator stalks, and when they realized that the New York city-state didn't have the budget, they stepped in." She squinted at her phone and asked, "Does anybody else have a blinking red light in the corner of their screen?"

"That's the thirty-second warning," somebody told her. "Our fifteen minutes are almost up."

"So I'll see you all on Tuesday at the regular time and we'll thrash out who is covering what," Ellen said. "And keep in mind that we're looking for stories about these issues from all angles, so you can focus on the arts angle, the business angle, the alien angle, it's up to—drat," she concluded as the video of herself talking on her phone was replaced by a black screen showing 'Time Expired.'

"Why didn't you just do the unlimited option and pay by the minute?" Fiona asked. "The Galactic Free Press is rich."

"The value of teleconferences is inversely proportional to their length," Ellen explained to the girl, and across the table, Gerald nodded in agreement. "Wait until you attend our regular meeting on Tuesday. The syndicated journalists are all professionals, but we get hundreds of people attending most of these calls. If you've taken a few hours out of your day to participate in a teleconference, it's human nature to want to speak even if you have nothing to say."

Fiona's phone beeped and she checked for the incoming text before realizing it was a voice call and putting it on speaker. "Hello?"

"It's me, with the backstage passes," Lena said. "Why do you sound so surprised?"

"I never use my phone for calling," Fiona admitted. "I thought you'd text or open a chat."

"Yeah, I usually do that too. But I went to my first press syndicate meeting last week, and everybody warned me that Ellen is, you know, and I figured since you're with her..."

"I know," Fiona said, "but I'm from here."

"You know what?" Ellen demanded. Across the table, Gerald was cracking up as he packed his things to leave. "I'm practically a smartphone expert now."

"We aren't laughing at you," Lena said. "Hexes can't help who they are."

"Did you just say that I'm cursed?"

"It's the latest slang for humans who are born and grow up somewhere other than Earth," Lena explained. "Human Extraterrestrials. Hexes."

"It's that obvious I'm a—Hex?"

"Not being fluent with smartphones is one of the biggest tells," Fiona said. "Another is the way you're always sniffing the air like you smell something funny but you're not sure what it is."

"That's because it's—"

"It's Earth," Fiona interrupted, and through her phone, they could hear Lena laughing.

"I'm going to get going," Gerald said. "Nice to meet you, Fiona. Enjoy your concert and I'll see you both on Tuesday."

"So, do you want to meet up before the concert or afterward?" Lena asked. "The real reason I'm going is to get some interviews with Atonement, the opening act. Cringe hooked me up, and the band wanted to talk before they go on because they aren't staying for the whole show."

"The opening act is leaving right after they play?" Fiona asked. "Is that normal?"

"They have a suborbital to catch to do a show in Australia tomorrow. Even though the flight is only a few hours, it's like a half-day time difference, so they want to get there and crash."

"I'd love to meet up beforehand and watch you do the interviews. I'm sure I'll learn a ton."

"I just try to be a good listener," Lena said modestly. "And the catering for shows at the Triple N is great, so don't eat dinner, and I'll meet you out front of the main entrance at six. Bye."

"Bye," Fiona said, and swiped the connection closed with a dreamy look on her face. "I can't believe I'm going to meet Cringe."

"Where's the Triple N?" Ellen asked. "I've been coming here for two years and I've never heard of it."

"Hexes call it The Garden, but it's the third complete rebuild, the New New New Garden, so we call it the Triple N, or Sixes."

"Because it's on Sixth Avenue?"

"I just know how to get there walking or on the subway," Fiona said. "Sixes is because it's the New New New Garden located in New New York, and three times two is six."

"Just be careful, okay? I've heard of things happening backstage at concerts," Ellen said.

"Things? Do you think I'll have a chance to sleep with Cringe?" Fiona asked. "What am I going to wear?"

"I know you aren't going to take my advice, but—"

"I'm kidding," the girl interrupted. "I just want to meet him and get a selfie. He's almost as old as you."

"I'm thirty-eight," Ellen said indignantly.

"You're right, Cringe is nowhere near that old yet," Fiona said, sifting through screens on her phone. "Hey, I can get a fake student ID for the New University delivered to the ship in under an hour. Will the Galactic Free Press pay for it?"

"Because you think that Cringe will ask to check your ID?"

"Don't be gross," Fiona said. "I want to get a job as a proxy shopper for the aliens. I've never been on a shopping spree in my life."

"You wouldn't get to keep any of it," Ellen said, looking at the girl speculatively. "If they deliver in less than an hour, you could stop by the New University campus in Manhattan on your way to the concert and see if the proxy shopping people are there recruiting. If Lena doesn't return to Europe right away, maybe the two of you can work on a piece together."

# Five

The willowy gallery assistant slid the empty eyeglass frames she wore for fashion's sake down her narrow nose and glared over them at Marco. "Have you been trained to keep your hands to yourself?" she asked coldly. "Where are your pa—oh, Hello," she cut herself off when Semmi entered. "Is the boy yours?"

The gryphon gave a noncommittal "Scraw," and keeping her wings carefully tucked in, moved past the assistant into the main room of the gallery. John, who had been holding the old-fashioned door for his two companions, entered last.

"The boy and the gryphon are with me," he told the woman, trying not to stare at her prominent collar bones, which in any other context would have indicated the final stages of starvation. "I'm in town for the month to do a little buying on behalf of an off-world client, and Hildy Grueun over at the president's office suggested this gallery."

"Then I'm sure you're in the right place," the assistant said, her artificial smile displaying equally artificial teeth. "This month we're showcasing works from Diana Hartberg, who recently passed away. As I'm sure you know, she was one of the original members of the Post Opening movement that was active from around seventy years ago up through the start of the last decade. Is there a particular—don't touch that," she screeched in horror as Semmi held up a paw with the claws extended in front of a painting of a desolate cityscape.

Marco waved to get their attention, pointed at one of the hidden light fixtures, and then pantomimed holding up a prism in one hand and observing the imaginary diffraction pattern on the floor.

"Whatever is he doing?" the woman asked John, her eyes going back and forth between the boy and the gryphon, who now seemed to be studying the back of her paw from different angles.

"I think Marco is trying to tell us that Semmi is using her claws to break up the light reflected from the canvas," John said. "The gryphon is an artist in her own right, primarily portraiture, and I trust her judgment implicitly when it comes to colors."

"Ah, so you're one of the new breed of buyer's agents who works with a team," the gallery assistant concluded. "If you tell me which species your buyer is from, I'll be able to serve you better."

"Human," John said, which drew a thin frown from the underfed woman. "My client has a very successful business translating alien novels into English and she's buying art for her headquarters."

"Maybe one of the smaller pieces we keep in the back. If you'll just—don't get so close," she called nervously to Marco, who was examining a painting of a burned-out skyscraper.

"Price won't be an issue," John said, recapturing the woman's attention. He handed over the programmable Stryx cred that Blythe had given him, and added, "Feel free to confirm it on your register."

To be fair, the gallery assistant's only visible reaction when she looked at the side of the coin displaying the current value was a slight widening of the eyes, but her voice underwent an immediate change.

"That won't be necessary, Mister…?"

"Just John," he said, and produced a plastic business card that he'd purchased at an instant printer down the street ten minutes prior. "Forgive me for not asking your name. I don't know where my manners are."

"Danika, with a K," she told him, stepping closer to get in range for the Drazen perfume she wore that was formulated to be unnoticeable by the human nose beyond arm's length. "Your boy is such a handsome little fellow, and quiet. Is he an artist as well?"

"Yes, he is," John said, accepting the programmable cred in return for the card and slipping it back into his pocket. He was so surprised when Danika took his other arm that he barely restrained himself from flowing into a martial arts move and throwing her over his back. Instead, he asked, "So what else can you tell me about Diana Hartberg? I'm afraid I'm not very familiar with the Post Opening movement."

"I'd be delighted," Danika said with a playful smile, leading him towards the largest canvas in the gallery. "These desolate cityscapes were painted in her early-middle period, approximately fifty years ago. When I was studying art history at the Sorbonne, we had a mnemonic for the order of emigration from Earth—RUSTED. First came the poorest Rural workers who signed up for alien labor contracts in agriculture, then the Urban poor taking labor jobs, followed by the Suburbanites as middle-class jobs disappeared. A generation later there was another round when people found out they could earn a decent retirement in thirty years or less, so the Technical workers and finally the Elites joined the exodus."

"What does the 'D' on the end stand for?" John asked her.

"Deniers," Danika said. "When the alien deniers began to come around and started taking jobs off-world, it signified the end of Earth's transition to a modern planet. Now the population flow has stabilized between emigrants to tunnel network worlds and retirees who choose to return home for the inexpensive real estate and rapidly improving services. Hartberg and her contemporaries started out by painting abandoned fields and collapsing farmhouses, but those pictures haven't appreciated in value as much as the condemned skyscrapers. Her empty villages also sell for a good price, particularly the ones with a leaking water tower or an overgrown cemetery, but she also wasted years painting run-down suburbs, which are just depressing. The final decade of her working life was given over to interior scenes from abandoned hospitals and empty bank vaults, but those are smaller pieces employing mixed media, so it's a different market."

"I see. So she and the other Post Opening artists basically documented the consequences of the Stryx opening Earth in the order that they saw them."

"Exactly," Danika practically purred. "Hartberg has always been very collectible, and her prices are achieving new highs with her unfortunate passing, putting her at the forefront of the movement."

"Her passing or her prices?" John asked.

Danika laughed and playfully punched his bicep. "Oh, you're so naughty," she said, and then lowered her voice. "Her prices, of course. Hartberg was always very fortunate in her timing. If she had died a decade earlier, there wasn't an alien market for contemporary human works, and if she had lived another decade, the peak might have passed."

"So you think if I wait, the price of this piece may come down?" John asked, waving his free arm at the post-apocalyptic image.

"Oh, no," Danika said, shaking her head vigorously to buttress her words. "All of her works will be in collections by that point, and from there they'll continue to appreciate with the overall market. It's the other artists from the Post Opening that I'm talking about. An artist's prices are always relative to their most expensive sale, so timing the markets is critical."

"I'll keep that in mind. What is it, Marco?"

The boy pointed at Semmi, who had moved to the door and was fiddling with her smartphone.

"Already?" John asked. He gently pried Danika's fingers from his arm and mustered up a fake smile of his own. "We have a list of galleries to visit today as we screen possible acquisitions, but I'm sure we'll be back once we complete our quick survey. You were our first stop."

"Take my card." Danika thrust a small plastic chit into his hand with a movement that seemed to start from her hips. She leaned in close at the same time to give him a final whiff of the perfume and whispered, "It has my personal contact information as well if you'd like to get together after hours and talk art, just the two of us."

"Er, thank you," John said, backing through the door.

As soon as they were all out in the street, Marco latched onto John's arm and started making eyes at him in a perfect imitation of the gallery assistant. Semmi snorted in amusement and took a picture with her smartphone. The EarthCent Intelligence agent heard a muted beep.

"Did you just send that to somebody?" he demanded, and then recalled that the gryphon already had her smartphone out before they exited. "Did you take a picture of me with that gallery vamp and send it to Ellen? What did I ever do to you?"

Semmi dropped the phone back in the flight pouch she wore around her neck and gave him an innocent look.

"Next time I'm leaving you both on the ship," John threatened.

Marco's smartphone played its ringtone, a riff from some Apologist band that Fiona had picked out for him. The boy looked at the phone, grinned, and passed it over.

"I never touched her," John said into the phone. "She was trying to sell me art."

"You should have bought something," Ellen said. "The poor girl looked like she hadn't eaten in a month, but that's not why I'm calling."

"Something come up at your syndicate meeting?"

"I have some good leads to work on, but nothing urgent. I'm calling because I got a message from Hildy that there's an impromptu reception at Disunion and the artists will be there. She called me because you didn't give her your number."

"I don't have a phone," John replied reflexively before realizing that he was playing right into her hand. "Disunion was on our list for later today but we'll head there now. Do you want to meet up, or are you still out at the elevator?"

"I came in with Fiona to visit a campus but I'll fill you in about that later. I'm only ten minutes away from you if I can find a floater cab. I suppose I better come in case you need somebody to watch Marco while you're getting busy with a salesgirl."

"What does that even—Hello?" John grimaced, passed the phone back to the boy, and scowled at the gryphon. "Thanks a lot. You got me in trouble with Ellen. And this next place is going to be crowded, so why don't you get a little flying in and find us later."

Marco tugged on John's sleeve and pointed at Semmi, his eyes pleading.

"No, you can't ride her, especially not in the city with all of the drones. We all agreed to wait until M793qK says that she's up to your weight. You know that in Tyrellian gryphon years she's not much more mature than you are."

Semmi shook her head, took a few bounding leaps, and launched into the air. The scattering of New York pedestrians who had grown blasé about aliens wandering around their city reacted quite differently to the gryphon when her wings were extended, whipping out their smartphones and capturing video. Semmi caught an updraft from a subway grate, let out an earsplitting, "Scraw," and disappeared over the buildings.

"I'm sorry, Marco, but she's getting too big to bring inside places that aren't set up for aliens, and a reception is likely to be crowded with people holding drinks," John explained to the boy. "I'm going to depend on your help with aesthetic judgments now. I could tell back in the tunnel that you learned more from that art book my boss gave me than I did."

Marco straightened up at John's statement and pointed across the street where a large silk banner featuring black capital U's crossed out with red X's was fluttering against a brick building.

"Is that it?" John asked, and it occurred to him that Semmi had been the one who had navigated the way to the first gallery. "Alright, let's take the underpass rather than waiting for the light."

The pair headed down the stairs into the short tunnel which was lit as bright as day by Verlock glow-stones embedded in the ceiling. A blinking message on a wall panel informed them that the next autowash would start in eleven minutes, which explained why it didn't smell like urine and there were no signs of even temporary residents. The stairway on the other side exited right in front of the gallery which featured another black U crossed out by a red X on the glass door, and in small lower case print, "disunion."

A heavily tattooed man who looked more like a bouncer than an art gallery attendant held out an arm to stop them. "Special event," he said politely. "Regular clients and invited guests only."

"We're with—we were told to come by Hildy Grueun from the EarthCent president's office," John said, handing over another of his new cards.

The attendant sniffed the card, grinned, and said, "Today's vintage, but I'll give you the benefit of the doubt and check the list." He stared off into space for a moment, a sure sign that he had an implant with a heads-up display, and then nodded. "John, Marco, Semmi, and Ellen. The other two will be along?"

"Ellen is coming. Semmi is a large Tyrellian gryphon and I was worried there wouldn't be room."

"We've never had a gryphon but we're set up for all of the tunnel network members weighing less than a ton. We even have an all-species bathroom. This gallery used to be a warehouse before the conversion."

"I didn't realize aliens were so important to the gallery business," John said. "Have you worked here long?"

"I'm the owner," the tattooed man said, and he smiled at John's surprise. "Long story involving Hortens, a gaming tournament, and a run of luck that scared me into returning to Earth. Go on in, and if the gryphon shows up, I'll tell her you're here. I've never seen one in the flesh, or the feather, as it were."

John led Marco into the foyer where a buffet was set up and aliens from all of the tunnel network species and beyond were jostling each other for the delicacies. The boy held up his smartphone and pantomimed drawing something.

"You want to send Semmi a picture message to tell her the place is full of aliens and she can come?" John asked. "Go ahead. She'll never let me live it down."

Somebody tapped the EarthCent Intelligence agent's shoulder, and he turned that direction to see a Drazen and a Frunge who appeared to be deep in conversation. Just as he was about to turn back, a greenish spike snaked around from behind him and tapped the shoulder again. This time he spun in the opposite direction.

"Myort," John greeted the Huktra, wondering how he had missed the bulky reptile when they came in. "What are you doing back on Earth?"

"Vacation," Myort said, retracting his claws and ruffling Marco's hair. "I still have some loose creds rattling around from our last adventure, and I thought, why not invest in some Human art?"

"Because your idea of art is sexy dragons painted on the prows of ships. How did you even get an invitation?"

"I always drop by Duncan's gallery when I'm on the planet to find out who's going to be the next big thing," the Huktra said. "Where do you think I got the pieces hanging on my bridge?"

"The pudgy purple fairies? I thought you had those printed somewhere just to put up as a joke when I came on board," John said.

"Those are Warhols, my ignorant Human friend, from his print series titled, *In the bottom of my garden*. I could sell them today for at least ten percent more than I paid, plus I've had the pleasure of looking at them for years."

John shook his head in disbelief. "Don't tell me what they cost. I don't want to know."

"And what are you doing here?" Myort asked. "If you're shopping for art you should have brought Semmi along. Visual art is a major part of early Tyrellian education."

"I thought the reception would be too crowded, but she's on her way now," he said, glancing at Marco for confirmation. "Do you know something about art? I can use all the help I can get."

"For starters, don't blow all ten million in one place."

"How did you know how much they gave me?" John asked, and then grimaced. "I just confirmed your information, didn't I?"

"I heard it from—" Myort paused, his eyes scanning the room—"her," he concluded, pointing at an elegant Vergallian. "Ballinth's cover job is at Astria's Academy of Dance, but she's the New York station chief for Vergallian Intelligence, and she was trying to find out how closely we're working together. It seems you're getting a reputation."

"As a triple agent working for you and M793qK," John said. "But how could she have known about my programmable cred? Is there a way to read the balance remotely?"

"I spoke with Ballinth just before you came in," the Huktra said. "Have you been flashing your cred around town?"

"Just at the gallery down the street, but now that you mention it, the attendant looked like a drama fan. Probably part of Ballinth's network of informants." He glanced at the Vergallian a second time. "I would have taken her for upper-caste if you hadn't told me her name."

"I'm not an expert on the species, but I believe the primary difference between the A's and B's is that the B's don't have the natural talent for producing pheromones that can influence half of the male humanoids on the tunnel network. It's not something that you can easily tell just by looking at them."

Somebody started tapping a wine glass with a spoon and the guests gradually fell silent. John found himself turning towards the entrance because everybody else was looking that way, and he saw that the owner had stepped inside and was preparing to speak.

"I wish to welcome you all again to our impromptu reception," Duncan began. "It happens that our featured artists were passing through on their way to London and I was able to convince them to drop by for a few hours to talk about their work. They agreed to wear carnations for easy identification as all humans look alike to some of our guests, so enjoy the buffet, and there's an open bar set up in the main gallery. Please, enjoy yourselves, and if you have any questions I'll be right here."

A pair of large doors were thrown open and the crowd immediately began flowing into the cavernous gallery, most of them heading directly for the bar. John and Marco followed the Huktra, who as the bulkiest alien in the room, cleared an easy path. They found themselves in a strange wonderland of metallic artwork, including sculptures on stands or hanging from the ceiling. The boy made a beeline for a construct that looked like a pair of tower clocks had collided at high speed, his jaw hanging down in wonder.

"It looks like something you'd make if you had the parts," John said, and then caught sight of a large display screen showing a grid of what appeared to be monetary sums denominated in eBucks. "Is that somebody's idea of art?" he asked Myort.

"An NFT board," the alien replied. "I thought Duncan had taken it down, but I guess there's still an interest.

"What's an NFT?"

"A Non-Fungible Token," Myort explained. "It can mean different things depending on how the smart contracts are written, but basically it's a token of symbolic ownership in a digital work or image. NFT's are generally separate from copyright, though I understand in some rare cases those rights were conveyed with the purchase. It's a funny sort of system that developed uniquely on Earth."

"I think my implant just glitched," John said. "Why would anybody pay real money for symbolic ownership in digital works that can be copied an infinite number of times?"

"I believe it was a grassroots response to your governments and central banks of the time actively undermining their own monetary systems. Currency is fungible by its nature, meaning five eBucks in your pocket is functionally identical to five eBucks in my pouch, and neither of us would lose by an exchange. A token that represents symbolic ownership in a piece of art is non-fungible because there's no mechanism on the blockchain to divide it among multiple parties. NFTs are an extra-governmental store of value, providing that the owner can find a counter party willing to buy."

John looked for a sign that the Huktra was having him on, but Myort appeared to be entirely serious. "So the gallery sells a piece of digital art, or the right to claim to be the symbolic owner of a digital piece of art, and then they put the sale price up on the board?"

"Those amounts represent the NFTs that Duncan is offering for sale. At some point, after the Stryx opened Earth and forced the planet through an economic reboot, the market for tokens dried up. Galleries and collectors gradually realized that it didn't matter which digital work was associated with the token since all of the images and videos were freely available on the networks. The sole figure of merit for NFTs became their last selling price."

"You're telling me that people are willing to pay," he glanced at the board, "over a million eBucks for a non-fungible token just because it's changed hands for that in the past?"

"That's pretty much how all art is valued," Myort told him. "Don't take this the wrong way, but I suspect that you might be better off buying reproductions to sell at the Aarden Arts Festival. It's a much more straightforward business."

"You won't get any argument from me, but I still want to understand this," John said. "NFTs are about the money and nothing else?"

"Well, the smart contracts were innovative. In some cases, whenever a non-fungible token representing symbolic ownership in a digital work of art changed hands, the original creator or the heirs received a cut, almost like a royalty payment. Before that, Human artists only benefitted from the initial sale of their work, and any subsequent appreciation was captured by the dealers and collectors."

"So, do you think I should buy one of the cheap ones?" John asked, studying the amounts on the board.

"Did you see that lovely old suspension bridge with the stone towers and all of the diagonal cables when you were coming into Manhattan?" Myort asked. "According to the tour I took on my first visit to Earth, it was the tallest structure in the Western Hemisphere at the time of its construction."

"Sure, the Brooklyn Bridge."

"I'll sell you symbolic ownership of it for whatever you're willing to spend on an NFT."

## Six

"Don't you think my mother is acting weird?" Georgia asked.

"She just met her first grandchild," Larry answered after a brief delay to swallow a mouthful of apple pie. "Within two minutes of our getting here, she wrestled Jimmy from your arms and headed out with your father to show him off to all of their neighbors. Seems like typical grandparent behavior to me." He took another bite of the pie and asked, "Why is this so good?"

Georgia turned away from the window where she had been watching her parents push the baby carriage in a slow circuit of the commune's main circular pathway. "I didn't try it because I'm on a diet and she always used too much sugar for my taste."

"The two of you really don't agree on anything, do you?"

"We agree to disagree," Georgia said, and then gave up her observation post to come over and take a small forkful of the pie. "It's the baking apples. I'll have to ask my dad which ones these are. The commune has some heirloom trees of varieties that have been growing in this region for at least four centuries. If you picked one off the tree and tried to eat it, you'd end up spitting it out, including any loose teeth you happened to have."

"They're that hard?" Larry asked.

"And tart. The hardness keeps them from turning into mush when they're baked, and subtle flavors don't come through in sweetened fruit pies. You know, I could probably get an article out of heirloom baking apples." She brought out her smartphone and took photographs from several different angles of the pie with the two wedges gone. "Don't tell my mother."

"She'd be thrilled to know that you used pictures of her pie for an article in the Galactic Free Press."

"How am I supposed to explain to a woman who doesn't believe in the existence of aliens that I work for a newspaper headquartered on a Stryx station?" Georgia demanded. "We still haven't told her that we live on a spaceship."

"She's not stupid," Larry said. "I'm sure she's figured it out by now. From what your dad told me, the commune's biggest customer for agricultural products is Drazen Foods, and—" he looked around the dining room and spotted the framed photograph of Georgia's mother standing next to a stunning Vergallian, "somebody must have told her that the doctor who fixed her eyes was here on an alien medical mission."

"You have no idea how stubborn my mother is," Georgia said, cutting herself a thin slice of pie. "Why are you bringing me the photo? I saw it last time I was here."

"I'm not," Larry said triumphantly, waving a familiar-looking book that had been hidden by the framed photograph on the shelf. "What does this look like to you?"

"Is that a *For Humans* book? I don't believe it."

"And look which one it is." Larry brought the large paperback with its familiar orange and silver foil spine over to the table and slapped it down.

"*Aliens For Humans*?" Georgia stared at the cover with cartoon art of several tunnel network species at a picnic. She glanced towards the window to make sure that her parents weren't returning, and then picked it up. "My mother always writes her name and date in—she bought it right after we left last time!"

"It can't have been easy for your mother to admit that she was wrong after all of those years."

"If she was going to change her mind, why didn't she do it twenty years ago before driving me half insane?" Georgia asked, blinking back a tear. "I know you're tired of listening to me complain about my childhood, but if I tried talking to her about anything she didn't want to believe, she pretended to be deaf. I mean, the commune had plenty of alien deniers, but she was, like, orthodox."

"Look at it this way," Larry said, gently massaging her shoulder with one hand while he took another forkful of pie with the other. "Where do you think a woman in her fifties finds the strength to put aside a whole lifetime of beliefs to start over again? It's because she loves you."

"Or you," Georgia said, suppressing a giggle. "Or you and James. She did buy the book after I told her I was pregnant."

"You have to admit that they're doting grandparents. I'll bet your mother is the one who cries when we leave. I wonder if they'd like to visit us at the long-term lot and see the ship."

Georgia suddenly stiffened, and then she handed the book back to Larry. "Put this away where you found it, and no matter what you do, don't bring up that we have our own two-man trader. Can you imagine what my mother will say if she finds out we've been putting her precious grandson in a centrifuge? She'd probably kidnap him and disappear."

"You have a point," Larry admitted, and he returned *Aliens For Humans* to its hidden spot behind the framed photo on the bookshelf. "Hey, there's also one of those pamphlets about living on Flower."

"The ones they give out at Flower's library? Bring it here."

"Maybe we shouldn't be snooping through their stuff."

"They're out there showing off our baby—the least we can do is look at their books," Georgia said, going over and taking the pamphlet out of his hand. She flipped it open, saw the writing on the inside of the cover, and froze.

"What is it?" Larry asked.

"This one is dated five months ago, the last time Flower was at Earth, and my mom wrote, 'From our visit.' Do you think my parents took one of those tourist junkets on the space elevator?"

"Wouldn't they have said something?"

"Here, put it back," Georgia said. "I think they're coming."

"Should I try bringing it up, casual like?" Larry asked. "I could mention that we just came from Flower. Where did you tell them you had the baby?"

"France. And I don't want to explain that my obstetrician is an alien beetle who complains that mammalian reproduction is extraordinarily messy." She peeked out the window again and added, "They're on the front walk."

George and Janice entered a few seconds later, the former pushing a pram that looked like an expensive replica of a centuries-old design.

"He's sleeping," Janice whispered before Georgia could open her mouth. "Let's go out on the patio and talk. Bring the pie, Larry. I'll make some hot drinks."

When Georgia sat down at the picnic table, her father shot her a conspiratorial wink, making her wonder what was happening. Larry came out with the pie, the dessert plates, and immediately helped himself to another slice. Then her mother returned with the tea service and a thick paperback on the tray. From the other side of the table, Georgia thought she was seeing an upside-down picture of herself from her press ID.

"What is that?" she asked, pointing at the paperback as her mother began pouring the tea.

"It's a publication on request book," Janice replied. "I assume you know all about such things."

"Print-on-demand," George corrected his wife. "You keep getting it wrong."

"Well, demand is such a harsh word. And I'm not sure it's fair to describe the process that produced this book as printing. I didn't see any type or rollers."

"Where did you get it?" Georgia asked, feeling a sudden chill even though it was just after noon and the sun was shining.

"Your father talked me into joining a group for—for people who were brought up the way I was brought up, and as a graduation exercise, we went on a field trip," her mother said. She grimaced and looked towards the sky. "It will be just like a long elevator ride, they told us. Bah. It took almost a whole day, and that Flower ship was spinning so fast I got dizzy looking at it."

Georgia felt Larry take her hand and reminded herself to remain calm and not start bringing up the past. Instead, she asked, "How did you like it?"

"The library was nice. A gorgeous man was working there, he might have been a male model, and I asked him if he could look up any newspaper articles you wrote. Dewey told me you work for some modern newspaper that only publishes electronically. Then he brought us to the publication-on-request shop just up the corridor and asked them to print your articles for me." She took the thick paperback from the tray and passed it across the table to Georgia. "I liked your restaurant reviews, but the interviews ran a bit long."

"They have a minimum word count for the column," Georgia explained reflexively. She turned the book over and read the title out loud, "Selected excerpts from the Galactic Free Press by Georgia, Larry's wife."

"I really don't understand why all you space people can't use last names like the rest of us," Janice said, and she took a sip of her tea. "The selection part is because they have a limit to how many pages they could bind in one book, and I didn't want it in a type so small that I couldn't read without a magnifying glass. I told the young man to just start with your most recent articles and work backward until he ran out of room."

"Did you have to wait long?" Larry asked, in order to give his wife time to recover.

"We went up a deck and had a nice walk above the reservoir while the book was printing," Georgia's father said. "I wish I'd brought my rod and tackle, but then again, I saw some alien fish swimming around in there that I wouldn't want to make angry."

"And I thought as long as we were in orbit we may as well splurge on a fancy café, but they served me blue tea," Janice complained. "Can you imagine? Blue tea. And it tasted funny."

"You must have gone to the Blue Tea Café, Mom," Georgia said, getting past the shock of her alien-denying mother visiting Flower much faster than she would have if Larry hadn't discovered the books on the shelf. "There's probably an interview I did with the owner in this book."

"Fandaz," Georgia's mother said. "She certainly had an interesting life. Personally, I can't imagine living for hundreds of years. How do those people stay married?"

"They're a little more careful about choosing their mates than we are," Larry said. "I understand that some of the tunnel network members rely on extensive testing and family compatibility meetings."

"Oh, that makes sense then." Janice gave a sharp nod in agreement with herself and took another sip of tea. "So you can stop pretending to work in Europe, Georgia. It's not nice to lie to your parents."

"But I didn't have a—sorry," Georgia cut herself short when Larry squeezed her hand.

"Actually, given the current reality, I can see where having a space-person in the family could come in handy," her mother continued. "Your aunt sent me a letter last week asking if I knew anything about a place called Earth Two. I wrote back to tell her I'd ask when you came."

"Aunt Ida? The one who makes her own soap and has a hand-powered pump in the kitchen? The first summer you sent me there she told me to wash the dishes and I couldn't figure out how to fill the sink. After she explained how they made the soap I didn't wash myself for a week."

"So you fit right in," Georgia's father said, drawing a stern look from his wife.

"Friends of ours spent some time on Earth Two and they're here for the month," Larry said. "What did Ida want to know about?"

"One of her children, your cousin Bess," Janice said, turning to Georgia, "joined an Old Way community. They're talking about emigrating."

"Little Bess is planning on moving to Earth Two?" Georgia asked, her voice rising a full octave. "But she was even stricter than Aunt Ida. She wouldn't ride a bicycle because the tire rubber was too artificial."

"She grew out of it, got married, and already has *three* children," Georgia's mother said, the emphasis making clear that she considered it a competition. "According to what Bess told my sister, Earth Two doesn't allow any people who rely on modern technology to move there. But Ida is worried that the planet isn't even attached to the space canals."

Georgia and her husband exchanged a look, and then Larry said, "You mean the tunnel network? That's true for now, but Flower has started going there four times a year to bring colonists, and as soon as the planet's population reaches fifteen or twenty million humans, the Stryx will connect a tunnel."

"And that means people will be able to travel there by way of one of those stations?" George asked.

"The Stryx stations are the hubs of the tunnel network, but ships don't have to stop at them unless they're commercial liners making connections. I don't have a clue how the physics works, in fact, I'm not sure anybody other than the Stryx really does. But once Earth Two is connected, even a little ship like mine will be able to get there in a couple of days."

"If they can bend the space-time continuum like the books say, why not instant travel?"

"I think it could be instant, or practically so if you have enough power, but biologicals like us tend to go batty if we cover too much distance too fast," Larry said. "At least, that's what everybody says."

"If Ida knows they'll only be a few days away she'll feel much better about it," Janice said. "After all, it takes her almost a week to walk to her oldest son's farmstead three counties away."

"I don't understand," Georgia said in a choked voice. "You think that Aunt Ida, the same Aunt Ida who wears out a pair of wooden shoes walking two hundred miles to visit her son because she believes it's cruel to make animals pull a carriage, will just grab an elevator up to orbit and book passage on—" she broke off and gave her mother a hard stare. "Did you volunteer us?"

"Well, I asked that nice librarian if he could look up Larry since you haven't been exactly forthcoming with us about his employment. Dewey told us Larry is very well known and has his own spaceship. Since you're already flying here and there to trade your collectibles and write about the local food scene, you could save Ida almost a day over taking the elevator. I'm sure she would insist on paying you whatever is fair."

"With what? Hand-carved salad utensils?"

"Tell your sister when the tunnel is open we'd be happy to take her," Larry said, squeezing his wife's hand again. "Just make sure she gets tested in Zero-G first so she'll know if it makes her sick. I've been told that one of the suborbital transportation companies runs flights that will let passengers experience weightlessness for a few minutes. On a small ship like ours, we're in Zero-G for the entire tunnel passage."

"Isn't that bad for the baby?" Georgia's mother asked, her eyes narrowing.

"We have—"

"—special vitamins," Georgia interrupted, nearly crushing Larry's hand. "The other tunnel network members figured out all of that baby-traveling-in-Zero-G stuff forever ago. You know I would never do anything that could harm James."

"Were they approved by that Farling doctor on Flower?" Janice asked. "He fixed your father's sciatica in two minutes flat while we were visiting and only charged—how much was it, George?"

"Thirteen Stryx creds, cash," her husband said. "It was exactly the amount of tunnel network money I had in my pocket. I still can't get over the coincidence."

"Try finding a doctor on Earth to even look at you for—what did it work out to—eighty eBucks," Janice said. "They'll laugh you out of the office."

"It's great to see how comfortable the two of you have become with the tunnel network," Larry said. "That must have been one great support group you went to."

"Actually, it all started with a traveling theatre company," George said. "You know how rare it is to see a professionally produced play this far from the closest city, so when ABE pitched their big tent at the old campus, I bought tickets without asking what the play was about."

"Imagine our surprise when we found out that ABE stood for Aaron and Barry's Extraterrestrials," Janice jumped in. "I saved the program inside somewhere if you want to see it, but I'll remember their story for the rest of my life. Aaron and Barry are actors who spent three decades acting in educational plays for humans working on alien worlds. When they grew weary of the tunnel network circuit, they returned to Earth and started doing outreach to people who were brought up the way I was."

"Alien deniers," her husband interjected.

"It's very similar to what they had been doing for workers from Earth who moved to alien planets all of those years."

"And that's all it took?" Georgia asked. "They put on a play about how to get along with extraterrestrials and all of a sudden you understood that aliens really exist?"

"Aaron and Barry were the only humans in the cast," Georgia's father explained. "They brought with them dozens of alien actors, and they invited members from the audience to come up and interact with them. It was more of a workshop than a scripted play, but it was very effective."

"The aliens were very nice, but I have my suspicions that they were in the theatre company because they couldn't get acting work from their own species," Janice said. "There was a fellow with four arms who whistled with a terrible stutter, one of those odd Horten females who couldn't settle on what color she wanted to be, and a Drazen with a tentacle that seemed to have a mind of its own."

"And you just accepted all of this without freaking out?" Georgia asked.

"It took some work, but between your being pregnant, and George benefitting so much from the group that he joined to work out his problems, I suppose I was ready for a change," her mother said. "I can laugh about those second-rate alien actors now, but it was quite a shock at the time. It's not like I walked out of there remembering which species was which."

"I bought her a book," Georgia's father told them. "Sort of a primer about alien cultures and the tunnel network. Very well written. Lots of helpful tips and review items to make sure you get the important points."

"You should tell them about your new assignment," Larry suggested to his wife.

"Can you get us a free meal at a fancy restaurant by writing a review?" her father asked.

Georgia laughed and shook her head in the negative. "I pay for the meals when I write reviews, though the paper refunds the cost to me if they run the story. When I was regular staff, they always picked up the tab, but as a freelancer, it's tricky."

"So what's your current assignment?" Janice asked.

"I'm working for my friend, Ellen, who's the Earth Syndication Coordinator for my paper," Georgia said. "The owner of the Galactic Free Press was worried about journalists on Earth not getting enough work because of all the alien stories that make the news here. She helped fund a syndicate to sell their stories, and since most of our readership is human, we buy a lot of them."

"And what does this Ellen have you doing?"

"I usually work the research angle since I went to university here and I have experience with Earth's library computer systems," Georgia said. "There's a species that produces popular documentaries—"

"The Grenouthians," her mother interrupted, demonstrating her mastery of the content in *Aliens For Humans*.

"—and they recently did one about Earth culture, in part to try to shame tunnel network collectors into returning some of our museum pieces that were sold under questionable circumstances. But it sparked a new interest in human arts and culture, and now we're worried about both the short-term effects on the market and the long-term effects on the direction of Earth's creative community."

"You should interview me," her mother said. "That play, or whatever you call it, changed my life."

If Georgia hadn't already become inured to shocking new behavior from her mother, she would have fallen out of her chair.

# Seven

"I told you the business had grown since the winter I worked for them," Fiona said smugly. "When Jennie texted me the new address, I couldn't believe it myself."

"This whole office building has been converted into a factory for art reproductions?" John asked in disbelief. "It must be over sixty floors."

"Fifty-nine, but it's one of the top ten buildings in Manhattan for floor space because it's much wider than most skyscrapers, especially the lower stories."

"But they'd need to employ thousands of artists to make the economics work."

Marco tugged on Ellen's sleeve and pointed at the ramp leading under the building where a floater carrying a container that barely fit through the opening was just emerging.

"Isn't that a Dollnick space elevator container, John?" she asked, pointing in the same direction as Marco. "They must be doing a high-volume export business if the Elevator Transit Authority is sending them containers to pack here."

"I just don't get how an art reproduction business goes from hiring street kids who sleep under the benches to this—" John gestured at the skyscraper, "—in just a few years."

"Did your friend tell you when they moved here, Fiona?" Ellen asked.

"Last year, so it was before the Grenouthian documentary was released, but after the Galactic Free Press started running stories about Earth's artifacts and artwork being sold all over the galaxy," the girl replied as she set off for the main entrance. "Come on. I told Jennie that you're rich, so the head sales guy is waiting for us. He was managing production when I worked for them."

Five minutes later, Fiona made the introductions to a man who had probably spent more on his suit than John had paid for clothes in his adult life. "Alex Burlingame," the sales manager repeated, offering handshakes all around. "It's always a treat when one of our alumni comes back for a visit, especially when she brings along a buyer. If you'll give me an idea as to your needs and your budget, I'll make sure that I don't waste anybody's time."

John caught the two-edged hint about wasting time and passed over Blythe's programmable cred. Despite his best efforts to force himself to buy expensive art, his only purchase to date was a non-fungible token he'd purchased so far below the asking price that he was sure it must have been a bargain.

"In addition to investing in premium art for my main client, I'm purchasing reproductions to stock a booth at the Aarden Arts Festival," John explained. "At the risk of sounding gauche, when dealing on my own account, I'm more interested in a reliable source and quality craftsmanship than unique works."

"Mister, did you ever come to the right place," Alex said. Then he turned to Ellen, his eyes going to the Galactic Free Press ID hanging on a lanyard around her neck. "Are you here officially? The way I see it, all publicity is good publicity, but wholesale pricing is a sensitive issue. I'll need your agreement to keep anything I tell you on that account off the record."

"How about the purchases I make?" John asked.

"You're free to share what you pay, of course, but I wouldn't want to be in your shoes at the Aarden Arts Festival when customers show you a copy of your wife's article and tell you how much they're willing to spend."

Ellen laughed at the mental image of John arguing with fairgoers about his markups. "I think our readers would be more interested in your suggested retail prices," she said.

"Is there a particular artistic movement or period you're interested in, or are you planning on wide coverage?" Alex asked as he led them to an elevator bank that had been retrofitted with Dollnick lifts. "We have packages ranging for every taste and budget, from Old Masters to Modern Art, and that doesn't even touch on the sculpture and installation art floors."

"You break up the art movements by floor?" John asked.

"In some cases we triple or quadruple up, mainly to keep art from the same period or region together. We need to save room for further expansion because we're currently hiring artists at a rate of more than fifty a week to keep up with demand. If you know anybody…"

"I could mention that you're hiring at the end of the article, though I can't guarantee the paper will run it," Ellen said. "Sometimes the editor cuts bits like that and tells me to pass along our standard advertising rate card for the Help Wanted."

Now it was Dan's turn to laugh as they entered a capsule. "I suppose I should look into advertising beyond North America since the talent here is getting a bit thin," he said. Then he added, "Renaissance," which seemed like a non sequitur until the lift tube capsule began rising and they all realized he had been giving it a voice command. "We try to match the artists we hire with their preferred styles, though that isn't always possible given the current craze for imitating alien cultures."

"You also do alien reproductions?"

Alex shook his head. "No. I meant that some of the local artists coming into their own these days have never worked in human styles. They grew up idolizing Vergallian Royalists or Drazen Medieval, and that's where they take their inspiration."

"I always thought that people became artists because they need to express themselves," Fiona said, and her face took on a slightly dreamy look. "I had a backstage pass to the Apologist concert at Sixes last Friday and I got to meet Cringe. He's so committed to his music, like, a total artist."

Marco rolled his eyes at Ellen, who gave a gentle shrug to indicate that Fiona was currently irrational on the subject and they'd just have to live with it.

"It takes all kinds," Dan said seriously. "Artists with families find a regular paycheck an attractive inducement, and all of our reproduction specialists work flexible hours so they can continue doing their own thing on the side. We offer an excellent employment package copied from the template that Drazen Foods made public, and if you don't mind a little bragging, we've created a fun and challenging work environment."

The capsule doors opened on a floor that was decorated in the fashion of fifteenth-century Italy with one rather glaring exception. A floor-to-ceiling hologram displayed the names of artists and the titles of the reproductions they were currently engaged in painting, including a sort of picture-in-picture video feed from cameras trained on each work in progress.

"Is all of the surveillance really necessary?" Fiona asked. "Are the pigments so rare that you're worried about theft?"

"We shoot authenticity videos to go with every piece," Alex explained. "You can't expect customers to pay a premium for hand-replicated masterworks if you can't prove the provenance. There are plenty of fly-by-night outfits knocking out paintings on sophisticated printers that can deposit any kind of paint you can imagine with synthesized brushstrokes and all. Our artists add a unique imperfection to every work to make it identifiable in the video, and we also code them with invisible serial number stencils."

Marco tapped on Fiona's arm and pointed at something on the holoboard. She nodded in understanding and asked, "Why are there so many Mona Lisas and Last Suppers in progress? Are they part of a standard Renaissance package deal?"

"The Mona Lisa is one of our most popular reproductions, but you would need abnormally high ceilings and thirty feet of unbroken wall space to display the Last Supper, the original version of which was a fresco," Alex said. "Most of the paintings currently on the holoboard are for an alien order that's going to keep us busy for years. All I can tell you is that if they hadn't been willing to let us space out the deliveries, we would have had to start turning away all other orders to keep up."

"You can't say which species has gone nuts over Renaissance art?" Ellen asked, and received a firm head shake in the negative. "Even so, why wouldn't they just reproduce it themselves?"

"I can't imagine they have artists who would do the work cheaper than humans living on Earth, and while I'm no interstellar traveler, I'm told that the aliens all have a thing about avoiding automation whenever possible," Alex said.

John nodded. "All of the tunnel network species would be living in post-employment societies if they didn't put strict limits on the use of robotics and artificial intelligence. I suppose it makes sense that they would prefer their reproduction art to be hand-produced as well."

Alex smiled broadly as he led them away from the holoboard out onto the production floor. "Which translates into more work than we can keep up with. We even have three floors dedicated to Imperial and Dynastic Chinese art, but we have to import the pottery reproductions from Asia. It's just not possible to do everything in one place."

"Do you think the reproductions are going into alien museums?" Ellen asked.

"There aren't nearly enough originals to go around, and many of those have disappeared into private collections around the galaxy over the last century," Alex said, not really answering her question. "In the long run—what are they all doing?" he interrupted himself as excited artists began shouting to each other, dropping their brushes, and crowding the windows.

Marco nudged Fiona and held up his smartphone. She saw the streaming video of city streets from a dizzying height, and then the view panned rapidly up a building to reveal a mob of people in Renaissance dress pressed up against windows and pointing directly into the camera.

"Semmi is out there," Fiona cried, and she ran ahead to get a place at the windows.

"Semmi?" Alex asked.

"She's a Tyrellian gryphon," John explained. "You know, head and wings like an eagle, body like a lion? Imagine a flying teenager who loves attention."

"In my encounters with alien buyers I've noticed that nature has a crafty habit of reusing the same evolutionary designs in different combinations," Alex said. He stood on his toes to get a glimpse of Semmi over the artists who had taken up all of the available window space in the area. "Are you shopping for her as well?"

"Semmi? No, she travels with us. It's a long story."

"Has she ever modeled?"

John looked stumped, the context escaping him, but Ellen jumped in with the answer. "Semmi has a healthy self-image and she's been known to pose for strangers on the street capturing video with their smartphones."

"Yes, she does seem to be hamming it up a bit," Alex said, watching as the gryphon held her position just outside the window, bobbing up and down with powerful wing beats. "If she was willing to come in and let us capture some 3D imagery to build a holographic model, I'll add her to the catalog and see if we get any orders. There's a ten percent royalty for live models who grant their image reproduction rights."

Marco was busily tapping away on his smartphone throughout this conversation, and a moment later, the gryphon opened her beak and a faint "Scraw," penetrated the thick glass. The boy showed the return text message to Ellen and nodded vigorously.

"Fifteen percent, plus treats," Ellen read off the screen.

Alex hesitated for a moment, considering a counter-offer, and then he offered Marco a handshake. "Deal," he said, and then took out his own smartphone and shot off a text. "I have a good feeling about how she'll look on velvet, and just seeing a live gryphon will be useful for our heraldic artists. Can you invite her in?"

Marco tapped out a message on his smartphone and then handed it to Ellen.

"Do you have rooftop lift tube access?" she read Semmi's question. "It seems she had an unfortunate accident with a security drone and some of the pieces may have scratched a parked floater. It's not convenient for her to return to the street level entrance at this time."

"We'll meet her up top," Alex said. The artists let out a groan as the gryphon turned away from the window and went into a climb. "I won't be surprised if half of them clock out early and start painting her from memory. One of the employment perks here is we let them use the easels and work areas to pursue their personal projects when the muse takes them."

"Any time they like?"

"You saw the holoboard tracking. The video also gives us an easy way to figure out how many hours they were working on the clock, since we combine piecework with an hourly rate. Plus, they all have the ArtApp on their smartphones."

"What does that do?" Fiona asked as she rejoined them. "I've never heard of ArtApp."

"It's a time and materials tracking tool for artists and artisans that integrates the phone's camera with the timekeeping software and voice notes," Alex explained. "It's popular for creative types, whether they charge by the hour or work on commission, because it lets them create a comprehensive log of their work to submit with the bill."

"I never realized that artists cared so much about accounting."

"I was an art history major at the New University and I did my thesis on the economics of second millennia art. Many of the works reproduced on this floor are religious in nature and were originally commissioned by wealthy patrons who were members of royalty or high up in the church. But by the twentieth century, it was hard to find a working artist who didn't know how to pinch a penny—that was the smallest unit of currency in these parts—until it screamed. Rooftop, override code da Vinci," he added for the lift controller.

"I guess I just thought that artists starved for a few years until they made it big and it was all part of the process," Fiona admitted. "I know that you hire the best copyists, but maybe—"

"Don't even think it," Alex told the girl. "In some ways, our artists have a tougher job than the original creators."

"That sounds like a reach," John said skeptically.

"When somebody creates an original work of art, there's no right or wrong, it just is. Creating an accurate reproduction requires total mastery of the media and techniques. My ten-year-old at home can knock out an original in a couple of hours that would fit right in with some twentieth-century museum pieces. We did an experiment once, mixing in a few of her works with shipments for festival sellers, and one of her pieces received more reorders than ninety percent of the Abstract Expressionists."

"Did it ever occur to you that she has talent?" Ellen asked.

"Oh, she's better than I am, but she doesn't take it seriously herself," Alex said. "If you really want to debate the difference between an artist and a technician, I don't believe there is a clear line. Objectively, aliens are better technical artists than any human, and some of them spend longer in apprenticeships than our lifespans allow, but subjectively? Meaning is in the eye of the beholder."

Semmi was already waiting when the lift tube doors opened, and she crowded into the capsule, looking rather pleased with herself. Ellen eyed the gryphon's beak for signs of chipping from the "accidental" encounter with the security drone.

"Studio," Alex informed the lift tube, and added, "Express." The capsule dropped so fast that for a few seconds it felt like they were back in Zero-G.

"What was that you mentioned about invisible serial numbers?" John asked. "It sounds like something I'll need to explain to customers."

"To be perfectly honest, I don't understand the technology involved. Oil paintings were traditionally varnished to provide a protective coating, though it can also improve the colors and help even out the sheen. Artists would have to wait six months to a year for the paint to completely dry before varnishing, but the Verlocks make a breathable spray that can be applied within twenty-four hours."

"You mean you don't need a special spray booth with respirators and ventilation?" Ellen asked.

Alex looked puzzled for a moment and then said, "Oh, I get it. I meant that the sprayed coating features something the Verlocks call 'time-limited unidirectional porosity' so the paint can continue drying. In the old days, the varnish was brushed on, which ran the risk of remobilizing the underlying paint if it wasn't fully dried. But the spray is miraculous stuff, and it's not tacky, which means there's no risk of locking in dust from the air."

"And the invisible stencils?" John prompted.

"It's a second application with the same spray but at a lower flow rate," Alex said. "The technicians who do the work have told me that the raised dots are invisible unless you look for them with high-resolution optics from at least three different angles at the same time, and then it still takes additional filters to bring them out. Given the clear labeling on the backs of our canvases, I don't understand the need, but our new owner insisted."

"Didn't you say that the artists also include a unique imperfection for the sake of the authenticity video?" Fiona asked as the doors slid open.

"Yes, but they can be surprisingly difficult to spot if you don't already know where to look for them," Alex said as he led the way into a large space that was reminiscent of a theatre. The overhead trusses were laden with all sorts of light fixtures and holographic imaging equipment. "The flaws are only flaws in the sense of photographic reproduction. If the original artists were alive today and noticed the imperfections, they might consider them improvements."

A number of white-coated technicians were waiting for them at a raised circular platform, but a woman in her thirties wearing a sharp Frunge business suit intercepted Alex along the way.

"Fifteen percent?" she demanded without any preliminary. "We've never paid more than twelve."

"It's nice to see you too, Vanessa," Alex said. "Did you prepare the contract?"

"Of course I prepared it, but I included a note that the royalty rate is on your authority." She offered a bonded legal tab to John to review the contract, but he jerked his head towards Semmi. "She can read."

The gryphon accepted the tab, scrolled through the contract, and then glared at the lawyer.

"It's just boilerplate," Vanessa protested. "Everybody gets the same contract."

Semmi did a gesture with her paw that shrank the contract so the entire text fit on the screen, and then she delicately extended one claw and traced a line under the fourth paragraph.

"You want me to cut everything after the reversion of rights clause? But what about action figures and subsidiary rights?"

"Just give her the bare bones contract that all of the aliens insist on," Alex said. "But with a fifteen percent rate and the treats."

"I already ordered those and the delivery drone is on its way," the lawyer said sullenly as she began manipulating electronic documents.

Five minutes later, a drone carrying a small package dropped out of the air shaft dedicated to deliveries. Semmi, who had been waiting for its appearance, tapped the blinking blue acceptance box of the new contract. A flat waveform appeared, and the gryphon let out a rather musical "Scraw." After the voice-print signature was verified, the white-coated technicians came forward and escorted Semmi onto the platform.

"She'll be busy for at least an hour, so how about we sit down in the observation area and get started on your order?" Alex suggested. "You mentioned that you're looking for festival quantity, which sounds like a good match for a few of our Century Squared packages."

"A hundred years at a time?"

"A hundred pieces from a hundred-year period. You can get it with or without weighting for popularity."

"Meaning if I took a Century Squared package for the Renaissance with the weighting, I'd get a dozen Mona Lisas and Last Suppers," John said.

"Mona Lisas, yes. Last Suppers are by special order only," Alex said. "In some cases, there's a discount for the weighted package, but with the Renaissance, it's two hundred thousand either way."

"That much for reproductions? I was going to guess fifty thousand."

"Stryx creds?"

"That's how I'm paying."

"Good, because I was quoting the price in eBucks. You'll pay a little less than forty thousand at the current exchange rate," Alex said with a wide smile. "Now, how do you feel about a hundred post-Impressionists for the same price?"

"Uh, I guess," John said. "I want to show up with a few hundred paintings because I don't have a clue what will or won't sell. But aren't some styles of painting harder to copy than others?"

"I'll bet you're thinking that pointillism would drive up the cost of our post-Impressionists package, but with a hundred paintings, it mainly averages out."

# Eight

The attendant for the archive that took up the subterranean floors of the Elevator Transit Authority offices vaulted over her desk and blocked the turnstile with her body before Georgia even extracted her pass from her purse.

"No babies in the archives," the woman declared. "You'll have to find a sitter."

"But James just fell asleep and he'll be out like a light for at least two hours," Georgia protested. "I called ahead to check with Yossi and he said it would be okay."

The attendant shook her head. "I don't know what you think you heard Yossi say, but it would be unfair to all of the other researchers. We can't start making exceptions or everybody in the reading room will want to start bringing their babies with them. It's bad enough that somebody trips over an emotional support animal every month."

"You allow dogs but not babies?"

"With a graduation certificate from a six-week emotional support animal course. Do you have one for your baby?"

"Of course not," Georgia said indignantly as she fumbled in her purse for her smartphone. "If you're so worried about noise, why not install some Dollnick acoustic isolation—Yossi?" she answered when the phone buzzed just as she fished it out.

"I got out of my meeting with the binding restoration expert early so I can stop by to show you the latest if you're here," the head archivist's voice spoke from her phone.

"I'm stuck at the entrance. Your guard won't let me come in with my baby."

"Did you tell her you're going to the Galactic Free Press room?"

The woman, whose ears were sharp enough to pick up the conversation even though the phone wasn't on speaker, relaxed visibly. "Why didn't you tell me?" she asked, moving back around her desk. "It's the reading room that's off-limits."

"I'll be there in a minute," Georgia told Yossi, dropping the phone back in her purse. On a hunch, rather than digging for her pass again, she took her press ID off from around her neck and swiped it through the card reader. The light turned green and there was an audible click as the turnstile unlocked. "Hey, you updated the card reader."

"Nobody asked me one way or the other," the attendant answered without looking up from the tab she had just swiped to life.

Georgia took the hall in the opposite direction from the main reading room and almost ran into a familiar figure at the junction of a cross corridor.

"Good timing," Yossi said, and he crouched a little to take a closer look at the infant in the baby pack. "So this is the male heir?"

"James, and he's very well behaved," Georgia said. "I was just asking the desk attendant why you don't install audio isolation fields in the main reading room."

"We could, but it's less about the noise than the fussing," Yossi said. "You know I have children, and I sympathize with parents wanting to bring their babies to work. But most of the researchers visiting the archive have traveled a great distance and are only here for a limited time. We do what we can to limit the distractions."

"I guess if I came from another continent for the week and had to share a table with somebody playing got-your-toes with a baby it would get old in a hurry. But what about the other researchers using the Galactic Free Press room? I thought it was out of Beta and open to the public now."

"Thanks to an unexpected grant from Astria's Academy of Dance, the digital archive funded by your publisher can now be accessed via a smartphone app. The only thing you gain by coming here is the ability to print off excerpts. I'm sure that everybody who works remotely is using screen grabbers, even though copyright laws prohibit it."

"You know that Astria's Academy of Dance is a front for Vergallian Intelligence, don't you?" Georgia asked as they entered the room.

"I've heard rumors, but my daughter has started taking classes at the local franchise, so who am I to turn down their money?" Yossi asked rhetorically. He settled into the chair next to Georgia in front of the familiar workstation and said, "Live performances."

"Don't you mean recitals?"

The archivist laughed. "I was talking to the upgraded voice controller. It uses a grid of directional microphones to determine when you're speaking to it. Just aim your voice at the top of the display and turn your head a little when you're talking to me."

Georgia turned to the archivist. "So what is it doing? Preparing to shuffle-play live performances at random?"

"It takes almost two minutes to load the index for the live performances data because it's so massive. When the Grenouthians gave us access to all of the archival performances of the music they've bought up from private sources, the database jumped to well over a billion hours of professionally produced audio and video."

"Versus amateur content," Georgia surmised.

"Nobody knows how much smartphone audio and video is stored on social networks, and I pity the archivist who tries to figure it out," Yossi said. "Our database includes some amateur content, but it's produced in the sense of being recorded from a live show."

"Index loaded," the workstation reported.

"So what kind of query can I try?" Georgia asked.

"Anything related to video or music," Yossi told her. "The Verlocks have been recording performances for seven million years, so digesting two centuries of our content only took a few weeks for the system they gave us. In addition to speech recognition on all of the decipherable audio, the software uses advanced image recognition algorithms to summarize all of the video for indexing."

"That's unbelievable. You mean if I ask for a mountain scene, I'll get back every hit from the last two centuries of recorded video?"

"And your baby would be an old man before you watched all of the results. Fortunately, we just installed the upgraded natural language interface with an intuitive inference engine. You can be the Beta tester."

"I'm supposed to be researching whether a sudden enthusiasm for Earth culture on the part of some aliens is having an impact on our creative artists," Georgia said.

"There's also some concern that one of the tunnel network species might take to producing their own version of some aspect of our culture which could then return to Earth and wipe out the local entertainment industry."

Yossi nodded. "I can see that happening already. My children watch *Let's Make Friends* every day, and I couldn't name a single children's show being produced on Earth."

"At least *Let's Make Friends* is a human—" Georgia began, and then broke off when she saw the archivist shaking his head in the negative. "Right. I forget that it's a Grenouthian show with a human host, and I'll bet everybody at the Galactic Free Press has forgotten as well."

"Do you know the reason your publisher funded this newspaper archive and supported the creation of a new reporting syndicate on Earth? It's because she didn't want to put our remaining newspapers out of business, which I have no doubt she could have done by adding a little local content to the Galactic Free Press for window dressing. As recently as a century ago, people around the world used to talk about the cultural imperialism of Manhattan and Hollywood, and a hundred years before that, it was Paris and London. Humans have a long history of herd behavior."

"I think I'll start by asking about alien performances on Earth because it has to be a smaller problem than artists here tailoring their output to the export market."

"Don't forget the Grenouthian news," Yossi said. "I saw an article the other day claiming that over fifty percent of people who regularly watch a news broadcast choose the Grenouthian news, even though their coverage of Earth is pretty much limited to natural disasters and industrial accidents. Somewhere around thirty percent watch their local Children's News Network, and whoever is left watches the streaming product placement channels."

"I didn't realize they did news," Georgia said.

Yossi shrugged. "It's cheap content because the announcer's script is reworded newspaper stories and press releases from manufacturers."

Georgia thought for a moment, carefully nuzzled the top of her baby's head so as not to wake him, and then spoke directly at the microphone array above the display screen. "I'm interested in alien productions being shown or performed on Earth, excluding the news, *Let's Make Friends*, sports, and anything related to the professional LARPing league or game tournaments."

"Nice query," the archivist said, leaning forward to see what the Verlock indexing system would come up with. "I'd forgotten about sports."

Georgia scanned the first screen of results and then pointed at a line. "Looks like the system was confused by the request. My parents went to a production of Aaron and Barry's Extraterrestrials, and they said it was run by the humans."

"Cross check result nineteen with the EarthCent Intelligence business database," Yossi instructed the system, and then added for Georgia's benefit, "The Galactic Free Press paid for the database subscription."

"Aaron and Barry's Extraterrestrials is a multi-species limited liability entertainment troupe chartered on Echo Station," the system responded. "Do you wish to print the database record?"

"That won't be necessary," Georgia said, making a mental note not to mention it to her parents. "Do you have any similar examples of recorded performances from Earth involving mixed companies of humans and aliens?"

"Nineteen theatrical companies including both human and non-human cast members are represented in the data, and the archive contains recordings of nine hundred and thirty-seven performances."

"Did you notice how the intuitive inference engine allowed the system to provide an answer that doesn't exactly match your query?" Yossi asked the freelance reporter.

"You're right," Georgia said. "I didn't ask about the number of companies at all." She squared herself to the display again and asked, "How many of the theatrical performances were educational in nature?"

There was a long pause, and then the system responded, "Please elaborate."

"I'm familiar with the work of Aaron and Barry's Extraterrestrials which I would define as a form of educational outreach rather than pure entertainment."

"Seventeen of the nineteen companies were formed on open worlds and toured Earth with the goal of attracting new settlers. Of the remaining two, Aaron and Barry's Extraterrestrials is subsidized by Echo Station's Council of the Arts, and the Academy Fun tour is sponsored by a Verlock foundation which funds math literacy for primitive species."

"Thank you," Georgia said, and she turned back to Yossi. "That software just saved me a lot of wasted time. If it's right, Earth hasn't attracted any for-profit competition in the performing arts yet."

"You only asked about mixed companies," the archivist reminded her.

"Do you think people would go to a show where all of the performers are aliens? I can't imagine an alien actor or singer going to the bother of learning to pronounce English for the sake of touring a backward planet where almost nobody has a translation implant."

"Don't ask me, ask the system."

"I'm interested in live performances featuring all-alien companies," Georgia spoke directly at the microphone array. "On Earth," she amended herself.

"Five traveling companies of non-humans are represented in the data and the archive contains recordings of two thousand and eleven performances. Displaying the list with the dates they were active."

"Most of these are from before I was born," Yossi observed as he studied the short list. "I wouldn't have guessed that."

"I should have thought of the Drazen Travel Chorus. They probably do a 'Welcome to the Tunnel Network' tour for every species that joins, even if they don't really mean it. And I'll bet you those Horten exhibitions had something to do with gaming. The only one active today is—" she ran her finger from the date range at the right to the description at the left, "—the Royal Vergallian Shakespeare Company?"

"I can't believe I forgot about them," Yossi said. "My wife took me to see King Lear when they were in Manhattan a couple of years ago, but they mainly work out of a restored theatre in England where some of Shakespeare's plays were supposedly performed when he was alive."

"So it's an example of alien actors putting human actors out of work," Georgia said. "But if you saw them a couple of years ago, they were here before any of the news about Earth's cultural treasures being ransacked."

"And I'm not sure they're putting human actors out of work," Yossi said. "Cultural centers need multiple attractions to make a go of it, and I doubt a playhouse ever went out of business because a new one opened up next door. My wife is involved in the business side of a theatre, and even though they compete over popular playwrights and actors, they generally work together in promotions and ticket sales."

"You know, I'm beginning to think I started off on the wrong track. If aliens were here in force taking human jobs in the arts, the syndicated reporters would already know it. I should be concentrating on whether there's been a change in the arts being produced on Earth to sell into the sudden alien demand."

"I'm curious to see how the system does with your request."

Georgia deposited a kiss on the top of her baby's head like touching a talisman and then addressed herself to the Verlock information system. "Has the percentage of human performances recorded primarily for export from Earth increased in recent years?"

"The portion of entertainment content produced on Earth for alien consumption has increased steadily in the years since the Grenouthians—"

"Cancel," Georgia said immediately. "I'm only interested in performances produced by humans."

"There has been a three hundred and twenty percent increase year-on-year in entertainment content produced on Earth specifically for the extraterrestrial market. Over eighty percent of that increase was financed by alien production companies. The funding source is given in the third column of the results listing."

"You see how it offered information that you specifically told it to exclude because the software inferred that it's important to the overall thrust of your questions?" Yossi said excitedly. "This system is going to help researchers save a tremendous amount of time."

"It's pretty impressive," Georgia admitted, scrolling through the text list on the display. "I suppose I shouldn't be surprised by these results. Some of these productions funded by aliens are based on historical novels that tie in to the recent Grenouthian documentary about our art, or older documentaries about how humans were living just a few hundred years ago. Look, there's a stage adaptation of *The Agony and the Ecstasy* about Michelangelo. I saw the movie at a retro night when I attended the New University."

"It was a book before it was a movie," the archivist said. "Looks like they went back to the same well for a play about Van Gogh."

"If they're being made for alien audiences, why record live plays instead of shooting immersives?"

"I'd guess it comes down to production values. The Grenouthians helped build some holographic studios on Earth as part of the deal for their monopoly on historical theme parks, but it's going to take a while before our people can produce immersives that are up to tunnel network standards. I'll bet expectations for the recording quality of live performances are lower because it's mainly a bunch of cameras pointed at a stage."

"And I wonder..." Georgia raised her chin a little and addressed the microphone array. "Have any of the dramatic companies on this list taken their shows on the road to other tunnel network worlds?"

"A play based on the battles surrounding William the Conqueror's ascension to the English throne in the year 1066 is currently being toured through Horten and Drazen space by six different troupes operated by the same production company."

"Could you show us a sample?"

The display shifted to a scene in which a small knot of men wearing chainmail and leather armor were battling against a similarly dressed group. Georgia didn't have a clue what was going on, but after a few minutes, an arrow pierced the eye of the tallest warrior on one side, and as he fell, his opponents began wielding their swords more like meat cleavers than military weapons.

"I guess I can see how that would appeal to the Drazens and Hortens who go in for battle reenactments from their own histories," Georgia said. "And it probably helps that one side favors axes and the other swords."

"I would guess that it was written specifically for the export market," Yossi said. "I wonder if the players are all professional actors or if they were recruited for the parts based on their size and strength."

"Do you have records for the casts of these productions?" Georgia asked the system.

"All of the cast members are listed in the playbills which are available from the newspaper and ephemera database."

"Can you cross-check the cast lists against the actors in previous unrelated productions and compute the percentage with prior stage experience?"

"Eighteen percent of the cast from the six troupes has appeared in older performances in the video archive," the system responded.

"It sounds like your hunch was right in the case of these productions," Georgia said to Yossi. They're expanding employment for human actors rather than cannibalizing other productions. I wonder if the same is true for the other performing arts."

"You're working with a pretty small sample size if we're talking about the sum of human culture," Yossi said with a chuckle. "Try another query."

"I'm going to ask about music," Georgia said. "Even though the aliens are all way ahead of us in music theory, I've heard Dollnicks on the street whistling our pop tunes." She faced the microphone grid and paused with her mouth half-open as she tried to formulate her request. "Are any musical acts from Earth currently touring off-world?"

The screen filled up with data, and Georgia ran a finger down the column giving the locations the acts were playing.

"You and I are in the wrong business," Yossi said, pointing at the bottom of the screen where the numbers showed page one of twenty-seven. "There must be close to a thousand acts listed here."

"There's no way the aliens like our music this much," Georgia said, skipping to the next page. "There's the Tokyo Symphony Orchestra and a folk singer playing on the same Frunge world, and here's a drumming collective and an Apologist band scheduled for a Drazen planet. What's chamber music?"

"Classical music that can be performed by small groups, most often quartets. Where are they going?"

"It looks like everywhere. No, wait." Georgia rapidly paged through the list, her eyes on a single column of the results, and then she looked up triumphantly. "I recognize nearly fifty percent of these destinations."

"You've been memorizing lists of alien planets and orbitals?" Yossi asked.

She shook her head. "I couldn't even identify the original homeworlds of any of the advanced species unless 'Prime' is part of the name. The only explanation is they have large enough human populations that I've heard Larry talk about them or seen the names in the Galactic Free Press." Georgia turned back to the microphone array and asked, "What percentage of the locations in the results list are open worlds with human communities?"

"Twenty-six percent," the system answered out loud.

"Oh, that's not as much as I thought."

"What percentage are worlds or space habitats with at least one group of human contract workers?" Yossi asked.

"One hundred percent," the artificial voice informed them.

"So none of these performers are going to play for aliens," Georgia said slowly. "They're just touring the human expat circuit."

"You can't say that for sure. It could be the host species for all those places have picked up a taste for Earth's music from the humans."

"Maybe, but I'm sure one of the music writers for the Galactic Free Press will know, so I won't waste time on that. What I'm more curious about is whether there's been an uptick in plays or immersives about interspecies romance, like all of the books."

Yossi popped up from his seat like a cork coming out of a bottle. "I'll be in my office if you need me. Just ping."

# Nine

"I couldn't pull the trigger," John confessed to Larry as the rented floater sped across the countryside of the New York city-state. "It wasn't a question of having the means or the authority, I just chickened out."

The head of the Traders Guild nodded sympathetically. "You wouldn't catch me spending millions of creds on a painting of dark matter. The whole canvas was black? Seems like a bit of a scam if you ask me, but I never understood modern art."

Marco broke off softly practicing on the flute he'd received as a gift from the Alt and reached over the seat to wave a hand between the two men. Once he had their attention, he mimed using his right index finger as a brush to swipe and mix different colors of paint on an imaginary palette held by his left hand.

"It wasn't just different shades of black paint?" John asked.

The boy began touching different colored items, like Larry's blue shirt, the tan seat upholstery, and John's red baseball cap. Then he pointed at the black emergency-hover handle and made an 'X' by crossing both of his index fingers.

"I wish Fiona was here to interpret," John said. "Do you mean that there are other colors under the black?"

Marco shook his head in frustration. Larry said, "Maybe he's talking about mixing paints," and received an affirmative charades response from the boy. "Georgia usually buys all of her educational stock from the Verlocks, but she came across this Horten game in Flower's bazaar that teaches kids how to mix colors. She said that if you get the proportions right, you can make any color except for white."

"Why buy a special game instead of using paint?"

"Everything is contained within a glass reactor. I thought it was some kind of musical instrument when I first saw it because the valves to add individual colors reminded me of a trumpet. Once the player matches the challenge color, there's a reset button, and all of the gasses separate out to their original state."

"Colored gases in a glass trumpet?" John asked. "It doesn't sound safe for kids."

"It's that special Horten glass that's nearly indestructible, and I'm not describing it well," Larry said. "There are settings where players can challenge each other to mix a certain color, and it has all of the basic combinations used for industrial processes built-in. You know how the aliens are. The same toy you use as a child may turn out to be a tool for a career professional if you put it on the advanced setting."

Marco waved to get their attention again, pointed at the black emergency-hover handle, and then did a horizontal circle with his forefinger as if to include everything in sight.

"So you're saying that the artist used every color except for black to create Dark Matter," John guessed.

The boy held one hand level and tilted it back and forth, first the thumb going high, then the pinkie, his standard way of expressing "so-so."

"Does that make the painting worth two million Stryx creds?"

Marco gave them a comical look and an exaggerated thumbs-down with both fists.

"So how much have you spent so far?" Larry asked.

"A few hundred thousand, and aside from the one non-fungible token, it all went on reproductions for my cover story as a dealer," John said. "I'm not cut out to be an art buyer."

"From what you've told me, the dealers and gallery owners in Manhattan have been talking your ear off about their alien clients."

"That's mainly thanks to showing up with Semmi. Maybe I'm getting old, but I was more comfortable back in the days of paying informants for information, cash on the barrelhead. Using Semmi as eye candy makes me feel like a pimp."

"I thought you said that Blythe was looking for original art to hang in her offices," Larry said. "You know she can afford it, and she probably had in mind supporting the arts on Earth."

"I let Myort talk me into going to an art auction with him before he leaves Earth and maybe I'll let him pick something out. Somehow, I doubt that Blythe will have the same taste in paintings as a Huktra intelligence agent, though I have to admit he has a pretty good ear for our music." John looked forward and pointed. "Hey, that must be the factory coming up."

"It's practically on the beach. I would have thought oceanfront property would be too valuable for industrial purposes, but maybe they need the seawater for cooling or something."

"Isn't glass made from sand? There's plenty of that under the ocean, and I see some sort of conveyer running out into the water."

"I don't know," Larry said. "I think I heard somewhere that Earth's beaches are more likely to have erosion problems than too much sand, but maybe it's a regional thing."

"Now that you mention it, a history book I read while on the exercise equipment a few months ago claimed that Earth was running short on sand in the right places around the time the Stryx intervened," John said. "It's one of the main ingredients in concrete, which was the principle construction material at the time."

"And then construction came to a screeching halt as people left Earth on alien labor contracts."

"Right, and what little building was done in the last century was mainly residential, and they started avoiding concrete for environmental reasons. We imported a lot of alien construction materials during those years because it didn't make sense for them to run empty ships to Earth to pick up laborers for one-way trips."

The floater came to a halt in the parking lot in a spot near the factory's entrance which was boldly marked "Guest Buyers." Marco ran ahead when they exited, waving his arms and looking at the sky, but the gryphon didn't appear.

"I don't think Semmi's coming," John called to the boy. "She was working on a painting when we left, and I think she's trying to finish enough to show in her own booth at the arts festival."

Marco nodded, but he couldn't hide his look of disappointment, and he kept glancing at the sky as they approached the entrance.

"He's close to the gryphon, isn't he," Larry said quietly.

"I think it's mutual, but Semmi is an alien, so who knows what she's really thinking," John replied. "We don't even have a clue how long she'll stay with us, but Myort implied it will be a few years yet. Both of the kids count on her to help with their homework."

"You've got them doing regular lessons?"

"With a teacher bot, and Ellen also signed Fiona up for a remote journalism course being taught through Flower's Open University campus. Fiona will have to show up in person for the occasional evaluation, but we seem to run into Flower every couple months without even trying."

"A correspondence course for a correspondent," Larry said. "Makes sense to me."

There was a faint glow over the entrance of the building, undoubtedly some sort of alien technology to keep the sand and salt air from invading. The doors slid open at their approach, and the three visitors all gaped at the giant logo constructed out of colorful glass beads in the lobby, which read, "EarthBeads."

"Are you Larry, Phil's son?" the attractive young receptionist inquired. "Miss Czendo asked me to ping her as soon as you arrived."

"That's me," Larry said.

"Your contact is Frunge?" John asked the younger man while the receptionist alerted the sales rep that her clients had arrived. "You mentioned they own a share in the business, but I didn't expect to come across any Frunge females out in the middle of nowhere."

"When I talked to her on Georgia's phone she sounded human. And I disabled my implant to make sure she was speaking English."

An auburn-haired woman, with skin so white that blue veins were visible beneath, hurried into the reception area.

"Larry, Phil's son," she offered the greeting as she approached, and held out a hand to shake to let the two men decide which of them was which. "I've been on the edge of my chair all morning waiting for you to arrive."

"I hope you understood that I'm buying stock for myself and not representing the Traders Guild," Larry said as he shook her hand. "Well, I suppose I'm always representing the Traders Guild, but not as some kind of buying agent or stamp of approval. I mean—"

"I understand that you're here on your own account. I'm just thrilled to have the opportunity to get my foot in the door with your guild as I believe our products are an ideal fit for independent traders," she said, and then offered her hand to John. "Please call me Evka."

"John," he replied, "and that's Marco with his nose pressed up against your display case." He let out a short laugh and added, "I hope you won't be offended, but when I heard your surname, I thought you were Frunge."

"Czechoslovakian," Evka said. "I can understand your confusion, and sometimes I think the main reason the Frunge invested in our new factory is that so many of us have 'Z's' in our names."

"I thought the building looked new. How long have you been open?"

"My family has been in the glass beads business for centuries. We broke ground for this location nine months ago, and we're still getting some of the bugs out of our production lines. You probably know that we sell two different grades, handmade and hand-finished, and the hand-finished beads involve some automation."

"Are the Frunge only interested in the higher quality handmade beads?" Larry asked.

"Exactly, so if you're interested in stock that you can trade with both humans and aliens, you might want to stick with handmade," Evka said.

"Does all of your production go into the craft jewelry market?

"Until recently, yes. But our Frunge partners have started making a line of textiles for the fashion market that includes beading. They have a customer who wants a product that can be certified as handmade-by-humans for a new brand concept."

"But the maker is Frunge?" John asked.

"The textile concern is located on a Frunge open world where they already employ thousands of humans in their factory. It's easy enough for them to segregate their manufacturing lines to meet the tunnel network certification requirements for origin claims. By partnering with us, they can source all-human beads, plus they get the benefit of our EarthBeads brand."

"Marco," Larry called to the boy who was still ogling the beads in the display case. "Tour is leaving."

"Does the boy craft with beads?" Evka asked.

"He crafts with everything," John replied. "I think somebody had him creating collectibles out of a recycling bin at some point because he can turn wire and tin cans into just about any animal you can imagine. I suspect where we see beads, he sees eyes."

The sales rep waited for Marco to join them, and then she said, "Before we go in, I have to give you a quick safety presentation. Molten glass is hot, and the furnaces that turn sand into glass are even hotter. Don't touch either of them."

"Do you get your sand directly from the ocean?" Larry asked as they entered the factory floor.

"Indirectly, it comes on ships," Evka explained. "The New York city-state doesn't allow beach sand to be removed for commercial purposes."

"Then why locate a new factory on the shore?"

"Our Frunge backers are a bit kooky about cutting down trees to make room for new construction, and you know how overgrown all of the abandoned industrial sites have gotten," she said, pushing through the double doors. "The beachfront property was already clear, and since the sand is delivered by ship, locating on the shore saves having to transfer the load multiple times. Land around here is surprisingly cheap because you can't get insurance for homes."

"And for the factory?" John asked.

Evka laughed. "You didn't recognize the Frunge architecture? It's one of their standard models and it would survive a tidal wave." She noticed Marco studying a rack with bundles of thin glass rods, no thicker than pencil leads. "Those are for adding color," Evka told him. "We have a wide assortment of special shaping dies that the glassblowers and lampworkers use to add the color canes into the process."

Marco tilted his head, clearly looking for a more detailed explanation. Evka led the group to where a woman dressed in casual clothing was just pulling a long rod out of a furnace with a bubble of molten glass on its tip.

"You employ glassblowers to make beads?" Larry asked in surprise. "I would have thought it was an extrusion process."

"The hand-finished beads are extruded, molded, and separated in a partially automated process, but the handmade beads are done by glassblowers and lampworkers," Evka said. "It's quite a painstaking process, but hobbyists are willing to pay a premium, as are the Frunge."

The glassblower rolled the molten blob back and forth on a steel table a few times to get a smooth cylindrical shape. Then she pushed the business end into a mold on the floor that might have been made out of carbon, and when she pulled it out again, there were thin glass rods of different colors embedded in the surface of the molten glass.

"That's how we add the colors to create non-random patterns," Evka said as the woman reheated the blob in a different furnace than the one from which she had gathered the molten glass. "Glass wants to be round. It's one of nature's miracles that as the molten glass cools, it naturally seeks to minimize its surface area, resulting in spherical or cylindrical forms. Our glassworkers have various tools to help them achieve different shapes, but the perfect spheres that Ava will create from cutoffs don't require much encouragement to take the shape as long as she keeps the mandrel turning."

Five minutes later, Marco pointed at the third furnace where Ava placed a tray with the finished beads, a questioning look on his face.

"All of the twisting and different colors create tensions in the glass that could lead the beads to shatter if they were left to cool at room temperature," Evka explained. "The annealing furnace is the lowest temperature of the three, and it keeps the glass soft overnight to allow the tensions to relax."

The tour continued for almost a half-hour, with Marco asking most of the questions using easily understood sign language. They ended in a combination warehouse/showroom with what looked like thousands of transparent bins of different types of glass beads.

"You don't worry about the beads damaging each other in those large bins?" Larry asked. "It would be a shame to have even a small percentage wasted after all the work that goes into making them."

"The beads are nearly indestructible unless you hit them with a hammer," Evka told him. "Keep in mind that most of the large ones are destined to be used in craft jewelry where they'll be naturally banging up against one another, not to mention occasionally falling to the floor and rolling around when a necklace or bracelet cord breaks."

"And you sell them by count or weight?"

"Weight. The prices on the bins include delivery to the elevator stalk, and—those are quality control rejects," she called to Marco, who had located a series of bins off to the side and was holding a bead up to the light as if inspecting it for flaws. "It's strictly an aesthetic judgment on the part of the sorters. Our Frunge partners supplied a high-tech imaging system that rejects any beads which still show signs of internal stress after the annealing process, and those get shunted off for recycling."

"Pick out whatever you can use," John told the boy. "We can square up after you sell whatever you make."

"We offer a ten percent discount for quantity when your order goes over a half-ton," Evka told Larry.

Larry nodded. "Do you think Ellen will take some off my hands if they don't move for me?" he asked John. "Last time I saw her spread a blanket it looked like she was back to arts and crafts."

"I was going to put in an order for a few hundred of the large beads for her just to see how they go, but I'd rather do a barter deal with you," John said with a grin.

"Barter is better," Larry responded reflexively, even though he had a pretty good idea of the stock his friend would try to unload on him in exchange. He turned back to Evka and said, "I'm a little worried that if I buy both the handmade and hand-finished, we'll eventually get them mixed up. I think I'll stick with all handmade."

"I would suggest splitting your purchase by size," she said. "Customers for large handmade beads often buy smaller hand-finished beads to use as spacers on the cord. Your customers may feel that you're pushing high-priced products if you don't have any alternatives."

"Good point, but I'm carrying a consignment this trip, so I don't have a lot of space on my cargo deck. What sort of sacking do you provide with purchases?"

"It's a Frunge weave, from one of our partner's factories. You could fill it with nails or knife blades without any fear of rips or punctures." She went over to the sack dispenser, pulled one out, and spread the mouth open with her forearms. "The weight per sack varies with the bead size, but on average, you're looking at forty sacks per ton."

"I forgot glass was so heavy," Larry said. "Does the discount go up if I take a full ton?"

Evka shook her head. "Two tons is the next break."

"Independent traders hate spending cash," John told her. "You'll have to consider barter if the word gets out and you start seeing large numbers of us."

"How about this," Larry said. "I bring my ship over to your parking lot after hours and load here rather than taking delivery at the Elevator Transit Authority. What kind of discount would that get me?"

Evka sighed. "It only costs us fifteen creds to ship half a ton to the elevator stalk because the Elevator Transit Authority has a pickup service running floaters all over the city-state. I can rebate you the fifteen creds, but is it worth the wear and tear on your ship?"

"Never mind." Larry took the sack from Evka and began filling it from a bin of handmade beads with a plastic scoop. "You may as well grab one of those and fill it for Ellen, unless you think she'll take two."

"They don't take up much space and the price looks right to me," John said. "If she doesn't want the beads, I'm sure I can barter them to another trader." He pulled out an extra sack and brought it to Marco, who was setting aside the individual beads he found interesting one at a time. "Do you think you can fill it?"

The boy held his hand halfway up his chest.

"In the next hour? I told Ellen we'd be back for lunch."

Marco nodded again, pointed at Larry, and then mimed tying something around his neck.

"Good idea," John said, and he returned to where Evka was helping Larry by filling a sack from a bin that he chose. "Do you sell cord for stringing the beads?"

"Funny you should ask," the sales rep said. "I wanted to, but our partners expressed a strong preference that we don't. It turns out that Frunge manufacturers are all specialists and they're suspicious of the quality of unrelated products sold by the same maker."

"But what could be more related than beads and cord?"

"Beads are glass, cords range from various elastics to natural silk, and every other fiber in between," Evka explained. "Our specialty is glass, but I can give you the names of some very reputable cord manufacturers. Just mention EarthBeads for a ten percent discount."

"Would you have given me another ten percent off if I had gotten your name from one of them?" Larry asked.

"Only if you didn't make weight. The Frunge frown on stacking discounts, they believe it cheapens the brand."

# Ten

"I can't believe we're actually doing this," Fiona said, struggling back into the straps of the trader's pack that looked ludicrously oversized on her small frame. "What kind of person pays somebody like me to go shopping for the latest fashions?"

"The kind who knows something we don't know and has the finances to prove it," Lena replied, hoisting her own much-smaller pack from the picnic table where they'd taken a coffee break. "And the supervisor who took our phones before handing over the eBucks was pretty smart."

"She didn't fall for my burner phone. Just glanced at it and said, 'Give me the real one.' But whoever she's working for…" Fiona twirled a finger next to her ear in the universal sign for batty.

"Why do you carry a burner anyway? You're not running drugs on the side, are you?"

"Having an extra phone to give up came in handy the last time I tangled with people working for aliens in Manhattan, so I thought I'd play it safe. But I still don't get why anybody would hand a stranger, much less two teenage girls, five hundred eBucks each to shop at a street festival."

"At least you were assigned scarves and gloves," Lena said. "I got stuck buying collectibles, and I hate cluttering up my space."

"Then it's a good thing we have to hand all of the stuff over to get our phones back from the Proxy Shoppers supervisor," Fiona said. "Did your friends who do this in Switzerland ever gain the trust of their supervisor to the point of being allowed to keep their phones?"

"No. But I've been thinking about that, and I wonder if it's intentional misdirection. Sure, taking our phones is a way to discourage us from running off with the cash, but I'll bet it has more to do with preventing us from *using* the phones while we shop. If we were running apps like PriceCheck and SeenIt, our employer wouldn't be getting our natural reactions or whatever it is they're hoping to achieve."

"I never really used shopping apps when I lived here because all I ever bought was food and phone chits," Fiona said. "What's SeenIt?"

Lena rounded on the younger teen with a look of shock. "Wow. If I hadn't believed you had a tough childhood that would have proved it. SeenIt is *the* fashion app for finding out if you'll be the first person in your circle of friends to buy something. You just do an image capture of whatever you're looking at, and if one of your connections has already bought something similar, the phone says 'Seen it,' in the voice of your favorite celebrity. I'm too cheap to buy a voice so I got Cringe to record his for free. It's pretty funny if you're with friends shopping through bargain bins and everybody's phones are saying, 'Seen it' at the same time."

"I guess that could be handy," Fiona said. "If you're going to pay extra for a new fashion it makes sense to find out whether you'll be the first or not."

"And our employer, who we're assuming is from one of the other tunnel network species, is interested in the latest thing that trendsetters might be interested in. Not whether our friends have already discovered it."

"How did you figure that out so fast?"

Lena shrugged. "It's just a theory. I've been covering the news since I was seven and it's all I've ever wanted to do. I started with the teacher bot newspapers and then I graduated to the Children's News Network until I aged out and went freelance. A tutor my parents hired told me about Occam's razor, and I try to apply it whenever I don't understand what's going on."

"I've heard Ellen use that. She said it means that the simplest solution is usually right."

"Really? The way it was explained to me, it's about shaving off the excess until you get down to the core. Sometimes the answer is still pretty involved, it's just that you don't want to report a story that's more complicated than it needs to be."

"Have we been down this way yet?" Fiona asked, indicating an aisle between a booth selling leather jackets and another one with art glass.

"I would have remembered the jackets," Lena said. "I'm keeping my eyes open for them because a guy I know bought a floater bike."

"Aren't you going to try one on?"

"We're not here shopping for ourselves, and leather jackets aren't collectibles." Lena sighed and headed for the next booth down with its display of figurines. "Who would collect action figures of professional LARPing league players? And they're not to scale. That Dollnick should be at least a head taller than the human, and the Grenouthian looks more like Peter Rabbit than an alien warrior."

Fiona laughed, and then looked thoughtful. "Uh, oh."

"Do you need to use the bathroom? There were some of those portable ones back near the picnic tables. Fair food is always a gamble."

"I was thinking about paring away at the complications like you said. What if the point of all of this isn't to find new fashions for aliens to copy but to figure out how our minds work? That way alien manufacturers wouldn't have to wait to copy a promising product, they could figure out what would be the next hit ahead of time by using artificial intelligence and stuff."

Lena frowned and put down the figurine of the Drazen brandishing an axe she'd been considering buying. "I've been doing a ton of business interviews because the Galactic Free Press will buy them all, and I've heard a number of smart people say that predicting the future is the Holy Grail of retail. But it's supposed to be impossible because there are too many moving pieces. And why would teenage girls be representative of anything an alien would care about, unless..."

"Unless what?" Fiona prompted.

"I haven't thought this through, but what if all of the interest in human culture is because the tunnel network species have gotten so accustomed to us that what we think *does* matter."

"I'm not sure I understand. I've been bumming around the tunnel network with Marco, Semmi, and the dolts for less than a year, but it's already clear that there are a lot more aliens who have never met a human than there are who have. The open worlds are one thing, but most alien planets have never been visited by humans. Ellen told me that the conditions on a lot of Verlock worlds would kill us before we got two steps from the ship."

"O-kay," Lena said slowly, "but what if alien familiarity with humans is really being driven by shows like *Let's Make Friends* and the Grenouthian documentaries? All of the tunnel network species have much longer lifespans than us, and maybe that means it takes longer for impressions to sink in with them. But let's say that human-style is becoming a thing, and by learning to quantify it, the aliens behind Proxy Shoppers can get a jump on the other species we've influenced."

"What does 'quantify' mean?" Fiona asked.

"To define something with numbers, with quantities," Lena explained. "Like, these aren't just collectibles," she continued, sweeping her arm to include the table full of figurines. "They're ceramic action figures of professional LARPing league players. And this guy would be further defined as a Drazen axe wielder or whatever gaming terminology they use—I'm not a fan. All of those definitions would be replaced by numbers, and then there would be a lot of other data, like how many shoppers bought the figurines, when we bought them, how many of each kind."

"Why not just make a grid on a big sheet of art paper?"

"This is where the computers come in. I only know something about this stuff because of the interviews I've done, but when you're working with a huge amount of data like you can collect from retail, you end up with what they call a layer of abstraction. The figurines and whatever are transformed into nothing but numbers, and then the computers look for patterns and do all sorts of weird math to make the interesting points pop out."

"But how will that help the aliens predict fashion trends?"

"The way it was explained to me, genuine machine learning is a sort of artificial intelligence without consciousness. It doesn't know or care why it's doing what it's doing, but it has the ability to make connections that people never would. Even the programmers don't understand how it's coming up with answers after a while, but they can transform those numbers back into the original stuff and say that Verlock mages will be the next hot figurine."

"I don't get it, but if the programmers don't either, I guess that's okay," Fiona said. "So let's say that our employer takes all this Proxy Shopper data and creates a computer program that tells them how human teenagers will react to new products. They would still have to create those products to test against the program, wouldn't they? Where are the savings?"

"They could simulate the whole thing, it's much, much, cheaper," Lena said. They walked on to the next booth, which was selling hand-woven scarves, and the older girl's face fell. "You know what? I forgot that aliens avoid automating this sort of stuff because they don't want to put everybody out of work."

"Ellen talks about that a lot, but I have a hard time imagining aliens sorting through trash for a living," Fiona said as she rummaged through the scarves. "How much is this one?"

"Fifty," the vendor said.

"eBucks? For a scarf?"

"You want to see video of it getting knit?" he asked, pulling out his smartphone.

"No, I can tell it's not machine-made, but that's almost ten creds." Fiona turned away to see if the vendor would call her back, but the price was firm, and she couldn't bring herself to spend that much. "I know that the aliens use advanced computer systems for stuff like tracking crime," she told Lena. "John uses ice-something, and Ellen's friend Georgia does newspaper archive research when she's on Earth with a system the Verlocks supplied."

"Ice-something is ISPOA, the Inter-Species Police Operations Agency," Lena said, perking up again. "And I'm planning on visiting the newspaper archive before I go home. Maybe our theory will hold water after all."

"You're saying that if all that computer stuff worked, instead of, like, doing fashion shows with models and all of that, a clothes manufacturer could just have a computer simulate a zillion designs. Then they could use the Proxy Shopper model to pick the one that we would buy the most of."

"I was thinking they would sell products to aliens, but I guess that wouldn't work because our bodies are different. And on Earth, the SeenIt app would stop people—women anyway—from all buying the same dress. Maybe I don't know enough about the tunnel network to come up with a solid theory."

"Why do you stay on Earth? You must be earning a ton with all of those interviews, and traveling the tunnel network is pretty cool."

"It's mainly because of my family," she said. "We're really close and—sorry."

"You don't have to apologize to me for having a family," Fiona said with a laugh. "Marco adopted himself as my little brother, and I bet right now he's nagging Semmi to fly here and check on me."

Back on the Grenouthian four-decker, Marco was waving his phone and trying to get the gryphon's attention.

Semmi steadfastly ignored him and kept working on her still life.

"Let Semmi finish her painting," Ellen told Marco. "I looked at the rules for the Aarden Arts Festival and one of the technical requirements for walk-on artists is a bowl-of-fruit still life. I guess it's something all of the tunnel network species agreed on."

The boy came over and showed her his smartphone with a whole screenful of unanswered texts.

"Fiona probably turned her phone off while she's working," Ellen told him.

Marco shook his head and used a small gesture with his fingers to zoom in on a little green dot next to the text. He tapped it and a box popped up with the message that the user's phone was active.

"I didn't know that's what the green dots meant, but I'm sure it's nothing," Ellen said. "I'll tell you what. I'll try calling Lena. She's on my contacts now." Two minutes later, after leaving a voicemail, she found herself accompanying the boy back to the area just inside the ramp where Semmi was taking advantage of the natural sunlight to knock out a painting of some carefully arranged fruit.

The gryphon exhaled in frustration, moved back from the easel, and stuck her brush in a glass of turpentine. Then she turned to them and let out a "Scraw" which fully conveyed the sense of, "What is it now?"

"Marco is worried about Fiona, and the reporter she's with doesn't answer her phone either," Ellen said.

Semmi picked up her own phone from the table that held her tubes of oil paint and opened the imaging app. Marco did the same on his, and Ellen watched as the image the gryphon drew on her screen materialized on the boy's phone.

"Yes, we know they went shopping, but where is she now?" Ellen asked.

The gryphon snorted and drew a circle around the previous picture.

"They're still shopping?"

Semmi bobbed her head and added a bored "Scraw."

"You're sure?" Ellen asked. "You'd know if she'd been kidnapped or something?"

"Scraw."

Marco stared at the gryphon for a moment. Then he turned back to Ellen and shrugged, as if to apologize for dragging her into it.

"There's nothing wrong with expressing your concern," Ellen told him. "We already knew that Semmi can find us at large distances based on her telepathic ability, and I guess she's saying she would feel something if Fiona was in danger."

"Hello on board," a woman's voice called.

"That's Georgia and her parents," Ellen told Marco. "Can you run up to the kitchen to get the picnic basket I prepared and bring it out to the table?"

The boy nodded and took off for the open shaft equipped with a gravity lift that ran through all four decks. He stepped in and began rising without any visible support. On her way out to meet the guest, Ellen reflexively glanced to the other side of the hold where a spiral staircase similarly disappeared up into the next deck. When the ship was on the ground, Semmi and the kids used the gravity lift, Ellen and John took the stairs.

Georgia's father was staring up into the hold as Ellen came down the ramp, but Janice was too busy getting her first close-up view of the space elevator to notice a mere spaceship. James was asleep in the old-fashioned pram his grandfather had restored.

"Thanks for inviting us," Georgia greeted Ellen. "This is my father, George, and the woman trying to catch flies in her mouth is my mother, Janice."

"When the alien-deniers group made our graduation outing to Flower, they brought us here and back at night so we wouldn't find the view too disconcerting," Janice said, her head back as far as it would go to witness the stalk disappearing in the clouds. "It must be the biggest manmade structure in existence."

"Don't forget the Great Wall of China," George reminded her.

"It's not manmade, Mom," Georgia added. "The Dollnicks installed it for EarthCent, and somebody told me it's second-hand."

"I just can't believe I managed to walk around for decades without seeing it," Janice said. "I must have been out of my mind."

"It's not always visible from the commune because of the curvature of the Earth and the clouds," George said, as if that excused his wife for denying the existence of aliens all of her life. He shook hands with Ellen. "So, our girl tells us that you've been to Earth Two."

"My partner and I were the first humans to visit, and we've been back again since," Ellen said, looking around to see where John had got to. "Marco is bringing out a little picnic I put together, and I'll be happy to answer any of your questions."

"We're not asking for us," Janice hastened to inform her. "My niece and her family are talking about emigrating, and I'm hoping to be able to put my sister's mind at ease about the conditions there. Is it true that it's just like Earth?"

"Settlers are only allowed on the small continent which the Dollnicks spent around eighty years seeding with Earth's flora and fauna. The climate isn't that different from around here, though the winters are a bit warmer and the summers a bit cooler."

"And the—" Janice lowered her voice, "—Neanderthals?"

"The Alts are human hybrids. By the time the Stryx concluded that the Neanderthals were facing extinction if they were left on Earth, there had already been tens of thousands of years of cross—of mixed marriages," Ellen amended herself diplomatically. "Marco," she addressed the boy who had just arrived with the picnic basket. "Do you have your flute?"

Marco handed over the basket, shook his head in the negative, and fled back into the ship.

"I think he's bringing it," Ellen said as she began unpacking the snacks and bottled juices. "I bought fruit at the farmers market this morning but it's currently in use."

Janice raised an eyebrow at this comment but didn't pursue it. "How is the boy progressing?" she asked. "Georgia warned us that he doesn't talk."

"Marco makes himself understood when he wants to, and he's a wizard with a smartphone. He's caught up with reading and writing for his age level so he can text us if he needs to express something complicated."

"I was going to offer to take him back to the commune and teach him farming, but we don't allow phones-of-the-hand," George said.

Janice nodded in agreement. "It was enough of a shock to me when I found out that Drazen Foods is owned by an alien. The commune has to draw the ideological line somewhere or there will be nothing left to keep us together."

"Plenty of nut cases," her husband added.

Marco returned on the fly, his flute clenched in one hand, and offered it to Ellen.

"The flute was carved by an Alt, one of the Neanderthals, as you call them," she told Georgia's parents. "Can you play something, Marco?"

The boy stood self-consciously straight and then began playing a piece that started by wandering gently up and down the scales. Ellen found herself holding her breath and wondering when he had found the time to become so expert with the instrument. Then the boy might have made a fingering error because he stopped, apparently annoyed with himself. He offered a shy grin and disappeared back into the ship.

"Debussy," George said. "Prelude to the Afternoon of a Faun. I have an antique HiFi system with a turntable that's the envy of our neighbors."

"I never understood why vacuum tubes were allowed and microwaves weren't," Georgia said. "It's practically the same technology, you know."

"Microwave ovens came at least fifty years after vacuum tube amplifiers, maybe more," her father replied. "And it's not like we don't have plenty of other options for heating food."

"I don't think any sort of amplification systems are allowed on Earth Two," Ellen told them. "It has more to do with the Old Way's distrust of long-distance communications and encouragement of musicianship than it does with the underlying technology, though the Alts have the final word on all of that."

"As long as somebody is in charge," Janice said. "We've seen what happens in communes where a simple majority is enough to ban this or that. It doesn't take long before people are back to the Bronze Age."

"Or the Stone Age," George concurred. "Luddite nut jobs."

"So, did you show your parents the nursery upgrade you had installed on your ship?" Ellen asked Georgia. "I'll bet they're the first members of their commune with a grandchild who—"

"Larry took the ship this morning to pick up another consignment from Flower," Georgia interrupted before her friend could mention the baby centrifuge. "And I've been putting off cleaning until we're ready to leave Earth."

"Some things never change," her mother said sagely.

# Eleven

"...but I couldn't come up with anything definitive one way or another," John concluded. He spent a few minutes staring at the ship's main viewscreen to read the text of the report for EarthCent Intelligence that he'd dictated and then made a face. "Delete all."

"Are you sure?" the ship's controller asked.

"Wait a second, let me read it," Ellen called as she floated through the hatch at the top of the gravity lift shaft she was only willing to use in Zero-G. "You must have a few thousand words there, John. It can't all be worthless."

"It's just a big mess, not that this assignment is any better. If EarthCent Intelligence had limited the scope of the investigation to the financial impact of the Grenouthian documentary on the prices of Earth paintings, I could have made some headway in a few weeks. I swear Blythe was laughing when she said they wanted a report about alien interest in Earth's culture in general. Sculpture, painting, music, plays, poetry—any one of those would keep an agent who actually knows something about them busy for years."

"Maybe that's why they assigned you," Ellen said as she grabbed the back of John's command chair to bring herself to a halt. "A specialist would have gotten bogged down in the details. You've got more experience than most at working with alien professionals and you can provide an outside perspective."

"That's a nice way of saying that I'm a cultural ignoramus. Are you reading and talking at the same time?"

"It's my journalism superpower," Ellen said. "Controller. Cancel deletion, revert to draft mode. I can save this with editing," she added for John's benefit. "Why didn't you say anything about the Ladies in Waiting? I thought that would have set alarm bells ringing at EarthCent."

"I put it in as a special report three weeks ago when you told me that drama fans were getting together to replace Earth's city-state governments with queens," John said. "And since we're officially on the same assignment, I sent along the draft of the piece you showed me about proxy shopping that Fiona worked on with that Swiss girl. The analysts on Union Station came up with a pretty interesting theory about why aliens might be interested in creating a model for how teenage girls shop. But I'm still waiting for you to fill me in on what your syndicate uncovered."

"Investigative reporting takes time, especially for people who actually know enough about the arts to say anything conclusive," she shot back. "Posing interesting questions isn't journalism."

"No, it's management, at least at EarthCent Intelligence."

"You tend to ramble and contradict yourself when you're dictating," Ellen said as she began rereading the draft from the start. "Have you ever considered getting an old-fashioned keyboard and typing your reports?"

"I do fine with dictation when I know what I'm talking about," John said. "Don't your syndicated journalists run their stories by you before they get too deep to make sure the Galactic Free Press is interested in buying?"

"They do, and some of them are investigating whether any of the arts and entertainment products that Earth imports from the tunnel network species are being specially tailored to influence us or out-compete us."

"Nobody wanted to investigate how Earth's cultural exports are doing in the wake of the documentary?" John asked.

"The syndicated journalists are all Earth-based, they don't have a clue what's happening anywhere else," Ellen said. "A few of them are working together to figure out whether that documentary made Earth's legacy art so collectible that deep-pocketed aliens are driving up the prices of whatever comes on the market, but that's basically a business story. They were going to send me something before we left, but some new data from a big auction house came in. I'll get their article when we arrive at Aarden."

"Legacy art?"

"From before the Stryx opened Earth. And Georgia spent the best part of a week doing archival research on performance art. She discovered that there's been a sharp increase in alien producers sponsoring troupes of human actors to put together extraterrestrial tours. She thinks that the historical-themed performances, including some of the Shakespearean plays with a lot of swordplay, are drawing aliens, but the music tours seem to be targeting Earth expats."

"That sounds fine either way," John said. "I think EarthCent was worried about alien performers and productions catering to our tastes and taking over Earth's market."

"Georgia didn't find any evidence of that happening, though the impact of Vergallian dramas and the Grenouthian news is growing more obvious by the year.

Keep in mind that the Vergallians have ongoing series stretching back millennia, so if somebody gets hooked, they can spend the rest of their life watching old episodes and never get caught up. The Grenouthians pull news from the entire galaxy so they always have a war or something blowing up."

"But it's all in translation, and I'd think the lack of lip-synching would put watchers off, even if the voices are perfect."

"You can learn to ignore it, sort of like suspension of disbelief, or choose subtitles," Ellen explained. "And before Georgia told me, I hadn't known alien performance troupes were doing cultural outreach on Earth almost immediately after the Stryx opened the planet. They may have had an impact on the number of people willing to sign up for labor contracts back then, but it's a nonfactor today."

"How about all the concerts Fiona went to? Is she writing up an article?"

Ellen shook her head. "Fiona has a great work ethic, stronger than mine when I was her age, but you put her in front of one of those Apologist bands and she turns into a fan girl. Now she's hitting the books hard to prepare for Aarden."

"If Fiona's that busy I should check on Marco." John undid the buckle on the four-point restraint he had automatically put on when taking the command chair, but Ellen reached around and pulled his shoulders back.

"Or, you could stay here and we could finish your report so it would be out of the way. Marco was doing teacher-bot homework when I looked in, and when he takes a break from that, it will be to work on one of his upcycling projects or to practice the flute."

"Did he tell you where he learned to play so well?"

"You mean, did I ask him and did he text me a reply?" Ellen shook her head even though she was behind John. "No. We agreed not to pry into his past, and M793qK said it was a surprisingly wise decision on our part."

"Semmi is sleeping in her crate?"

"I can't get over how she prefers that old thing to the cabin we set aside for her, but she only took a quick nap before getting back to painting."

"I thought painting required gravity. I can't see it working in the tunnel without drops of paint going everywhere. I hope she's keeping a lid on the turpentine."

"Fiona said that Semmi bought a Zero-G painting kit from a Grenouthian in Flower's bazaar," Ellen told him. "The brushes have a battery in the handle that gives them some kind of charge, and the powered palette puts the opposite charge into the paint so they attract."

"Then what makes the paint come off the brush and stick to the canvas?" John asked.

"A third charge? I don't know anything about Grenouthian technology. It makes sense that they'd have worked out a solution for painting in Zero-G given how much time their traders spend in weightlessness. Semmi hates getting paint spots on her feathers so she's being really careful," Ellen added, steering the discussion away from physics as quickly as she could. "I'm just happy to see her doing something other than watching anime all the time while we're on the ship. I was afraid she was going to turn Marco into an addict, but now I worry that he doesn't get any downtime at all."

"Playing the flute makes him happy, and so do his upcycled art projects. If he didn't give them all away I would have planned to rent a space for him at the arts festival."

"I think that with Marco it's more about the process than the result. If you give him a table in your booth and some bits and pieces to work with, I bet he'll attract more attention than if you just showed the finished works."

"All right," John said, relaxing back in the chair and reflexively buckling the safety restraints. "How are we going to edit this?"

"Give me the tab from your armrest," Ellen said, and then instructed the ship's controller, "Link tab." She used her finger to highlight around sixty percent of the text and tapped the recycling bin icon. "There. You did fine on the general outline, but your recommendations for follow-up were all over the place, and your conclusion just raised more questions."

"That's because I don't know what to do next. As near as I can tell, the other tunnel network species are making more work for human artists than they're taking away. And at the craftsman level, I'll bet that a higher percentage of humanity is working with their hands today than a century ago because of the premium the aliens place on labor over automation. Most of the employees at the bead factory I visited with Larry were artisans doing handmade work, and the Frunge who financed the operation employ human weavers in their textile factories on the open worlds."

"So you think this is turning out to be another false alarm, like when our bosses had us chasing reports of forced child labor?"

"It feels like there's something more to this than there was to that, but the scope of what they asked me to report on is too broad to make any sense of it. Does the Galactic

Free Press have any of their staff reporters on Stryx stations or open worlds looking into whether humans working in the arts outside of Earth have been affected?"

"I didn't ask," Ellen admitted. "That's a good point though, and—what's up, Fiona?"

The teenager, who now maneuvered in weightlessness like an old pro, brought herself to a halt at one of the grab bars John had installed on the ceiling of the bridge and hooked an arm through it to remain in place.

"I've been studying the guide to the Aarden Arts Festival like you suggested," she said. "Did you know that there's a featured species each week?"

Ellen nodded. "The Galactic Free Press timed it to get us there before the start of Human Week, and Georgia is looking forward to writing about the food offerings."

"Nobody told me," John said. "I was sort of hoping to see all of the alien arts at the same time."

"You will,' Fiona said. "Human Week just means that's when the juried show for our arts will take place. We'll be arriving around the mid-point of the overall festival. I think it works out to eleven weeks on our calendar, but it's hard to say with the different length days and all. Anyway, it's supposedly our first time."

"It's definitely our first time," Ellen said. "None of us have ever attended the festival before."

"I mean, it's humanity's first time getting our own category at a major tunnel network arts festival, at least according to the brochure. I think the basic requirement was a thousand registered artists, performance groups, or dealers, unless it was *and* dealers. The wording isn't clear."

"How many booths and events are there at this show?" John asked.

"Over ten thousand," Fiona told him, and then read from her tab, "The Aarden Arts Festival takes its place among the major tunnel network cultural events for the first time with juried awards for ten species. All winning works will be automatically entered into the open-species category without paying an additional fee—they charge artists to get judged?" she interrupted herself.

"It makes sense," Ellen said. "If anybody could enter at no cost, everybody would, and that would make the job impossible for the judges."

"A real-time schedule for ongoing events will be available on the standard information channel for implants, and all food vendors will conform to tunnel network best practices for menus identifying which species can safely eat what items. All performance venues will offer ear-cuff translator rentals for individuals without implants, and permanent venues with stadium seating will offer screens with closed captions on seatbacks."

"Sounds like the Fleet Vergallians are going all out," John said.

"Wait," Fiona told him, and read the next sentence in a louder voice, spacing between her words. "Alien intelligence agents must register with festival security or attend at their own risk." She looked up. "What does that even mean?"

"Myort mentioned that arts festivals draw lots of intelligence agents. I think it's because they give everybody from every species a reasonable excuse to be there. Maybe that's why he was on Earth buying, but I know that he's sort of in charge of keeping an eye on humanity for Huktra Intelligence, so it could have been coincidental."

"Are you going to register?" Ellen asked.

"I'll play it by ear," John said. "I have legitimate cover as a dealer, even if it's strictly reproductions, but I wouldn't have fooled anybody trying to sell original art."

"I doubt you would have bought anything other than those reproductions without Myort and Semmi pushing you. Have you seen her latest painting? She's making tiny points of color with the tip of a brush rather than doing strokes."

"Pointillism," Fiona said. "At least, that's what it's called on Earth, but like most things, we weren't the first species to invent it. Marco told me that it's one of Semmi's elective styles for the contest, whatever that means. And there isn't a Tyrellian Week at the festival so she's entering as human."

"What do you mean she's entering as human?" Ellen said. "Did she ask Marco to front for her?"

The girl scrolled through the brochure with rapid finger flicks and then read, "Artists whose species are not represented at the festival may participate in the juried contests of an alternate species, provided they can demonstrate first-hand knowledge of the culture. In the case of an artist winning a prize in the competition of a species other than their own, a special mention and ribbon will be given to any native artist displaced from the rankings."

"That could be a problem for us," John said. "If you were an alien artist from outside the tunnel network or from a species that didn't qualify for their own week, whose competition would you show in?"

"You think that all of those artists are going to crash Human Week?" Ellen asked. "Wouldn't they have to imitate our style of art to have a chance of winning?"

"Judges will recuse themselves from voting on the works of artists from their own species," Fiona read from the tab. "Does that mean they don't get to vote?"

"Exactly," Ellen said. "It also means that the artists who win may turn out to be unknowns within their own species. I've been exposed to a lot of ideas about how the arts can cross cultural barriers in the last few weeks, and while everybody can name some prominent examples, those are generally the exceptions to the rule. The tunnel network species all have their own sense of aesthetics. We usually only see alien art that happens to be similar to our own."

"Why is that?"

"I can answer that one," John said. "Money. Art galleries show works in order to sell them, performers go on stage to earn a living. Even on Stryx stations, each species has its own deck. Compared with planets inhabited by a single advanced species, space stations are cosmopolitan melting pots, but plenty of the sentients living on board rarely venture out of their own areas. When band promoters arrange tour dates, the goal is to sell out shows, not to do interspecies outreach."

"So you're right that alien artists whose species aren't separately represented at the show are going to pile into Human Week," Fiona said.

"They'll have to pass the culture test," Ellen pointed out.

"It's got to be easier to pass our test than for a species with millions of years of recorded history," the girl countered. "The human questions will probably all be from Grenouthian documentaries, like, about indoor plumbing or wastewater treatment."

"I forgot about all of those Grenouthian documentaries," Ellen admitted.

A loud "Scraw" echoed through the ship. John struggled a moment with the buckle on his safety harness while Fiona kicked off the bulkhead and beat Ellen to the open hatch by a length. She pulled herself through before the older woman could grab her ankle.

By the time John caught up, they were all three decks below in the cargo hold where Semmi had appropriated the open space as her studio. The first thing he noticed was Marco in the act of handing Ellen something that looked like a metal mixing bowl with two spikes improvised from aluminum foil. Fiona was scowling and holding a plastic shield that looked suspiciously like the lid of a small Drazen cargo container in one hand and extending a Grenouthian fire axe to him with the other.

"Is there a fire?" John asked, sniffing the air as he scanned the hold. He clicked the heels of his boots together to activate the magnetic cleats and let go of the grab bar when he got his feet in contact with the deck. "What are you doing with that bowl, Ellen?"

"Putting it on my head, of course," she replied. "We've been drafted as models."

John clicked his heels again to turn off the cleats and prepared to launch himself back up through the shaft, but Marco had expected him to flee and locked onto his leg.

"Semmi promises it won't be more than twenty minutes," Fiona told him. "She needs a Viking family."

"Get over here," Ellen called to him. "If you don't do it, I'll have to stand in for you after she finishes roughing me in as the wife."

"But I modeled for Semmi on Earth," John said, wincing when he heard his voice come out like a whine. "I must have spent twenty hours hunched over that table staring at those stacks of coins while she scrawed instructions at me."

"Like what?" Fiona asked, extending the axe to him again.

John accepted his fate with a sigh and took his place in the Viking family group. "How should I know? I don't speak Tyrellian and it's not in the translation table for our implants. I asked M793qK about that, and he said the Tryrellians requested their language data be limited to high-level diplomats."

"She didn't send you any telepathic projections?" Ellen asked.

"She's sending me one now," John said. "It's a mouth covered by a piece of tape."

"I'm being serious."

"So am I. Semmi sat me down in front of the table with the coins and had Marco pantomime counting them to show me what she wanted. The scrawing was to keep me from dozing off. Do you have any idea how boring it is to count the same stacks of coins over and over again? I ended up assigning them all values for things, like the shares in our ship, our inventory, and the expenses. If she hadn't finished the painting I would have gone into a deep depression over our recent lack of profits."

# Twelve

"No, I am not an intelligence agent," Larry repeated for the two Vergallians in an even tone. "I thought the whole point of answering questions in front of a truthsayer was so you'd know whether or not I'm lying. You've already asked me the same question three different ways."

"But you admit to delivering a sealed consignment for—" the woman in the Vergallian Fleet officer's uniform glanced down at her tab before continuing, "—Next Stop Deliveries."

"Is that what Flower is calling her package network? I thought she liked using her own name in everything."

"Don't you check the cargo manifest when you accept transfer shipments?" the officer asked.

"Not when they're from Flower," Larry said. "If she wanted to trick me, she could trick me. She said it was art."

The Vergallian leaned forward and asked, "But did Flower tell you whose art you were carrying?"

Larry shook his head. "Only that they trusted me and that it had to be here on time."

"He believes what he's saying," the truthsayer confirmed.

"And you had no idea at all that you were working for M793qK," the officer said, making the question sound like a statement.

"I didn't even know he was an artist," Larry said.

Both Vergallians looked at him in disbelief. "How could he not be an artist?" the truthsayer demanded in exasperation. "Mastery of three or more of the Seven Arts of Farling is a requirement to move up in their hierarchy. M793qK is known to have mastered five, and as for the other two, it's probably just that he hasn't been caught yet."

"Let's take it again from the top," the Vergallian officer said, redirecting her desk lamp so that the light was shining in Larry's eyes. "How do you know the Farling?"

"He's our family doctor," Larry said in frustration. "He delivered my son."

"Unbelievable," the truthsayer said. "The rumors were true."

"What rumors?" Larry asked, trying to shield his eyes from the light and see his interrogators.

The officer tilted the light back down again and held up a tab with a high-resolution image of John lying dead on a stretcher as he was being loaded into a stasis pod. "Do you know this man?"

"Of course I know him. I was with him at Rendezvous here when he got poisoned, and our wives both work for the Galactic Free Press. We're all friends," Larry added.

"Were you aware that he's a triple agent working for both M793qK and Huktra Intelligence?"

"No, and as a matter of fact, I'm sure he isn't."

"He believes what he's saying," the truthsayer told the officer.

"What's this all about?" Larry asked. "Maybe if you explained what you want, I could help."

"It's nothing," the officer said, sounding rather disappointed. "You can go now."

"That's it? After having me detained and giving me the third degree about delivering a consignment of artworks for Flower, you aren't going to explain why?"

"You aren't an intelligence agent so you wouldn't understand. As compensation for your inconvenience, I'll inform the parking authority to give you a twenty-five percent discount."

"Enjoy your visit to the Aarden Arts Festival," the truthsayer added. "See you again next time."

"So it was you who interviewed us after Ellen's ship got firebombed," Larry said. It struck him for the first time that upper-caste Vergallians were so beautiful that they all looked alike to him. "Am I on a watch list now or something? Are you going to bring my wife in?"

"That won't be necessary," the officer told him. "If you should see your previously deceased friend, please inform him that we would appreciate it if he voluntarily came by for a chat."

Larry nodded and tried to appear nonchalant as he exited the office. He surveyed the giant festival with over ten thousand booths, tents, and food carts, and every direction looked pretty much the same as the others. He couldn't locate the short-term parking area where Georgia was waiting in the ship and realized he hadn't been paying attention to where he was going after the festival security guards, who were clearly Vergallian ex-military, had intercepted him returning from the consignment delivery tent and escorted him to the interrogation room.

"Larry, Phil's son," somebody said behind him, and he turned to see an older trader who he recognized as the winner of the Tall Tales competition held at Rendezvous when it took place on Aarden.

"Marshall," Larry greeted him when the name clicked into place. "Am I glad to see a familiar face. Another minute or two of not being able to choose a direction and I was going to cheat and check the map on the public information channel."

"And then you would have to resign as the head of our guild," the older man said. "Traders never get lost—we just don't always know where we are."

"I wasn't going to tell anybody I cheated," Larry said with a laugh.

"None of us ever do. Where are you trying to go?"

"If I don't get back to the ship before dark and move it out of short-term parking I'll get dinged with the overnight rate."

"You're in the central lot?" Marshall asked, a note of disbelief creeping into his voice. "I thought that was only for yachts and ships making deliveries."

"All right," Larry said. "I'm not proud of it, but I accepted a consignment from Flower. You know how persuasive she can be. That's how I ended up here," he added, hiking a thumb over his shoulder at the security building. "Turns out the shipment included Farling art, and these Fleet Vergallians assumed that I was in the intelligence game."

"You do associate with a known spy, and the Vergallians were hardly going to forget either of you after the splash you made the last time we were all here." Marshall glanced around to get his own bearings, then pointed into the distance. "See where those green tents end?"

"The Frunge section, right? I'm pretty sure we marched through on the way here."

"The ground starts sloping downhill after the Frunge section, that's why you can't see the ships. You'll cut across the corner of where the Verlocks are set up, and then it's Drazens all the way down until you get to short-term parking. Probably a twenty-minute walk if you keep to the middle of the paths and don't stop to look at anything."

"Thanks, Marshall. I better run if I don't want to pay for another hour or whatever the time unit is for short term. I know my wife wants to get out and start looking over the food stands to see if she can pick up some easy money with a few freelance stories. Baby needs new shoes."

"I heard that Georgia was expecting. Congratulations," the older man said, offering Larry a handshake.

A few seconds after they parted, it occurred to Larry to invite Marshall for a meal, but when he turned around, the older trader had already disappeared. Now that he wasn't being marched along by armed security, it took a real effort for Larry to resist getting caught up in some of the alien art he passed. During the final stretch through the Drazen area, he had to put his implant into the sound-cancellation mode to keep from being drawn in by a choral performance. An image of Ulysses tied to the mast to resist the song of the Sirens came to mind, and he wondered how the ancient Greeks would have fared as traders on the tunnel network.

"Where have you been all this time?" Georgia asked when Larry stepped off the ladder onto the bridge of their ship. "I would have put out the camping table and chairs to sit with James in the fresh air, but I knew you would want to get out of short-term parking as quickly as possible."

Larry only caught the end of what his wife said for not turning off noise cancellation quickly enough, but he could easily guess what she had asked.

"I got picked up by festival security, though the officer was clearly Vergallian Fleet. Do you remember the interrogation the last time we were here and Ellen's ship got firebombed?"

"They're still investigating that?"

"No, but it was the same truthsayer, and maybe the same officer as well. I didn't ask." Larry headed for the command chair and strapped in. "It turns out that consignment Flower had us bring included pieces from M793qK. The Vergallians assumed I must be working for him, or at least, for EarthCent Intelligence."

"But he's our family doctor," Georgia protested. "You could show them those check-up reminders we keep getting on the ship's controller if they don't believe you."

"They believed me, I think," Larry said, and then requested the fair's traffic controller for a transfer to a long-term lot with camping hookups. "And we get discounted parking now, so it wasn't a complete waste."

"Ellen messaged me when they came out of the tunnel. They'll be landing in time for supper."

"Hopefully they can get a spot near us. The Vergallians are convinced that John is a triple agent and they want to see him when he gets in. Aren't you going to put James in the infant seat?"

"I can hold him while we're just changing lots," Georgia said. "I've watched those floater tugs moving ships, and it's not like the Vergallians are going to run us into something."

"Just do it," Larry said. "Flower probably slipped a clause about bridge surveillance video in that user license for the centrifuge."

Georgia sighed, knowing that there was a chance the baby would wake up when she put him in the infant seat strapped to the side of her own acceleration chair, but he slept through the transfer. Once she was belted back in herself, Larry informed Parking Control they were ready.

"The festival is pretty overwhelming, what I saw of it," he said as a tug locked onto the two-man trader with manipulator fields and smoothly lifted it from the ground. "I put in for a temporary booth assignment next to John's, and the two-week rental cost half as much as if we had come for the whole fair."

"But that's more than a three-hundred-percent markup!"

"Arts festivals aren't enthusiastic about vendors cherry-picking which times to show," Larry explained. "They expect a fairly steady stream of off-world visitors, and plenty of those who come make three months of it and try to take in every exhibit. Nobody likes to see empty spaces in the aisles, so they fill them with pop-up performances or information booths."

"I told Ellen I'd help her if I have time, and I want to store up some food articles for when our income is thin," Georgia said. "I was wondering…"

"I'll keep James in the booth with me as long as you make it back for feeding times. I'm sure the festival provides nursing stations for mothers with babies. It's probably another good use for empty booths."

"Didn't I tell you I bought a Horten modesty cube?"

"One of those holographic devices that projects a big potted plant you can hide inside?" Larry asked. "How much did it cost?"

"Just a few creds in Flower's bazaar, they're practically throwaways," Georgia said. "I tested it on my parents and they were very impressed."

"Sometimes I think you're trying to shock your parents with new alien experiences to make up for them denying you access to technology when you were a kid."

"Anyway, it's kind of cool, because you can see out of the hologram but they can't see in."

"It's surprising more people don't use holograms for privacy," Larry mused. "Maybe we should look into stocking some cheap projectors for trade."

"You can buy special glasses that see through them, and I remember hearing from somebody, maybe Dewey, that they don't work on artificial people," Georgia said. "And they don't really fit with your usual line."

"Main viewscreen on," Larry instructed the ship's controller. "Ground view."

"Viewscreen off," Georgia countermanded a few seconds later. "We're too high up to see anything, and if you zoom in, I'll get motion sick."

"I figure that today is our chance to wander around a bit, because starting tomorrow, it's going to be dawn-to-dusk beads for me. I'm glad I went for a half-ton of the handmade ones because I doubt the festival administrators would be happy if I started selling children's shoes and clothes to make the booth rental."

"I finished reading the rules while I was waiting for you, and selling manufactured shoes and clothing is expressly prohibited in the display areas," Georgia told him. "There's a big area set aside for regular fairgrounds out past the Grenouthian section, but the booth rentals are even higher."

"Figures," Larry said. "It's a good thing Flower paid extra for—"

"Navigation released," the ship's controller interrupted. "Please make a note that our new location is Lot 61, Campsite 17.12. A twenty-five-percent-off coupon has been applied."

"I didn't even feel when the ship stopped moving," Georgia said. "Those tugs are super smooth. I wonder how far we are from the festival grounds now. You've got a lot of weight to carry."

"I reserved two glass showcases with the booth and I'm only going to set a hundred or so beads out at a time," Larry told her. "If I displayed them in bins like at the factory, they'd just look cheap. I picked up some velvet scraps before we left Earth and I'm going to do my best to make each bead look like a treasure."

"If you have extra room, maybe you can show some of Marco's upcycled pieces if he hasn't given them all away. From what you told me, John's booth is going to be crammed with canvases."

"He's not happy playing art dealer because he doesn't know the first thing about it. Last I heard he's sticking with the reproductions. John just wasn't comfortable with the idea of trying to buy and sell paintings that cost as much as spaceships."

Georgia released her safety harness, stood up, and headed for the ladder to the cargo deck. "You bring James down, I'll get the carriage ready," she said over her shoulder.

To Larry's surprise, it turned out that the Vergallians had laid temporary moving sidewalks to the long-term lots. At the edge of the fairgrounds, the conveyor carrying visitors went into a tunnel, and then popped up right in the central plaza.

"They've really thought this out well," he told Georgia. "How often does Aarden hold the festival?"

"They only started after they got the tunnel network connection when the growth of the human community qualified them, and that makes it the only Fleet world that's connected," she said. "I think the locals are investing big to make Aarden into the Vergallian culture capital."

"What about the imperial worlds?"

"The tech-bans make it too complicated to host a giant festival like this. There are thousands of ships on the ground if you include the yachts, and shuttles are running continuously for well-heeled aliens who don't want to waste a day down and back on the space elevator."

"I guess it would be pretty tough for the queen of a tech-ban world to just pretend she didn't notice the way they do with individual traders," Larry said. He saw that his son had partially kicked off the quilt and moved it back up under the baby's chin.

"Oh, look," Georgia said, pulling excitedly on Larry's arm. "A troupe of Horten mimes."

They watched as the aliens struggled to get out of a glass box, walked against the wind, and pretended to climb an invisible rope.

"Looks like pretty standard stuff," Larry said. "Why don't—" his jaw dropped as the music started and the mimes began doing a circus act. A petite young female was thrown from one group of mimes to the other, and she managed to give the impression that she was swinging on a trapeze during her hang-time. Then the whole troupe mimed wrapping themselves in aerial silk and then spinning as the ribbons unwound.

"How are they doing that?" Georgia asked. "There must be some technology involved. Are they using miniature floaters?"

"Take that back!" a voice squeaked in translation, and they looked down to see a Horten boy, around the right age to be appearing on *Let's Make Friends*, holding a collection jar. "Nobody has ever accused my family of using technology. We're mimes!"

"But how do they hang in the air like that?"

"See the couples dancing?"

"How could I miss them?" Georgia asked. "The dresses are lovely, though the dancers are all moving so fast it's like a waltz on high speed." Then understanding sank in, and she said, "The acrobats are getting their feet down and jumping in the air again every time a dancer screens them from the audience. I've never seen that level of body control."

"Practice time is expensive," the boy said, and he shook the jar significantly.

Georgia got a cred out of her purse and dropped it in the jar. The Horten boy moved on to a Verlock who had stopped to watch.

"Tough way to make a living," Larry said sympathetically. "Though on the bright side, it's an easy setup with low overhead, and they'll probably clear a hundred creds for a ten-minute performance."

"I watched the Verlock," Georgia said. "He dropped in a five-cred piece. Do you think I should give the boy more?"

"Better we move on before we're broke." Larry turned away from the mimes and his blood froze as he saw a horde of zombies approaching. "You take the carriage and run. I'll buy you time."

"Don't be a baby, Larry. They're just teenagers who got make-up jobs at the booth there. You know the Hortens are cosmetics experts." Georgia cast a critical eye over the last zombie hurriedly shambling forward to catch the others after stopping to tie a shoelace. "She's human, but I definitely saw an extra pair of thumbs on one, and hair vines on another. They're probably the children of artists or vendors, and it's nice to see teenagers from the different species hanging out together."

"I never got the whole dressing-up-as-living-dead thing," Larry complained. "And what does it have to do with art?"

"It's a festival, visitors come to enjoy themselves. I give them credit for making themselves part of the show rather than just observing."

"Hey, aren't zombies a human thing? Is this an example of human culture influencing the aliens that you can write about?"

"A Horten face painter doing zombies?" Georgia asked. "I can't see stretching it to a story, and now that I think about it, I remember reading an article about the professional LARPing league that went into all of the monster types. It turns out that most of the tunnel network species have reanimated corpses in their gaming mythology."

"I thought the advanced species grew out of all of that millions of years ago," Larry said, pushing the baby carriage towards a group of jugglers. "Who wants to be scared?"

"You could learn a lot from watching *Let's Make Friends*. Whenever they play Storytellers and Aisha starts them off with something happy, the children bring in a witch or a space monster. One of the educational games I saw at the Verlock wholesaler was basically a build-your-own-monster kit."

"I hope you didn't buy any."

"No, it was way too complicated for human kids," Georgia said. "Maybe our scientists specializing in genetics could play, but they're probably too old for that sort of thing."

"I'll never understand aliens," Larry told her, and he turned the baby carriage sharply to the right.

"You don't want to watch the jugglers?"

"They're Drazens, and it's all knives and axes. Look how far up they're throwing them! I don't want James anywhere near there."

"I can't believe that I ever thought traders were adventurous people," Georgia said. "You and John behave more like shopkeepers, and he's an ex-mercenary and undercover intelligence agent."

"He's not that undercover, and I have you and James to worry about," Larry said. "I've never known a trader or anybody else who made a profit on being dead."

# Thirteen

John stepped back to view the reproductions hanging on the booth's walls and the pair of free-standing partitions that left just enough room for members of the thinner species to squeeze through. "Do you think I have the Renaissance too close to the Impressionists?"

"You hung all of the paintings way too close to each other," Ellen said. "I would have gone with three on each side and maybe five on the back wall. No more than two on each side of the partitions."

"I'm trying for volume sales. If I display the paintings like a gallery, people might think they're originals and be afraid to ask about the price."

"Nobody is going to believe you have the original *Three Graces* jammed in that little spot left between the four different Venus paintings that aren't quite the same heights and widths. Did you plan it that way to make a perfect rectangle?"

"I wanted to get the most out of the space," John admitted.

"And you grouped those five paintings because they're all naked women?" Ellen followed up.

"Well, I wasn't going to put them next to the scaled-down version of *Last Supper*."

"Come for a stroll with me and let the kids rearrange everything," Ellen said. "I want to take a look around before we buckle down to work."

"But the kids are still working on Semmi's booth," John objected. Then he lowered his voice and added, "If I had thought it out ahead of time, I never would have rented her the space next to mine. I'll bet most buyers would rather have an original than a reproduction, and she really is talented."

"It's pretty clear she's had professional training, the same as Marco with the flute. But I don't think you have to worry about Semmi under-pricing you. Fiona showed me what they're going to be asking."

"How much?"

"The still life with the fruit is two thousand creds, and that's the cheapest of the lot," Ellen said.

"Semmi would be lucky to get two hundred creds for that painting," John exploded. "It doesn't matter how talented she is. It's a work by an unknown artist."

"It's a good thing she's off stretching her wings because I don't want her hearing you say things like that. I think you forget sometimes that she's around the same emotional age as Marco, and that it's easy to hurt young egos without even trying."

John grumbled something and took a dozen steps to his left to survey the gryphon's exhibit from the common aisle. "I still can't believe she got all of those painted in such a short period," he said grudgingly. "And the kids did do a good job hanging them. I guess taking them to those galleries on Earth paid off."

"Are you finished, Fiona?" Ellen called to the girl who was taking pictures with her smartphone. "John could use some help arranging his reproductions."

"I'll do it if you take him away," the girl replied. "He's got no aesthetic sense whatsoever and I'm not going to argue with him."

John hesitated for a moment, and then said, "I don't care about the order, but keep them all showing, all right?"

"No," Fiona said. "They look like crap all jammed together."

"Marco?"

The boy was clearly uncomfortable about being asked to referee, but he put down his flute and came into the aisle to view John's booth. Marco's wince on seeing the crowded display told the EarthCent Intelligence agent all he needed to know.

"Put the spares under the table with the others so I can fill in the spaces as there are sales," John said. "I don't want to hire another mulebot just to take them back to the ship."

"How about overnight security?" Ellen asked.

"The Vergallians put the entire festival grounds on lockdown after close," John told her. "I wouldn't want to be a thief on this planet."

Ellen pointed. "Let's go that way. I'm more interested in crafts than paintings, and you ended up right on the border of the high-arts section."

"I hope it works out for Larry's beads," John said as they passed the trader's yet-to-be-filled display cases. "He's right on the border too."

"Based on the beads you bought for me I'm sure they'll sell," Ellen said. "It's just a matter of pricing. If they don't move for him, I'd be happy to take whatever he wants to give me at the wholesale price. They're a good fit for my art supplies and I'll use them up eventually."

"What's that smell?"

Ellen came to a halt and sniffed. "I smell it too." Then she remembered Fiona making fun of her at the syndicate meeting and exclaimed, "It's Earth!"

"You're right, but why would Aarden smell like Earth?" John asked, sniffing at his shirt. "Is there something wrong with the ship's sterilizer?"

"It's not our clothes, John. There!"

"EarthScent Candles," he read off the placard on the partition of the booth. Then he saw the pricelist and almost jerked Ellen's arm out of her socket as she went to look at the mosquito candles. "Don't even think about it."

"But they're so pretty, and you know how I hate it when we have the camp table out on Earth and the mosquitoes swarm," Ellen said. She rubbed at her wrist and looked at the pricelist that John thrust at her. "You've got to give them credit for asking. Maybe Semmi is onto something with her pricing."

"Wait a second," John said, looking at the name card again. "EarthScent? Aliens who don't read English will hear 'EarthCent' when they ask who the maker is. Hey, you!"

"Me, sir?" the young man sitting on a camp chair behind the table full of candles asked. "I don't set the prices if that's what you're mad about."

"Who owns this booth?"

"Parents of a friend. For me, it's a cheap way to attend the Aarden Arts Festival. You wouldn't believe the cost of a ticket from Cold Iron."

"That's one of the Drazen Open worlds with a large human population. Doesn't Flower stop there?"

"Only once a year," the young man said. "My friend's parents paid for my ticket and I only have to work the booth every other day. I'm Dorv," he added, offering a handshake.

"John, and my wife Ellen. I don't suppose you know anything about tunnel network trademark infringement."

"Is this about the EarthScent thing? A couple of people have asked us, but my friend swears that his parents checked it all with a lawyer. They've been making candles for like forty years and they thought they came up with the name first, but it turns out the diplomats did."

"And you don't think alien diplomats could be confused by the identical pronunciation in English?"

Dorv shrugged. "They're all a lot smarter than us, so I doubt it. It's more likely they'd have trouble with these guys." He shuffled through some plastic business chits in a pile on the desk and extended one to John.

"EarthSent? You've got to be kidding me."

"Most of our candles are handmade by my friend's parents on Cold Iron, but they import the mosquito repellant ones from Earth. That's the delivery service that brought them."

"It's kind of funny," Ellen said, looking at the plastic business card. "The logo looks sort of like EarthCent's as well."

"Are you guys with EarthCent?" Dorv asked. "We've got one that's sort of a gag gift that's been selling like crazy. It's supposed to make you smarter." He pointed to a black candle on a little display pedestal labeled, "EarthScent Intelligence."

"Somebody isn't going to be happy about this," John said. "Can I keep the card?"

"Sure, but it would be polite to buy something."

"Can't afford it. Come by my booth and I'll swap you a painting for one of those smudge pots."

Dorv hesitated for a moment, thinking about what kind of art he could expect in return for a mosquito candle, even an expensive one. "I think I'll pass."

"If you change your mind, we have the booth next to the Tyrellian gryphon," Ellen said as John tried to move her away. "Everybody will know where she is, and I really want one of those candles."

"You can buy one on Earth for a tenth of the price," John said as they moved away. "It's not like you're going to encounter mosquitoes anywhere else."

"There are mosquitoes on Earth Two. They weren't out when we were there, but that was just the season. With all of those beaver dams, I'll bet they're bad in the summer."

"Half of the people in the Old Way movement make candles, so you can buy something that will work on mosquitoes the next time we go there. I know I'm not the galaxy's sharpest trader, but these prices are ridiculous. Look what they're charging for knit scarves in that booth!"

"Oh, those are lovely," Ellen said. "I should get one for Fiona. A girl her age should have something nice."

"There's no difference between these scarves and what we could trade for anywhere there are knitters," John said. "It's like everybody here is willfully confusing the value of things with the prices charged."

"But that's always the case with art. How else could you justify paying what you did for the one painting you bought for Blythe?"

"I can't, and I wouldn't have without Myort and Semmi twisting my arm. But at least that was art. All of these booths are selling crafts."

"You know, ever since Semmi ran up a big bill on your programmable cred renting anime last year you've been funny about money," Ellen said, coming to a halt and turning so she could look him in the face. "Yet with Myort cutting you a piece of the action on his shady dealings, and the prize money that bought us the Grenouthian four-decker, you've never been better off."

"But we're cash poor," John protested. "And even if I had thousands of creds burning a hole in my pocket, that doesn't mean I'd fork over a hundred for a chicken dinner that would be expensive at five creds."

A well-dressed Sharf stepped in front of the couple just as they began to walk again. "I beg your pardon," the skeletal alien said. "Are you the guy?"

"What guy?" John asked.

"The Human," the Sharf said, glancing at something he held cupped in his free hand, and then back at John again. "*THE* Human," he repeated.

"I'm a human, but there are lots of us here. You're in the human section, you know."

Without taking his eyes off of John, the alien suddenly stuck out his hand, showing Ellen a small screen that was strapped to his palm. It was displaying a man's face as a sort of topographical map, like the 3D images formed by a laser measurement system. "What do you think?" the Sharf asked her.

"You know, it does look like John, but it would be easier to tell with the skin and all," she said. "I'm not an engineer."

"This is taking too long and we're exposed here. Follow me."

"What are you doing?" John asked Ellen as she set off after the gaunt alien.

"Following him. Don't you want to find out what this is all about?"

"Not if it ends in him mugging me for Blythe's programmable cred," John hissed as he took a jog-step to catch up. "It's still got over nine million on it."

"You know that the Stryx voice authorization is foolproof," Ellen said. "Nobody even bothers stealing programmable creds."

"I'll follow him. You go back to the booth and wait."

"I'm an investigative journalist, John. This is what I do."

"The last time we were on this planet, I got killed and your ship was destroyed," John said. "This guy must know I'm with EarthCent Intelligence. Either he wants to sell me information, which would be fine, or he thinks I know too much about something already, which would be bad." The Sharf, who had gotten several paces ahead, turned sharply into a curtained-off booth with a banner embroidered to advertise a fortuneteller. "Just wait outside at least, okay?"

"Pull the curtain aside when you enter so I can see it's not an ambush."

"It's going to be a lot more subtle than that. We're in the middle of the Aarden Arts Festival and the Vergallians have security all over the place." He pulled open the curtain enough for Ellen to get a glimpse at a group of aliens sitting around a folding table, and then stepped in and jerked it closed behind him.

"That's no way to treat your mate," Myort said. "Why didn't you invite her in?"

"Because she works for the Galactic Free Press, and this looks like a mini-convention for intelligence agents going rogue," John said. "Why didn't you come to get me yourself?"

"Yaelk wanted to see if he could find you with a vector kit. It's the same mapping technology the Gem put in microminiature surveillance trackers."

"We had a bet about how many unique data points it takes to identify a Human face," the Sharf said. "I thought I could do it with a handful of vectors in three dimensions, but Balri," he jerked his pointy chin towards a tough-looking Vergallian with a prominent Imperial tattoo on the back of her hand, "claimed it's easier to render your type of face on a two-dimensional plane and measure between seventy or eighty nodal points to get a mathematical model."

"My type of face?" John asked.

"You know, Vergallian derivative. And I did find him," Yaelk said to Balri, "but you were right about all of the loose skin and wrinkles making it iffy."

"Can we get down to business before security shows up and busts us all for unlicensed espionage?" demanded a Grenouthian who John was pretty sure he had seen at least once on Earth, though it was hard to tell with a species that resembled rabbits grown to the size of brown bears. "The Evil Farling Mastermind isn't paying me enough to take that sort of chance with my pension."

"Who?" John asked.

"He doesn't watch anime," Myort explained to the other spies. "That's M793qK's nom-de-guerre on *Everyday Superheroes,* the series that Flower produces."

"So you're all working for the Farling?"

"He's playing innocent because he suspects the booth is bugged," an undersized Dollnick spoke up from the chair at the end of the table. "Don't worry, Human. With the hardware the five of us are carrying, it would take the Stryx to listen in on this meeting."

"But I don't work for M793qK," John protested. "Sure, I've done a few errands to pay back favors, but—"

"No buts," Balri said. "Do you think I have a signed contract with him? I'm Imperial Intelligence and we have some shared interests with the Farling for which I'm the cut-out. You're EarthCent's semi-official connection with M793qK. It's on the Fellow Travelers list."

"I never heard of that list."

"How do you think we keep track of who's working for whom?" Myort asked. "If it makes you feel any better, it has me as working for Flower and EarthCent, in addition to M793qK. I had to do some fast talking at my last performance review to keep from getting promoted to a desk job."

"Since when does Flower have her own side?" John asked. "She works for EarthCent."

"If that's your logic, then by extension M793qK works for EarthCent as well," the Sharf said with a dry chuckle. "Get with the program, Human. Everyone has their own interests, and where they overlap, we work together. Does anybody have a quiver of arrows on them?"

"If you're going to show me the thing where one arrow can be easily broken but a bundle of arrows is strong, I've seen it," John told him.

"Am I the only artist here who's worried about what's going on back at his booth?" the Grenouthian demanded. "For all I know, my assistant may have just lost a major sculpture sale by getting her gold alloys mixed up—again. We've shown you who we are, Human. What message did M793qK send with you?"

"He didn't tell me a thing," John said, "and despite what you all think, we really don't have that kind of relationship. Other than a couple of errands, the only times I've worked for him I thought I was helping Myort."

"He's good," the Vergallian said. "You have to give him credit."

"It's because I'm telling the truth."

"I was talking about M793qK, not you. Running agents who don't even know that they're being run is something that only the best spymasters can manage. When was the last time you saw him?"

John thought for a moment. "Around a month ago, before we left Flower for Earth. I took Fiona, a girl who—"

"She's on the list, get on with it," the Sharf interrupted.

"I brought her to M793qK to get a translation implant."

"What did he say while you were there?" Myort asked. "It could have been completely innocuous if it was intended for us rather than you."

"He started with something about my weight, asked Fiona a bunch of questions about her health, and prattled on about the importance of letting Semmi develop as an artist while he was installing the implant. When it was done, he played a recording of aliens speaking a dozen different languages to calibrate the volume levels."

"What did he charge?" inquired a Frunge female sitting at the end of the table. She had kept so still to this point that John had almost taken her for a potted plant.

"Nothing," John said. "Fiona owes him one."

"Weight, the girl's health, Semmi's art," Myort ticked off on his talons. "You're sure there was nothing else?"

"We were in and out of his clinic in less than five minutes. Oh, he knew we were going to be on Aarden when Flower arrives and asked me to keep an eye open for Farling art. I guess he misses home or something."

This last statement was met by a chorus of groans and curses, and John realized it probably should have been his opener.

"All right, Farling art," the Grenouthian bellowed over the other speakers. "Each of us will cover the section set aside for our own species, plus one other that's not represented in our group. I'll take the Verlocks."

"Drazens," the Frunge woman said immediately.

"Hortens," the Dollnick whistled, and to John's implant, it carried the intonation of a curse.

"I guess I can cover the Fillinducks, but I'll be seeing triple by the end of the week," the Sharf said.

"All right, if that's the way you all want to play it," Myort growled, and he blew a short flame out his nostrils. "We don't meet again until somebody figures out what we're supposed to be doing. You all know the signal."

"I don't know the signal and I didn't get another section to cover," John said.

"I'll be doing Humans in addition to Huktras. You sit this one out."

"You dragged me in here to tell me I'm working for M793qK but you don't trust me to get it right?"

"We don't trust you to know Farling art from a hole in the ground," the Vergallian told him. "We're all artists and you're here selling reproductions. To each according to his abilities."

"We'll leave at ten-minute intervals so it's not obvious," the Sharf said, and then he dove through the curtain before any of the other aliens could move.

"It's out the back for me," Balri said, and she ducked under the rear curtain into the utilities path that ran between backing rows of booths.

"I was browsing next door," the Frunge said, and after untying a few loops, she slipped into the adjoining booth without causing any alarm.

The Dollnick shook his head at the antics of his colleagues. "Feels like ten minutes to me." He walked out the front, holding the curtain aside for Ellen to enter.

"Well, that was interesting," John said. "How much could you hear from the outside?"

"I cranked up the gain on my implant, but all I heard was you asking a fortune teller for help picking winners at a racetrack."

"That's my standard interference," Myort said, tapping a pendant he wore around his neck. It went from a glowing blue to a dull stone, indicating he'd just disabled it. "The real fortune teller won't be back for another hour in case the two of you wanted a little privacy."

"Wait a second," John said to the Huktra. "What was that about you being an artist?"

"Mixed media, glass and metal constructions. I was rather famous before I was recruited. Being known in the arts is a great cover for intelligence agents when they're first starting out."

"You gave up a career as an artist to be a spy?" Ellen asked.

"I'm older than you think," Myort replied. "One of the tricks to staying occupied through a long life is to remain open-minded about career options."

# Fourteen

"Without onions," Georgia told the owner of Burrito Planet. "The baby doesn't like them."

"Nursed four children myself and none of them could stand onion or garlic," the woman said as she started spooning ingredients from the steam table onto the large tortilla. "The girls refused my milk outright, the boys were fussy afterward."

"Is that your son making tortillas?"

"My youngest, the only one who doesn't look down on the family business. The other three all went off to universities as soon as they were old enough to be on their own. Running a food truck wasn't good enough for them."

"Is that what you call this kind of ship?" Georgia asked, looking past the counter to where the young man was cooking tortillas in a kitchen that would normally have been cargo space. "My husband owns a Sharf two-man trader, but this is the first festival we've gone to, other than Rendezvous, and I didn't see any food trucks there."

"The Traders Guild discourages food vendors from attending Rendezvous because there are cafeteria tents to raise money for charity," the woman explained. "Chicken dinners and burgers cooked by volunteers sell a lot better if there's no professional competition." She glanced up at Georgia. "Do you want sour cream instead of the house sauce?"

"Is the sauce spicy?"

"Drazens like it."

"I'll stick with sour cream," Georgia said hastily. "Do you mind if I ask how long you've been in the business?"

"Going on thirty years," the woman said. "Did I see a press ID hanging around your neck?"

"Galactic Free Press. I'm actually a freelancer, but I used to be the food reporter on Union Station and—"

"I thought I recognized you from the profile picture in your articles. I'm Josephina. Let me know if you need help with the spelling. I love the way you write about food."

"Would you be willing to do an interview?" Georgia asked. "I'd have to come back because it takes a few hours. I ate at food trucks every day when I attended the New University on Earth and I'm embarrassed to admit that I hadn't realized they were a business model on the tunnel network. My husband has been so busy working for the Human Empire that we've spent most of our time visiting human communities on alien worlds."

"Carlos," Josephina called back into the ship. "You're on the line for five minutes. I'm taking a break." Then she lifted a section of the counter and stepped out to join Georgia. "I'll give you a quick rundown while you eat and maybe that will save time when you come back. I'd love to see Burrito Planet reviewed in the Galactic Free Press, but I don't think I could manage a few hours of free time while the festival is going."

"I understand," Georgia said, taking a seat at one of the ubiquitous carbon fiber dining sets found all over the Aarden fairgrounds. "I guess part of your business model must be long stretches of travel followed by days of dawn-to-dusk work."

"In the case of the Aarden Arts Festival, it's going to be months of working flat out, but then we're planning a six-week vacation. Can I get you something to drink?"

"I have a water bottle in my bag. So what kind of ship is that? I don't recognize the type."

"It's a converted Frunge space bus," Josephina said. "They mainly use them at orbital construction sites or for the daily commute miners do to claims in asteroid belts. The design makes landing on planets very expensive, a stop at Earth takes a tenth off our fuel pack. That's why we look for long-running festivals or fairs. Anything less than three weeks and we'd be hard put to break even, but my understanding is that even though your Sharf fuel packs last longer, they're more expensive to replace. The bus has just enough oomph to be accepted as a tunnel craft, but it sleeps six in comfort, plus the kitchen and walk-in fridge."

"This is very good," Georgia responded after a moment's delay to swallow. "What other festivals do you work? Is there a circuit for long-run events with strong human attendance?"

"The Aarden Arts Festival is both new and the exception to the rule for the number of humans living locally and coming in from the tunnel network to participate," Josephina said with a smile. "All of the events we've worked since changing our focus to the festival circuit have catered to aliens. We're usually the only ones selling Mexican-style food. The trick is to incorporate local ingredients, even if we can't eat them ourselves."

"How do you test the recipes?" Georgia asked between bites.

"On the aliens. Don't laugh, you'll choke," she hastened to add. "When you're selling novelty food, it's more about presentation than taste. The trick is showing up early and testing combinations by offering free meals to the permanent fairground staff. Burritos, enchiladas, and tacos are ideal for experimenting with fillings as long as we stay away from Frunge worlds. And the new version of the All Species Cookbook is changing the business because now we can tap into the database of tribute recipes submitted by humans working on alien worlds."

"I didn't know aliens were so open to human cuisine thirty years ago."

"They weren't. The first two decades we were in business, our customer base was humans working on labor contracts. The aliens welcome outside food vendors to come in and spice things up for the contract workers, and we had a ten-year run working for a Dollnick caterer who covered our costs moving from world to world where they had humans employed. We only stumbled into the festival circuit after a six-month invited stint on a Drazen mining world."

"Did you hook up with one of their traveling choruses? I've heard that there are so many music festivals happening on the tunnel network that there's always one going on somewhere."

Josephina laughed again, the skin around her eyes crinkling. "There are always a hundred music festivals happening somewhere, maybe thousands," she corrected Georgia. "There's probably one happening all the time on any reasonably populated world. But they tend to run for an extended weekend or a holiday, which isn't long enough for our economics. What we learned on that Drazen world is that you can make a living selling human food to aliens, at least to Drazens, if you just punch it up a bit."

"They like heat," Georgia said, keeping it short so she could continue eating.

"I thought there was something wrong with my implant the first time a Drazen ordered an Aztec burrito and told me to hold everything except the chili sauce. Carlos was working with me, and he thought he was being funny asking the customer if he'd like to skip the tortilla and just get the chili sauce in a cup. The Drazen, you're not going to believe this, asked if he could get that with a straw." Josephina paused to give Georgia a chance to react, but the reporter had just taken another bite and was chewing. "It didn't take long to realize that we couldn't sell at our regular prices doing that, but it turned out that the Drazens will happily eat rice and beans as long as there are enough chili peppers thrown in."

"These are the best refried beans I've had in a long time," Georgia said. "Do you fry them in fat?"

"Olive oil, it reduces the bad cholesterol. I'll give you the nutrition sheet the next time you come. The Grenouthians and the Frunge won't eat anywhere without one, and the Vergallians always ask. Some fly-by-night operators have given food trucks a bad reputation, though the aliens seem to worry less about the kitchen and more about the ingredients. The Frunge don't eat grains and the Grenouthians don't eat meat. According to the introduction of the All Species Cookbook, it's a matter of tradition with both species, and they can safely digest almost everything we can eat."

"As the newest species on the block, we're kind of a least common denominator, or maybe it's most common—I get the two confused. All I know is we can't tolerate alien food, other than Vergallian vegan."

"Momma," a male voice called loudly, and both women looked over to see a line backing up in front of Burrito Planet.

"He's still not up to running the counter alone," Josephina said, rising from her seat. "I could give you a whole hour if you arrange with me ahead of time, but otherwise, this is the reality of my life."

"I'll stop again and we'll schedule something," Georgia said, carefully wrapping the loose foil over the remaining half of her burrito. She held it up and added, "I promised to bring my husband something."

Rather than exploring the rest of the independently operated restaurant ships that she now knew were properly termed food trucks, Georgia decided to head back to the booth to make sure that Larry was managing with James. She walked past Semmi and John's booths with a polite nod and a wave, and slipped in behind a couple of Drazens, perhaps a mother and a daughter, who were examining Larry's beads. Each of the aliens had a string of beads artfully wrapped around her tentacle.

"When you say handmade, do you mean handmade-handmade or Human-handmade," the older Drazen asked Larry.

"Handmade by humans," Larry replied.

"That's not what I meant. Humans have a reputation for labeling goods handmade if any part of the process was done by hand."

"I think it has to be fifty-one percent," the daughter chimed in.

"I can assure you that these beads are one hundred percent handmade," Larry said. "I visited the factory myself. They also sell hand-finished beads, which are smaller and less expensive, but I'm not displaying any of those here."

"Do you have an authentication hologram?" the mother asked. "If not for each bead, just a basic proof-of-process would do."

"I didn't realize that was a thing. Do other bead vendors have them?"

"The ones in your price range do. Without some sort of supporting evidence, I can't see paying more than half of what you're asking."

"Georgia," Larry called, spotting his wife behind the Drazens. "Can you check next door and see if Marco is there? I think I saw him taking video on his smartphone when we visited the factory."

"There's that word again," the daughter said. "The translation I get is an industrial facility full of machines. That doesn't sound very handmade."

"As I said, they also make hand-finished beads in the same building. It's a joint venture between human glass-workers who have been producing handmade beads for centuries, and a Frunge textile manufacturer that—"

"Frunge?" the mother interrupted. "Then they would be in the certified handmade directory. What's the name?"

"EarthBeads," Larry said. "I'm sorry, but I've never heard of the certified handmade directory."

"You can access it from any implant or information kiosk—it's one channel up from the booth directory," the daughter told him while the older Drazen stared off into space, obviously checking a heads-up display. "All of the big arts and crafts festivals subscribe to the database. It covers the large cooperatives, brands, and member listings from crafts organizations. It's cheaper for unaffiliated craftsmen of high-end handmade goods to capture holo or video of themselves making the pieces."

"Got it," the mother said, her eyes coming back into focus. "They just registered last cycle which means they haven't passed a review yet."

"Are all Drazen bead stringers as knowledgeable as the two of you?" Larry asked. "It's a new line of trade for me and I'm beginning to wonder if I'm in over my head."

Marco came running into the booth, pulled up a video on his smartphone, and passed it to the aliens. The pair of them watched for several minutes, at one point exchanging a significant look as a panning shot took in Larry and John, and at the end, the mother nodded.

"I'll accept it, though a holo would be better. Can I make a copy?"

"If you can figure out how," Larry said. "You track the provenance for every bead you buy?"

"We're professional bead stringers," the daughter explained as she did something to her own tab and held it close to Marco's phone. "We sell most of our creations, and a handmade necklace is only as authentic as the provenance of its weakest bead."

"Strings by Shinka and Tinka," the mother said. "We specialize in tentacle ornamentation, though I don't suppose you would know anything about that."

"Your little tab is so cute," the daughter said as she returned the phone to Marco, and even though the boy didn't understand Drazen, he intuited what he heard as a compliment and blushed. "Oh, I didn't know Humans changed colors like Hortens."

"So, do the beads come with their nests?" the older Drazen asked.

"Do you mean the velvet squares?" Larry asked. "They're only there to accentuate the colors with the case lighting. I don't have enough for all of the beads back at—"

he cut himself off, but their smiles told him that it was too late.

"Let's talk quantity," the mother said. "Now that I've seen the quality in person, I could put in a wholesale order with EarthBeads, have them delivered by EarthSent, and they'd be here before the end of the festival. But I have a weakness for helping a fellow entrepreneur and you're on the spot. Ten percent above cost?"

"I haven't put any thought into becoming a distributor, and I'm sure that EarthSent would charge a lot more than ten percent of the wholesale price to ship the beads halfway across the galaxy," Larry said. "I bought factory direct, and I had to sign a pledge not to sell below the catalog price, even if I'm having a liquidation sale. Besides, are you really willing to purchase a large enough quantity to get the wholesale pricing?"

"We should try them first to see how they sell," the daughter said to the mother. "I brought up the EarthBeads catalog while you were talking and the retail prices aren't that bad. Why don't we take a selection to string tonight and we can put them out tomorrow as a test?"

"Did I offer them the retail price?" Larry whispered to Georgia. "I was going to start at double and see where we ended up."

"It's a good markup for you, and they save on shipping," she whispered back.

"All right," the mother said. "We'll take all of the beads in this case with red highlights. And if that's a mini-register under the cloth, you don't have to worry about anybody doing a snatch and grab. Vergallian festival security is top-notch."

"I didn't notice it was covered," Larry said, removing the spit-up cloth draped over the mini-register and hanging it over the handle of the baby carriage. "How many beads do you make it?"

"Seventeen," the daughter said. "Why is the retail price point nine three creds? They should have rounded up."

"That's one point nineteen creds savings to us on the order," the mother said. "Don't complain."

"The prices must be translated from eBucks," Larry said. "I can't imagine it's on purpose so I'll drop them a note." The total of fifteen point eight one creds appeared in a hologram projected by the mini-register, and the older Drazen handed over her programmable cred and completed the voice authorization.

"Are you alright with paper?" Georgia asked, removing a small brown lunch bag from the supply under the table. "We have plastic, but we try to save them for the Frunge."

"I'll just string them," the daughter said, plucking a silvery object out of her sleeve. "I always carry a few threaded beading needles at festivals because you never know."

Larry opened the case and the Drazen girl deftly threaded the seventeen beads she'd identified with red highlights.

"You know," her mother said. "That would almost do as a major necklace as it is if you added some of those obsidian spacer beads the young Verlock couple were selling."

"Handmade spacer beads?" Larry asked. "Those must be expensive for the purpose."

"Verlocks have a way with working lava using the traditional volcanic method. If you've never seen them dancing around a lava flow with mandrels and making beads, it's a treat. They sell the least interesting ones as spacers."

As the Drazens moved off, Larry pulled a handful of new beads from the bucket under the table and began replacing the seventeen that had been sold. Georgia checked that the baby was still sleeping and moved the spit-up cloth to the pouch on the back of the stroller.

"How are things going in your booth?" she asked Marco, who had remained to watch the transaction.

The boy shook his head in the negative.

"No sales yet?" Larry asked, grabbing another handful of beads. "It looked like Semmi was getting plenty of interest, and I know I've seen visitors entering John's booth."

Marco sighed and pantomimed painting a picture. Then he stepped back and began pointing at different areas of the imaginary finished work while looking at his smartphone and moving his lips.

"You mean he has trouble describing the works to customers and he's reading from a cheat sheet?" Georgia guessed. "I wondered how he could manage to sell art."

"But they're reproductions," Larry said. "Wouldn't people shopping for that sort of thing already recognize them?"

Marco shook his head, and then in rapid succession, feigned a tentacle behind his neck with one arm, did a bunny-hop like a Grenouthian, and then took a few waddling steps holding his hands with the fingers interwoven in front of his waist like he had a big belly.

"You're saying that the shoppers are all aliens and they want to know about the originals."

The boy nodded again, and then he reached a little higher than his head, brought his hands down as if he was smoothing long hair, and tried to take a few steps with his hips swaying.

"And the female aliens all want to know more, like the Drazens who were just here," Larry said.

"No," Georgia jumped in when Marco shook his head. "He means that Fiona could do a better job but John isn't letting her."

Marco nodded energetically, grabbed Georgia's hand, and started pulling her out of the booth.

"You want me to tell him? It's not that simple with adults. John is older than I am and an experienced trader. I don't want to hurt his feelings."

"You're such a girl," Larry said with a laugh. "Come on, Marco, I'll tell him. Watch the store, Georgia."

"Hey," Fiona greeted them when they reached the front of John's booth with the whimsical 'Repro Man' signage the factory had provided. "If you're looking for his majesty, Myort just stopped by and led him off somewhere. It's just as well because he was scaring all of the customers away. I bet I sell a half a dozen paintings before he gets back."

"That's what Marco wanted me to talk to him about," Larry told her. "You know something about art?"

"I crammed it on the way here, and Ellen has been making me do a sort of high-school equivalency thing on Marco's teacher bot, so I've also had the Great Art of Earth Civilizations. John only knows about war history and stuff like that."

"What's that one?"

"*Girl with a Pearl Earring*?" Fiona answered without hesitation. "It's Johannes Vermeer, second half of the seventeenth century or thereabouts. Oil on canvas, Dutch Golden Age, and somebody made a movie of it in the film age."

"They made a movie of a painting?" Larry asked. "Like an authenticity thing?"

"You're getting your centuries mixed up. Film came way after oil paint, though some people think that Vermeer used a camera obscura in his work, which is kind of a stepping stone between the two media." Fiona took the canvas down from the wall and held it up right in front of Larry by the edges of the stretcher. "The movie was a dramatization of Vermeer's family life and that of an imagined model for the *Girl with the Pearl Earring.* The original went missing from a museum in the capital of the old European super state at some point after the Stryx opening and is referenced in the recent Grenouthian documentary. Would you like me to wrap it for you?"

Marco shot Larry a smug grin.

"Uh, that won't be necessary, but if you have any free time, you're welcome to take over at my booth. I can give you an hourly rate or commission."

"I think commission will be fine. Those beads will practically sell themselves."

# Fifteen

"I don't see what's so great about it," John said with a scowl. "Counting creds is something all traders do at the end of a busy day at a fair. I'll bet you could find billions of similar images with a simple search, and I can't even tell the denominations of the coins from those stacks."

"It's not supposed to be photorealistic," Myort told him. "We gave it a ribbon because of the way that Semmi captured the mix of worry and avarice in your expression. I'm not even a mammal and it comes through as clear as crystal."

"You think it's funny, don't you. Ellen already told me that the prize-winning art is going to be reproduced in a special supplement of the Galactic Free Press. They're pooling their resources with the news coverage of a dozen other species for the arts festival. I'm going to be famous around the galaxy as the face of greed."

"I wouldn't have recognized it was you if I hadn't known you were the only adult human male she had available as a model," the Huktra reassured him. "The interplay between the two emotions, the way she blended the light and the dark, that's what makes the portrait compelling. I won't be surprised if Semmi gets an honorable mention for Best Newcomer."

"You mean out of all of the representational paintings from all of the species displaying? I thought you said she's just a teenager."

"In terms of Tyrellian gryphons, she's not even old enough to speak in council, and in many ways, she acts like a typical teen. But making age comparisons between species is always tricky."

"She certainly eats like a teenager." John watched glumly as yet another alien posed for a selfie with Semmi and the painting. "And the title, what's that supposed to mean?"

"An Abundance," Myort translated into English. "You can't read it literally. Tyrellian includes prefixes for negation and reversal, and that's the closest I can get in Humanese. The title expresses that one man's pile of coins may be another man's partial payment on a debt. Think aerobic versus anaerobic, a prefix reversal like that. Semmi is saying that the dividing line between abundance and insufficient funds is all a question of context."

"I think she's just trying to get back at me for complaining about all the money she blew on renting anime last year. And you still haven't explained how you ended up as a judge."

"Just for Human Week. Festival organizers try to find judges from different backgrounds so that the prizes don't end up going to artists who merely represent the latest social movement popular in academia or with critics. I'm considered something of an expert on the culture of your species even though painting isn't my specialty."

"You told us you were famous in mixed media, but I'll believe it when I see it," John said. "Why aren't you showing at the festival?"

"I will be, and as a matter of fact, you can help me set up," Myort said. "A young relative of mine cleaned out my old studio and is rushing here in a borrowed ship. There was a delay finding a jump-carrier to a tunnel-network world, but she's landing in the short-term lot as we speak."

"What about my booth?"

"Fiona has things well in hand, and she can always ask Larry if there's a problem. From what I've seen, your reproductions sell better when you aren't there."

"Her implant is new enough that holding a conversation with aliens is still a thrill for her, and the enthusiasm comes through in her sales pitch," John said.

"Either that, or she did her homework and you didn't," Myort said, pushing John in the direction of the girl. "Tell her where you'll be, Larry too, and I'll congratulate Semmi while she's free."

It took the Huktra and the EarthCent Intelligence agent almost a half-hour to work their way through the crowds to the short-term parking area and locate the ship piloted by Myort's relative. They arrived just in time to see a delicately built version of Myort with pale blue skin engaged in a vociferous argument with the Vergallian military officer and her truthsayer partner who managed fair security. John couldn't recall ever seeing upper-caste Vergallians so close to losing their cool.

"How can I be of help?" Myort asked, interposing himself between his hissing relative and the Vergallians. "Is this about my unpaid parking tickets? I thought I cleared all of that up the last time I visited."

"What are you trying to pull here?" the older of the two Vergallians demanded as she pointed up at the impressive artwork on the side of the ship. "That's a Farling coat of arms, and now that I know the two of you are involved, I can guess whose it is."

"And is it against Vergallian law to transport art in a Farling ship?" the younger Huktra demanded belligerently, a few flames escaping with her words.

"Kyor, let me do the talking," Myort remonstrated his relative. "It's like this, officers. When M793qK moved his medical practice to Flower a few years ago, he called in a favor and asked me to mothball his old Sharf cabin cruiser at my place in the desert on Huktra Sixteen. It's a mere pleasure ship, completely unarmed, and the only Farling thing about it is the paint job."

"I've never heard of any Farling owning a second-hand alien ship, much less one of M793qK's rank," the officer said. "I know Sharf cabin cruisers, and that's an obsolete interplanetary model from the generation where the fuel packs became unstable on depletion and had to be recalled. I think somebody painted that Farling coat of arms on there recently and did a little artistic sandblasting to make it look old."

"Are you accusing me of lying?" the young Huktra female growled, struggling to break free of Myort's restraining arms and tail like a child whose sense of honor had been offended. "I've never even met a Farling."

"She's hiding something, but her emotions are too strong for me to get a fix on it," the truthsayer said in frustration. "I suspect she's worked herself up on purpose just to screen me."

"Why all of the excitement over a paint job?" Myort asked calmly. "You're welcome to inspect the ship, of course, but you won't find anything other than a collection of mixed-media works that I held out from the market when I changed careers. My clutch-mate's granddaughter has been pushing me to free up the studio space for years, and I finally decided that the time has come to let go of the past."

"And I was sick of looking at this stupid ship parked out in the desert," Kyor added.

"Let's do that inspection," the officer said. She stared off into space for a bare second, obviously informing her subordinates of her status over her implant, and then gestured for the younger Huktra to lead the way.

As a family excursion craft, the Sharf cabin cruiser was smaller than a two-man trader. The command chair looked like it might have been modified to accommodate a Farling resting on his carapace, but John thought that the Vergallians were probably right about Myort pulling a fast one. The officer obviously thought the same as she strode directly to the chair and jumped on the backrest, which had been lowered to almost parallel with the deck. It held her weight, barely.

"I hope you packed all of these in foam," Myort said to his relative as he released the cargo netting rigged to enclose half of the small ship's cabin space. "Where did you find all of the boxes?"

"Old cactus flower crates," Kyor said. "And I used dried grass rather than foam. You only sent enough money to cover the jump carrier and tunnel fees."

"Two hours," the Vergallian officer declared. "I've arranged for this ship to be moved to the long-term lot, and if you don't have your cargo unloaded by then, you're out of luck."

"Which long-term lot?" Myort asked.

"There's a space next to your Human minion's Grenouthian four-decker that we've been holding open against your relative's arrival—it makes it easier to keep an eye on you both. If you don't get this sorry excuse for a ship and its provocative paint job off this planet the day that Flower arrives, your parking fee jumps to five hundred creds a day. I don't know what you and M793qK are up to, but if you think you're going to involve us in the affairs of the Farling hierarchy, I've got a prison asteroid waiting for a mixed-media artist and his Human assistant."

"I don't know anything about art," John protested, and then realized this didn't sit well with his cover as an art dealer.

"My file on you makes that eminently obvious." The Vergallian officer headed for the exit ramp, accompanied by the truthsayer. "Two hours, gentlemen."

John waited until the Vergallians were out of the ship before turning on Myort and his now-giggly relative. "What was that all about? I'm already in enough trouble with security just for knowing you and M793qK. I'm going to end up banned from Fleet Vergallian space."

"I can understand why they're so upset," Myort said, passing John a crate. "Kyor has that effect on everybody."

"Do not," the young Huktra said, settling down on the sagging command chair that now resembled something closer to an acceleration couch. "Let me know when you finish."

"You aren't going to help?" John asked, shifting the heavy crate to get a better grip.

"I did all of the packing and loading, and I'm sure he's going to stick me with the unpacking as well."

"There seem to be more boxes than should have been necessary to move my remaining works," Myort said, hefting four crates in one go.

"I brought a few of my own pieces," Kyor said. "You didn't think I was going to come all the way to the Aarden Arts Festival and not show."

The Huktra spymaster shook his head in mock despair as he and John tramped down the ramp. A floating cargo sledge had materialized next to the ship, undoubtedly ordered by the Vergallian officer to keep them moving, and in less than an hour, the job was finished. Only then did Kyor rise from her nap and join them.

"I recognize the beetle in the center," John said, pointing at the Farling coat of arms, "but what's with the shark guys, the dragons, and the lobster-looking things around the outside?"

"Members of the Farling Empire," Myort explained. "M793qK was high enough in the hierarchy to have allies at the governmental level from all of the species shown in his coat of arms. It's more complicated than what you see, just like his name is a much-shortened form of his life history."

"He made me listen to it once," Kyor said. "It went on for days."

"But you just told the truthsayer you've never even met a Farling."

"I lied. The best way to keep them confused is to lie about everything so they can't create a baseline for comparisons."

"It's been a while since I used one of these," Myort said, peering at the sledge's control yoke. "John?"

"Not a type I've ever seen before," the EarthCent Intelligence agent replied.

"Hopeless," Kyor said, grabbing the yoke with her tail and heading for the Verlock section of the festival grounds.

"Why aren't you showing in the Huktra section, or our section, like Semmi?" John asked. "Were all of the booth spaces taken?"

"Art requires the proper context to be appreciated, and Humans aren't there yet with mixed media," Myort said. "My primary materials are molten stones and metals, and the Verlocks are the only other tunnel network species to accomplish much there, though their works are a bit abstract for my taste."

"Maidens on their first mating flight is more his style, and he got a deal on sharing a Verlock booth," Kyor said over her shoulder.

"I do appreciate the female form, but as usual, your generation completely misses the point of action art. I never once worked from a hologram or video."

"I hope that doesn't mean you were some weird Huktra who flew around in a long raincoat peeping on young lovers," John said.

"Raincoats are a Human thing," Myort said. "Unlike Kyor, I did my rough work on the spot, returning to the studio only for the finishing touches. Do you imagine it's easy working with molten metal while flying alongside an amorous couple on a stormy night? I can't tell you how many times I've been struck by lightning. Now that I recall, it's one of the reasons I took a break from art to concentrate on intelligence work. Spying is safer."

"You mean you created your mixed-media whatever on the spot?"

"Wherever my subjects were found. I did a series about miners on the job that left me feeling claustrophobic for decades." Myort let out a nostalgic sigh. "One of my biographers hypothesized that the reason I sculpted so many bakers in the latter stage of my career was that they work inside where it's warm and dry and I didn't have to chase them around."

"The truth hurts," Kyor contributed. "Which aisle?"

"Look for Brynsal, I sublet space from her. She does the skinny Verlocks with elongated arms and legs in sintered pumice."

"I've never seen a skinny Verlock in my life," John said.

"One suspects they see themselves differently than you do," Myort said. "Think Alberto Giacometti."

"Doesn't sound like a Verlock name."

"Twentieth-century Swiss. You could at least read the *For Humans* book about Earth's art."

"Fiona read it so I don't have to," John said. "Is Brynsal in the game?"

"Do you mean is she in the intelligence business?" Myort asked. "She was, but then her sculptures got so popular that she couldn't afford to split her time. You never know how long the public's attention will last."

"So speaks the voice of experience," Kyor commented, drawing an involuntary laugh from John.

"I was at the height of my popularity when an old friend recruited me to join Huktra Intelligence," Myort said indignantly. "It's typical for the prices of living artists to go through cycles, and a few failures to sell out the gallery or meet pre-auction estimates do not spell the end of a career."

"No, but you could read the writing on the wall."

"Isn't that one of our expressions?" John asked the young Huktra.

"Your translation implant probably picked an appropriate idiom to substitute," she replied. "I take it that's Brynsal."

The sculptures on display in the Verlock's booth were so visually compelling that John stopped in his tracks and stared. He hadn't expected that the sintered pumice representations could capture the essence of the species, but somehow the slender elongated figures gave the impression of moving and talking in slow motion, and the proportions spoke to a mastery of mathematics that he could only guess at.

"She's not half bad," Myort said to John, and then moved past the sledge to greet the Verlock. "Brynsal, it's great to see you. How long has it been?"

"Long enough for the hundred creds you borrowed from me in the Imperial Bar to have little grand-creds, or great-grand creds, depending on their fertility," the artist replied at an acceptable cadence. "Did you bring it, or just your leftover inventory?"

"This is my young relation, Kyor, who will be showing my work and a few pieces of her own, and this is—"

"John," the Verlock interrupted. "I may be on extended leave but I still keep up with the known-associates lists for a select group of troublemakers. So, do you have my hundred creds?"

Myort reached in his pouch and removed a strange-looking coin with five holes of various sizes around the edge. "Can you break a Huktra Double Dragon? I've been meaning to go by one of the currency exchanges but I haven't had the time."

"Let me see it," Brynsal said. Moving in the ponderous manner of Verlocks, she accepted the coin from Myort, held it up to the sun, and then bit it. "When you pay me for the sublet, you can have this back," she said, dropping the coin in a purse worn crossways across her body. "Your timing is terrible, as usual. As you can see, the festival porters haven't moved my pieces to the featured artist display area yet, but you can unload your sledge and put all of the crates under the tables."

"When do you expect the porters?" Kyor asked. "I arranged ahead of time to be discovered by a few critics and I need to get set up."

"Sounds like somebody in the family understands the art business," the Verlock said. "The porters are on their lunch break and will be here soon. You'll be set up before the evening rush."

With Kyor helping, and the sledge parked right in front of the booth, it only took ten minutes to unload. As he placed the last crate under a display table, John noticed that each of the sculptures had a small blue stone resting on the base.

"What's the significance of the little blue stones?" he asked the Verlock.

"They indicate that the piece is already sold," Brynsal told him. "To be a featured artist at the Aarden Arts Festival, you have to be present in person and sell over eighty percent of your work without pre-arrangement, though some aliens have been known to cheat," she added with a sidelong glance at Myort. "I sold all but one of my pieces during Verlock Week, during which I also received the Best Sculptor award."

"Where is it?" Myort demanded.

"My award? I only brought it up to annoy you," she said. "I don't believe in showing prizes and ribbons for fear they will prejudice the first impression visitors have of my work."

"I meant, where's the piece that didn't sell?"

Brynsal shuffled over to a table holding elongated Verlock figures which stood as tall as a grown Dollnick and returned with a much shorter piece that had been concealed behind one of the legs of a full-sized sculpture.

"It was an experiment," she admitted. "I visited an open academy world to give a lecture some time back and I saw a Human pointing up at the sky when a volcanic plume was overhead."

"Your model was too skinny to start with," Kyor said, her reptilian eyes squinting as she tried to make out the details. "What do you use as a binder for the sintered pumice?"

"A six-part epoxy," Brynsal said. "The result is almost as workable as sandstone, but with a custom color profile and no crumbling issues. It's as hard as iron when the epoxy is fully set."

"It looks like a short spear with a face that's been squeezed in a vise," Myort said. "It's never easy working with other species as models."

"I like it," John said. "It reminds me of the way I felt as a boy when I saw a storm rolling in."

"Then it's yours," Brynsal told him, thrusting the sculpture into his hands. "Here come the porters, so hold onto it while they get my exhibit moved."

A minute later, John was still trying to figure out if he was more amazed by the Verlock's gift or the speed at which the Vergallians had emptied her booth. There was a white-gloved porter for each piece on display and they all knew their assignments. The smallest Vergallian, a young teen, was left empty-handed by Brynsal's impulsive gift, and shot John a nasty look before leaving. The Verlock sculptor followed immediately after.

"Thank you," John called after the departing Verlock, realizing that there was no point in arguing with the alien over a gift, especially an alien who had been involved in intelligence work. "I owe you one."

"You're going to owe everybody one the way you're going," Myort said. "Now put that down and help us get my work set up. We have a meeting to attend afterward."

"What meeting?"

"The known-associates-of-M793qK meeting," the Huktra said, allowing an amused belch of flame to escape his snout. "I made the first move, the Vergallians have responded, and now we need to coordinate his grand arrival."

"What grand arrival? Would you mind telling me what this is all about?"

"I'd have to figure it out myself first and that wouldn't be any fun. Sometimes in this game, all you can do is act according to everyone else's expectations and wait to see what happens."

"That doesn't sound like much of a strategy to me," John said. "Whatever happened to planning ahead?"

"We do that too," Myort told him as Kyor began setting out her own pieces in the prime aisle-facing locations. "Nobody likes surprises in the intelligence business. When the other side has it wrong, it's best to adjust your operations so they get it at least half right. Saves everyone involved a lot of pain."

# Sixteen

The Drazen completed his close examination of Manet's *A Bar at the Folies-Bergère* and asked, "Can you guarantee that this was produced without automation or holographic aid?"

"I can show you the authenticity video on my tab," Fiona offered, looking around to see where she'd left it. "And I've never even heard of holographic aid. How does that work?"

"You know, projecting a hologram of the original work and then filling in the spaces with the right colors."

"Paint by numbers?" She located the tab leaning against the side of John's mini-register and swept it to life. "No. I was in the factory and the artists all worked from full-size photographic prints. And they were real artists, not just copyists."

Fiona used the tab's camera to capture the code on the back of the canvas which brought up the associated authentication video. The Drazen watched for a couple of minutes, nodded, and asked, "Where's the flaw you told me about?"

"The top hat of the gentleman behind the barmaid's shoulder in the far background is tilted to the right instead of the left," Fiona said, pointing without touching the canvas. "It was Manet's last major work, and many consider it his best."

"How many of them do you have?"

"Six. We started with seven but I sold one yesterday."

"Quantity discount?"

Fiona shook her head, smiling gently.

"Well, the reflection is perfect for my purposes, though it would have been better if all of her fingers were visible. Wrap it up and I'll take the spares as well. Now, what's with this one showing the woman facing the wrong way in a boat?"

"Renoir, *La Yole*, or *The Skiff*," Fiona told him. "And that's how rowboats work on Earth—you face the opposite direction."

"So the second woman is there to tell the first woman where she's going?" the Drazen asked. "It seems like an inefficient design."

"I think they're friends taking a pleasure trip. There are plenty of representations of a single person rowing a boat in Earth's art. I guess they check over their shoulder when they get near shore."

"Strange, but unquestionably Human. How many of them do you have?"

"Just the one on display."

"Wrap it up," the Drazen said. He moved on to the last painting he hadn't viewed and turned away immediately with a sour expression on his face.

"Botticelli," Fiona told him. "*Pallas and the Centaur*. You're the third visitor today who's reacted that way so I'm thinking of replacing it with something else."

"You can't please everybody," the Drazen said, producing a programmable cred. "You can deliver the paintings today?"

"The duplicates are all back on our ship, but for a three thousand cred order, I'm sure we can work something out," Fiona said, keying the amount into the mini-register. "If you need more copies we can probably have them delivered before the festival is over, though we won't be here that long."

"The way your stock is selling, I'll be surprised if you last another week," the Drazen said. He gave the mini-register his voice confirmation and passed a business chit to Fiona. "I'm always looking for gallery assistants who know how to sell. If you're ever on Void Station, look me up."

"Sounds like you made another conquest," Ellen told the girl after the Drazen left with his paintings.

"I didn't see you come back," Fiona said, turning away to hide her blush at the compliment. "How was your meeting?"

"Not worth the Stryxnet charges, but I'm not the one paying, so I shouldn't complain. Georgia isn't back yet? She left before me because it was time for the baby to eat." Ellen did a quick circuit of the booth, marveling at all of the empty spaces that used to hold paintings. "Did you send John back to the ship to get replacements? He's going to want to keep you in the booth full-time when he sees how many paintings you've sold. I'll tell him that I need your help with the piece I'm writing."

"Thanks. I enjoyed today, and the paintings have been selling themselves, but it's all getting a bit weird. A Dollnick acting as a buyer's agent for some prince bought all of the nudes."

"Why would a Dollnick be interested in Human nudes?"

"I'm glad I missed the first part of that conversation," Georgia said as she approached, bouncing a little on her feet in an attempt to get a good burp out of the baby over her shoulder. "Maybe the prince does business with humans and thinks they would make good gifts."

"Did he understand that they're reproductions?" Ellen asked Fiona.

"That's the first thing I explain to everybody who enters the booth," the girl said. "And none of them have bought without checking at least one authentication video first, though nobody has watched the whole thing."

A Frunge with her hair vines twined in a fashionable updo on an elaborate trellis entered the booth and checked the tab she was carrying for instructions. "I'm looking for pre-Raphaelite reproductions," she said.

"All I have left is a scaled-down Waterhouse, *The Lady of the Shalott*, and technically, the pre-Raphaelite Brotherhood had broken up before it was painted," Fiona told her. "That's the only reason I still have it, because an artificial person who cleaned me out of that school earlier wasn't sure it qualified as pre-Raphaelite."

"Was he working for one of us?" the Frunge asked.

"He mentioned being employed by another species but didn't say which." Fiona removed the tablecloth disguising a large shipping box with internal dividers that held twenty canvases on stretchers when it was full. There were a scant half-dozen left, and she easily located the Waterhouse she hadn't had a chance to hang in an open space after serving several customers in rapid succession. "It's a scene from a famous Tennyson poem that—"

"Human art isn't my thing," the Frunge interrupted. "I'm just doing a favor for somebody." The alien made a cursory examination of the painting and asked, "Do you have authentication video?"

"Right here," Fiona said, capturing the code from the back of the canvas and handing over her tab.

"All right," the alien said a few minutes later. "I'll pay the suggested retail price. When will you be getting more in?"

"I'm afraid this is it for our trip to Aarden, but if you want to place an order for—"

"My friend will have to do that," the Frunge cut her off, and then checked her instructions again. "Are you sure you don't have a Cowper or two in the back? I was specifically asked to look out for a work titled *Vanity*."

"We had two of those, but the artificial person bought both of them," Fiona said apologetically. "He offered to pay double if I could get him another Rossetti titled *Lady Lilith*, but we only had the one."

"Do you have an image of it on your tab?"

The girl swiped back a few screens and showed the pre-Raphaelite painting with its highly detailed depiction of the model's luxurious hair being combed out in front of a hand mirror.

The Frunge shook her head in frustration. "That would have been perfect," she said, handing over a programmable cred. "I'll make a note of it and tell my friend."

Fiona keyed in the amount and was surprised when the buyer responded to the voice authentication prompt with, "Temporary user, I'm on the list." The transaction went through, Ellen wrapped the painting in plastic instead of paper in deference to Frunge sensitivities, and the three women watched as the buyer disappeared into the crowd with *The Lady of the Shalott* held high.

"Have they all been like that?" Georgia asked. "I didn't get the impression that she had much interest in art."

"Varies," Fiona said with a shrug. "Some of the buyers, like that Frunge woman and the artificial person, were clearly acting on instructions. I suspect the only reason they came in person was to confirm the authentication video. Others seemed very interested in the art, but more in the subjects than the technique. There was a Horten who got really excited by the religious-themed Renaissance art, and a Dollnick who bought a cricket painting carried it off in all four arms like he was afraid somebody was going to try to take it from him."

"Cricket?" Ellen asked.

"The one with the guys in the field dressed in white uniforms playing a game that looked kind of like baseball."

"Baseball?"

"You had to have grown up on Earth," Georgia said. She gave James a final jog on her shoulder to see if anything else would come up, and then moved the drowsy baby to the carrier she was wearing. "I must have gathered enough material for a half-dozen easy food articles and I've got two interviews scheduled. How's the art story going? Did the syndicated journalists on the Stryxnet call say anything interesting after I left the meeting?"

"Lena, the girl who was working with Fiona on the Proxy Shoppers story, was able to figure out that all of the purchases were being held in a container at the elevator stalk for shipment. She learned from an employee there that the first container they filled went up to orbit two weeks ago, but she couldn't determine what happened to it next."

"What about all of the other syndicated journalists?" Georgia asked. "Did any of them follow-up on the archival research you had me doing?"

Ellen shook her head again. "A few feel-good stories for the Arts section, but nobody uncovered evidence of the aliens trying to break into the culture markets on Earth by imitating what our own creative people are doing. If anything, the most successful cultural imports from the tunnel network species have been products like the Grenouthian news and Vergallian dramas that didn't exist on Earth before the Stryx opened the planet."

"Earth didn't have news channels featuring wars and disasters a century ago?" Fiona asked skeptically.

"From what I've seen in the archives, they mainly talked about politics and culture wars, a twenty-first-century thing where everybody got angry at anybody who didn't agree with them, and it repeated endlessly," Georgia said. "The Grenouthians will report from anywhere in the galaxy as long as they have compelling visuals. There are always wars happening somewhere, stars going nova, space stations spinning out of control."

"How about the trademark issues that you guys were talking about the other day, like with EarthScent candles and EarthSent package delivery?"

"As near as we can tell, those are designed to cash in on aliens who are sympathetic towards EarthCent," Ellen explained. "John already heard back from his boss about the legal standing, and we never registered for sound-alike trademarks, which are critical when translations of proper names come into play. They've retained an alien intellectual property attorney to get the claims in for the Human Empire before somebody starts selling HewMan Empire T-shirts showing a guy with an axe, or HueMan Empire body paint."

"So all of that talk about aliens taking over our culture to conquer Earth with soft power was just paranoia?" Fiona asked.

"It looks that way at the moment, though prices of art produced on Earth have been on the rise, and we'll be publishing a few stories about that. It's the famous pieces that have seen the greatest price jumps, but according to one of the draft articles from the news syndicate, alien visitors are the primary buyers of contemporary art in all of the main tourist centers."

"Larry got tickets for the Human Roast in the central food court tonight," Georgia said. "He says they do one for each species in their corresponding week. If you're still willing to watch our booth, Fiona, could I hire you to babysit for a few hours at the same time?"

"You're willing to pay me for both?" Fiona asked.

"Of course, they're two different jobs."

"Is it okay if I invite Marco and Semmi?"

"Doesn't Semmi have to watch her own booth?" Georgia asked.

"She sold out after getting the Best Human Newcomer prize, and the festival is sending staff later today to move all of her paintings to Winner's Row, or whatever they call it," Fiona said. "I think Semmi is kind of burnt out from all that rush painting and posing for selfies with buyers so she'll probably just sleep."

"You have to come along and bring John," Georgia said to Ellen. "He can help Larry explain the alien jokes to me."

"Sounds good, but I may be late getting there myself," Ellen said. "There's another press conference this evening, and I'm hoping to talk with some of the alien arts correspondents who attend about extending our cooperation after the festival. The Galactic Free Press has a good relationship with the Grenouthian Network, thanks to their presence on Union Station, but this fair is the first time we've clubbed resources with news services of the other species."

"Can I help you?" Fiona asked, jumping to her feet as an alien who resembled a giant beetle strutted into the booth, balanced upright on its lowest pair of limbs. "All of our reproductions are hand-painted by human artists on Earth, and I have authentication video for every piece."

"As you're working for M793qK, I'll give you a little piece of advice," the Farling rubbed out on its speaking legs. "It's all fun and games when you've got the Stryx to hide behind, but let me remind you that Aarden isn't a member of the tunnel network, even though the infestation of Humans on this world was enough to establish a connection. And tell that Huktra joker that the Fleet Vergallians take a dim view of intentional provocations staged in their space."

"Who are you?" Ellen demanded, but the alien had said its piece and strode off without a backward glance. "I wonder what that was all about?"

"Maybe it mistook you for John," Georgia said. "We probably all look alike to a giant beetle."

"I got an image of him with my implant," Fiona said. "Ugh, I wish I hadn't because it's superimposed over my vision now. How do I send it to storage?"

"It's an option on your heads-up display," Ellen said. "Good job, I didn't even think of that."

"I got the impression he was speaking to all of us, not just Ellen, so I don't think he had her confused with John," Georgia said. "Maybe he thinks all of the humans at the art festival are working for M793qK."

"How do you know it's a he?"

"Didn't you see the blue fringing around the green carapace pattern?" Fiona asked. "M793qK pointed it out to me when I asked him how to tell the difference between male and female Farlings."

Marco ran into the booth, skidded to a halt, and began rubbing his forefingers together under his chin as if they were speaking legs.

"He's gone, and he wasn't friends with M793qK."

The boy nodded, did a quick count of the remaining canvases, and looked in the shipping crate to see how many were left there. He turned back to Fiona with a wide grin and began clapping.

"And she sold a number of the copies back at the ship that we'll have to deliver today," Ellen said. "Have you seen John?"

Marco flapped his arms, wagged a non-existent tail, and then exhaled while moving his hands away from his mouth and spreading his fingers widely.

"Flying, long tail, fire-breathing," Fiona interpreted. "He's with Myort."

"Did you just come from them?" Ellen asked.

Marco nodded, thought for a moment, and then shaped an invisible mound of sand on the floor before making a sort of rumbling sound and miming something coming out of the top and running down the sides.

"Verlock," Fiona said. "They're both at Myort's booth in the Verlock section. I still feel kind of bad about asking John to leave this morning, but it's easier for me to work if he isn't watching."

"I'm sure he understands," Ellen said, "and he'll be thrilled with the results. Maybe art sales is your natural calling."

"I just crammed a bit of art history, and selling to these aliens is as easy as pushing out ice cream during a heat wave in Manhattan. He seems so worried about money lately that I'm glad I can help."

Marco nodded his agreement with this statement and made an imaginary stack of coins.

"You're referring to Semmi's painting," Ellen said, taking the obvious clue. "I want both of you to understand that John isn't worried about money for its own sake, and we both have well-paid jobs. He's just afraid that if you decide to leave us, Fiona, he won't be able to pay you for your share of the ship all at once. The same is true for Semmi, and she gave Marco half of her share. We want you all to stay with us, but not to feel that you're stuck because of your investment in the ship."

"That's—may I help you?" Fiona interrupted herself as a Fillinduck entered the booth. The other two members of the alien's trio remained outside, their duller feathers a contrast to the leader's brightly colored covering.

"Renoir, *La Yole,*" the Fillinduck demanded, though if he had been consulting notes, they must have been on his heads-up display.

"I'm sorry, I sold the last one just before you came," the girl told him. "Do you have a particular interest in the Impressionists, or perhaps boating scenes?"

"How much is that one?" the alien asked, pointing at Wood's *American Gothic,* with its iconic presentation of an aging pair of Midwestern farmers, the male holding a pitchfork like a soldier on parade.

"I'll just have to check the catalog," Fiona said. She found the piece without difficulty and seemed surprised by what she learned. "It's only three hundred and twenty-five creds, and I have the authentication video loaded if you'd like to see it."

The Fillinduck grunted, accepted the tab, and continued increasing the playback speed until it seemed impossible to the humans that he could be processing the visual data.

"I suppose that's a fair price," he said, and gestured to the second tallest member of his trio, who then entered the booth. The female rummaged in her purse for a moment and produced a few hundred-cred coins, a twenty, and a five. "We'll take it with us."

"Can I interest you in any other Modernist paintings?"

"Galaxies, no! One is more than enough." He shot Ellen a disgusted look as she began wrapping it in plastic. "Do we look like Frunge to you? I want the opaque paper wrapper so nobody sees us with it."

The Fillinduck watched closely as Fiona and Ellen wrapped the reproduction of *American Gothic* in brown paper, perhaps worried the humans would pull a switch. He accepted the package and then quickly passed it to the smallest of the trio to carry as if he couldn't get it out of his hands fast enough.

"He was even weirder than the Farling," Georgia said after the aliens left, unconsciously nuzzling her baby's head as if to remind herself that the universe hadn't gone mad. "How much do you want to bet he's going to burn it?"

"Three hundred and twenty-five creds to burn a copy?" Ellen asked. "Not a chance. He started by asking for a Renoir, and even I know that the Impressionists and Modernists had completely different philosophies. There must be a connection that we're missing."

"I've been keeping a list of who bought what, so by the time all of our inventory is sold, maybe a pattern will come clear," Fiona said. She turned to Marco. "Can you tell John there are orders to deliver and that we're closing the booth early?"

The boy nodded and fled at full speed into the crowded aisle the way only a thirteen-year-old could run.

"Can John interpret Marco's version of sign language as easily as you do?" Georgia asked the girl. "How is he going to relay the message?"

"Myort's there, and he's pretty sharp. If worse comes to worst, Marco can type it out on his smartphone and show the screen to John. He just doesn't like to for some reason."

"And still not a word?"

"You heard him do an impression of a volcanic eruption earlier, and he laughs pretty easily now," Fiona said. "M793qK said he'll start speaking again when he's ready."

# Seventeen

"Is this the first time the two of you have let somebody else watch the baby?" John asked. "You both look like you could use a drink."

"We let my parents babysit when we were on Earth, and Larry is probably more worried about his beads," Georgia said. "No alcohol for me while I'm nursing."

"I'm not worried about the beads," Larry said. "Fiona will probably get a better price than I could. I don't know if she has what it takes to be a trader, but when it comes to selling for cash, she's a closer. And Georgia brought her smartphone so Fiona can use the walkie-talkie function to call us if something goes wrong."

"I keep forgetting they can do that," John said, shifting uncomfortably on the stackable carbon fiber chair at the small table. He looked around the central food court at the other guests waiting for the action to begin and didn't see any other humans. "I wonder what's keeping Ellen? The Vergallians run a tight ship, and the press conference should be wrapping up by now."

"She mentioned to me that she was hoping to spend a little social time with the journalists covering the arts festival for alien news organizations," Georgia said. "I think she's jealous of the relations you have with intelligence agents from the other species."

A ripple of snorts and laughs flowed through the audience as the worst-dressed Vergallian any of them had ever seen took to the improvised stage. He wore a yellow sports jacket over a black button-down shirt, white pants with a blue stripe running up the leg, and open-toed sandals with high heels. The amateur comic stood silently with a tragic look on his face, milking the initial reaction to his appearance. Then he launched into a story about how he was just back from a visit to Earth because somebody had told him it was the place to shop for cheap custom-tailored suits.

"So the Humans have this thing that goes around the neck," the Vergallian continued, pulling a rolled-up silk tie out of his pocket. "The guy who sold it to me didn't know exactly how it worked because he had a clip-on himself. Being an artist, I thought, 'Easy enough. I'll look at some portraits from Earth and find out how this thing goes.' So here are the options I came up with, and I want you to help me choose."

"He's even better than the clown I saw making balloon animals at a birthday party," Georgia said as the Vergallian somehow twisted and knotted the tie to look like everything from a ruffled collar to the choker-bow of a racy cocktail waitress—all to the loud appreciation of the audience. "Is it really the same tie every time, or is he doing sleight-of-hand?"

"It's black on one side and white on the other, and I think he turned it inside-out once to get the red," John said. "I saw a Drazen do a similar shopping-on-Earth act at the last ISPOA convention I went to, but she did it with hats."

The Vergallian wrapped up by fashioning the tie into a leash and leading himself off the stage to the thunderous reaction of the audience.

"I get the humor, but when I bought the tickets for a Human Roast, I thought we were going to an Earth-style cookout," Larry said. "I've noticed quite a few of the aliens looking our way and pointing."

A heavily tattooed Horten took the stage carrying a guitar with a harmonica mounted on an attachment. He looked around the small stage, then turned to somebody out of sight in the wings and asked, "Where do I plug in?"

"Your instruments are acoustic," a slender Horten female who was obviously part of the act called back. "That visit to Earth rotted your brain."

"I keep forgetting," the musician said, and then went into a routine about visiting Earth on a fact-finding mission for the tunnel network subcommittee responsible for an obscure corner of musical copyright law. The problem, he went on to inform the audience, was with the other aliens in the group, all of whom had difficulties pronouncing various sounds in Humanese. They insisted on attending live performances and then competed on singing what they'd heard.

"There was a Frunge who prided himself on mastering Human pronunciation, but he always made a 'gee' sound for 'be,'" the Horten continued, and then performed a credible version of a cover artist singing *Tangled up in Glue*. When the applause died down, the comic drew a small glass tube of white powder from his pocket and shook it out on the top of his harmonica. "And we couldn't help noticing how many performers relied on stimulants." He snorted the line of whatever it was, sneezed, and then crooned a soulful *Coke Gets in My Eyes*.

"I can't believe how good everybody's translation implants are," Georgia said. "They must be mapping the routine to something in context for each alien culture or it wouldn't be funny at all."

"Preloaded," Myort told her, settling heavily onto the seat next to John. The chair flexed under the Huktra's bulk but didn't give. "Stand-up performances for a multi-species audience like this always have a data dump available on the implant's local color channel. And Ellen is going to be late."

"You were at the press conference?" John asked.

"The journalists nominated me as the 'Blast from the Past' artist of the week," the Huktra said as a nervous-looking Drazen female took the stage. "It's not exactly a compliment, but all publicity is good publicity in the art game. Isn't anybody drinking?"

"I was just offering to buy a round," John said. "Juice, Georgia?"

"Or tea, whatever they have."

"One beer," Larry said. "I want to refill the display cases before we turn in. Fiona has probably sold half of the beads by now."

"Can you loan her to me?" Myort asked John. "It's not dignified for an artist my age to sell his own works, and Kyor is only interested in pushing her pieces."

"You can ask her, but I don't think we'll be staying much longer," John said. "I expect the stock of reproductions I bought to be gone by lunch tomorrow. We may just head back up to Flower and save on the tunnel toll."

"—and that's when I realized that every woman in the boutique was trying to pass as Vergallian," the Drazen concluded her story, her eyes on the only table whose occupants had talked right through the performance. "But I see we have some Humans here tonight with something important to say, so why don't we find out what it is?"

"Drinks are on me," Myort said, rising from his seat and disappearing with surprising speed.

The Drazen arrived and thrust her fist with the top thumb out like a microphone in front of John's face. "First time at the Aarden Arts Festival?" she asked.

"Uh, yes," he said into her thumb, and was surprised to hear his amplified voice coming out of hidden speakers.

"I've got a joke for you. Knock, knock."

"Who's there?" he asked reflexively.

"Interrupting Drazen."

"Interrupting Dra—"

"SHUT UP WHILE I'M DOING MY BIT," she shouted before he could finish his response, drawing a huge laugh from the audience. "Humans," the Drazen continued on her way back to the stage. "Can't live with them, can't kill them all because the Stryx will get upset."

"Well, that was pretty funny from the other side of the room," Myort said when he returned to their table with a tray holding a pitcher of beer, two empty glasses, and a juice. He passed the glass of juice to Georgia, poured John and Larry each a mug of draft beer, and then took a deep sip from the pitcher. "That hit the spot. Drazen got your tongues?"

"I figure I'm in enough trouble with Vergallian security already for being your known associate," John said. "I don't want to get picked up for heckling."

"It's part of her routine," Myort said. "Even though they're all amateurs, you can tell how much preparation they put in. She'll probably track you down after the show and thank you for getting her a big laugh."

"Either that or she'll strangle me with her tentacle."

A Grenouthian hopped up on stage holding a colorful wad of paper folded up under one arm. He reached in his pouch and pulled out a pair of oversized black eyeglass frames that hooked over his large fluffy ears. Then he unfolded the paper, and even from the distance, Georgia recognized an old print edition of the Gotham News.

"So on Earth, they print their newspapers on paper," the alien began, holding it up over his head and turning from side to side so that everybody in the food court seating area could see. Then he brought it back down, cleared his throat, and read, "Famous Actor Caught In Booze Fueled Orgy – Claims Aliens Made Him Do It." He waited for the audience to stop laughing and pushed the glasses further down his snout so he could look out over the frames. "Let me clarify a few things here. First, nothing any Human does while drinking alcohol can possibly be newsworthy."

"He's got a point there," Myort said, and he puffed a short flame at the night sky.

"Second, we all know that the last place any of us would want to be is in attendance at a Human orgy, much less encouraging participation. Third," he flipped through several pages, shaking his head, "that was the whole thing. They don't have a story, and the only picture is the one on the front page with the faces blotted out so you can't tell who the supposedly famous actor is—unless you've got all of their private parts committed to memory." The Grenouthian paused for a moment as the audience noisily showed their appreciation. "What I discovered on my visit to Earth is if you wanted to find out what was happening, the only option was the Children's News Network, and believe it or not, it really is run by schoolchildren."

"There's that sound again," the Vergallian reporter said when the distant audience applauded the Grenouthian. "I'm sure it's coming from the direction of the food court."

"They're having a Human Roast tonight," Ellen said. "My friends invited me, but I thought it was more important to get to know some of you."

"Why is that?" a Frunge asked suspiciously. She pulled out a stylus that was poked through her tightly woven hair vines and tapped her tab to life. "Let's see. According to your bio in the festival's press directory, you're the common-law wife of an EarthCent Intelligence agent and you work for the Galactic Free Press."

"Yes, and I'm also our Earth Syndication Coordinator, so I'm in close contact with journalists from all over the globe," Ellen told her. "I used to be a lone wolf in the news game, but I've since learned that working with others can be very rewarding."

"You're missing the point," the Frunge cut her off. "It's not cooperation between journalists that we oppose. It's the way you work hand-in-hand with governmental agencies. There's such a thing as separation of press and empire."

"Humans haven't evolved to that point yet," the Vergallian reporter said. "She's not even embarrassed."

"Why should I be embarrassed?" Ellen asked. "For what it's worth, we barely have a government, so there's no issue there. You know that EarthCent was set up by the Stryx so that your governments could have a point of contact with humanity, but most of our people and their dependents are contract workers living on alien worlds. The Human Empire is supposed to represent the billion or so of us living on open worlds and space stations, but the whole organization consists of a couple of twenty-somethings and their Cayl advisor."

"Don't - underestimate - the - Cayl," contributed the Verlock journalist who had joined the impromptu group at Ellen's invitation. They all waited to see if she would add anything further, but the slow-spoken alien had said her piece.

"We understand the concept of the Fourth Estate," Ellen picked up again when she was sure the Verlock was finished. "We thought we had invented it until the Stryx opened Earth and we found out the rest of you existed. The Galactic Free Press is completely independent of EarthCent."

"Completely independent?" The Frunge looked down at her tab again. "The owner and publisher of your paper, Chastity Papamarkakis, is the younger sister of Blythe Oxford, who in addition to being the wife of Clive Oxford, the Director of EarthCent Intelligence, funded the startup of that organization."

"But that doesn't mean there's an official relationship," Ellen argued.

The Vergallian produced a small device that proved to be a holographic projector. "This was forwarded to me from a friend on Union Station," he said, and hit the play button.

A hologram of Clive Oxford and John sitting in the former's office appeared, and the EarthCent Intelligence agent was just starting to speak. "The way Ellen tells it, journalists are a good fit for a spy agency, and your people are happy to let the Galactic Free Press pay their salaries while they report to EarthCent Intelligence on the sly."

The Vergallian glanced at Ellen, whose mouth had fallen open, and the hologram blurred into fast forward. It dropped back to normal play just in time for Clive to say,

"That's why I advise getting Ellen and her syndicated journalists involved."

The Verlock sighed, a sound like crushed stone being dumped from a truck, and began to rise to her feet.

"Wait, let me explain," Ellen said, grabbing the alien's arm and finding herself lifted half out of her chair before the Verlock even noticed. "This is the first time—maybe the second—at most the third time that I've ever worked on the same story that John is investigating. And he's more of a policeman than a spy, he's even presenting at the next Inter-Species Police Operations Agency conference. Besides, a source is a source, and trading information with a trusted party is more reliable than buying it."

The Verlock sat down again and pointed at the holographic projector. "A – friend – on – Union – Station?"

"An anonymous friend," the Vergallian muttered. "It's not like we work hand in hand or sleep together that often." He put away the projector and turned to Ellen. "I've been reporting on the festival circuit since before the Stryx invited your world to join the tunnel network. Arts journalists are at the bottom of the pecking order because our editors know that most of us would pay to go to the performances and shows if we didn't have press passes. The last thing any of us need is to lose a story to a couple of freelancers from a backward species, or worse, to get scooped by you."

"It doesn't have to be a zero-sum game," Ellen protested. "The Galactic Free Press shares bylines all the time, and we don't have any problem with publishing news when we're not the first to report it. Our owner and her sister grew up on Union Station and they're very multi-species-minded. When Chastity and her sister are concerned about something that could affect the future of humanity, of course they ask us to investigate."

"The daughters of the EarthCent embassy manager," the Frunge read from whatever source was now on her screen. She stuck the stylus back in her hair vines and made a show of switching off her tab. "Let's say the four of us hard-working reporters are having a little chat and nothing we say will go beyond this table. What is it that your multi-species-minded publisher is worried about this time?"

"The impact of that last Grenouthian documentary about our arts on Earth's creative community and whether any of you might, well, take advantage."

The journalists exchanged a look, and then the Verlock began to tremble with repressed mirth. Between her weight and the vibrations, the carbon fiber chair gave out and deposited her on the ground, and then all three aliens exploded with laughter.

The Vergallian was the first to recover, perhaps because he had visited Earth to report on the art missing from museums and was more familiar with the self-aggrandizing tendencies of the planet's inhabitants. "So, it's the old fear of cultural imperialism," he chortled. "We figure out what makes you tick, take advantage of our backlist art to out-compete you, and the next thing you know, Humans are all walking around pretending to be Vergallians. But you're doing that already."

"We're well aware of the impact your dramas are having on addicts," Ellen said. "Some people watch them twelve hours a day. But what was that backlist thing you mentioned?"

"Art that may only exist today as stored images," the Vergallian explained. "I suppose Humans are too new to civilization to have encountered the problem yet, since your museums never would have noticed their vaults and archives being ransacked otherwise. Take oil paintings, for example. How far back do they go?"

"Maybe seven or eight centuries," Ellen said. "Fiona would know." She took out her smartphone, intending to try the walkie-talkie function, but the alien gestured for her to put it away.

"Let's say a thousand years. Vergallians have been producing oil paintings or the equivalent for over two million years, the same with the Frunge. And the Verlocks..."

"Seven – million," the bulky alien said, looking up from where she was repairing the carbon fiber chair using a tube of some sort of quick-setting glue she must have carried for that exact purpose.

"And there are a lot more of us than there are of you," the Vergallian continued. "Based on the Grenouthian documentaries I've watched about Earth's history, I doubt there were anywhere near a billion of you living on the planet when oil painting was introduced, and most of those would have been too busy trying to feed themselves or fend off cannibals to have time for the arts."

"Not to mention the cost of the pigments," the Frunge put in.

"I'm not sure I understand what you're getting at," Ellen said. "Are you saying that we're so far behind in the arts that we'll never catch up?"

"Our artists have produced many thousands of times more paintings as yours since the time we discovered interstellar travel, and images of all of the works of artists who achieve any level of recognition are in digital storage," the Vergallian explained. "If we were trying to take over your culture, we'd just check our backlist for the closest match and look at what came next. Then we'd have our artists start creating works in that style, and to Human critics, it would appear we were always one step ahead."

"Oh," Ellen said. "Are all of those images, your so-called backlist, available to everybody? I'd hate to think that one of our starving art students might stumble on it and then sell her soul for success."

"Arts – are – not – the – same – as – technology," the Verlock pronounced slowly. "Possible – to – skip – steps."

"That's true," the Frunge said. "Discontinuities in the arts are often seized upon as the most important breakthroughs precisely because they seem to leave the past far behind. But as our distinguished colleague pointed out," she continued, inclining her head to the Vergallian, "none of our artists have designs on your markets. And while one never knows exactly what intelligence services are up to, I'm sure there are far more effective ways to get whatever they want from Humans than trying to influence you through the arts."

"We thought that you, I mean, one of the tunnel network species, might be inclined to try it just to show they're more sophisticated than we are," Ellen said.

"Kids, maybe," the Vergallian said. "Our intelligence people tend to think in more forceful terms, especially when dealing with primitive species." She paused for a moment as if an idea had just occurred to her. "I'll ask around and see if I can come up with anything, provided you answer one question for me. As you said, information sharing is a two-way street."

"What do you want to know?"

"These non-fungible tokens I keep hearing about in reference to Earth's arts. I've read all of the descriptions and I still don't understand the point."

The Frunge and the Verlock both nodded their heads in agreement, and the latter even said, "I'm – in – on – that – deal."

"It's like this," Ellen said, wracking her brain for everything she'd been told about NFTs and trying to put it in some semblance of order that would make sense to advanced aliens. "I don't understand it either."

# Eighteen

Larry checked the festival map on his implant again and turned into the Dollnick section. Most of the works on display reminded him of a technical manual, though he had to admit that a three-dimensional rendering of a colony ship would look great on the bridge of his two-man trader. Then he overheard somebody inquiring about the price of a small schematic print signed by the engineer and almost fell over. After that, he didn't look left or right until he arrived at the booth displaying the art he had delivered for Flower.

"Mister Phil's Son," the four-armed proprietor greeted him. "I was wondering when you would stop by. Most couriers insist on seeing the packing cases opened in their presence to document that the artworks were delivered undamaged, but you did me the honor of trusting my integrity. Are you here to capture images for the Thark underwriter?"

"I don't believe there is one," Larry said. "Do you mean that art couriers usually find a Thark bookie to take bets on successful delivery?"

"The regular insurers make you fill out a mountain of forms and charge an extra fee just to get you set up in their systems," the Dollnick told him. "Unless you're going to make a career out of fine arts deliveries, it's far more efficient to lay off your risk with the Tharks."

"It never occurred to me that I was taking any chances," Larry said. "Flower assured me that the packing cases were indestructible, and if my ship had blown up, the last thing I'd be worried about is the delivery. I came because I was in the neighborhood and I was curious to see M793qK's art. I didn't even know I was carrying his work until the Vergallians pulled me in for an interview."

"The Fleet Vergallians are very sensitive about anything related to the Farlings. The two species occupy a number of star systems that are in close proximity to each other yet they have never established official relations. Did you bring lenses?"

"Do you mean a magnifying glass? I don't want to sound ignorant, but I don't know anything about art at the technical level of brushwork and all of that."

The Dollnick shook his head and reached under the counter with one of his lower arms. "I don't have lenses certified for Humans because it's never come up before, but your facial structure is nearly identical to the lower cast Vergallians. If you feel a sharp pain in your head, take them off immediately."

Larry accepted the goggles which reminded him of an overblown version of the kind he had once seen swimmers wearing in a pool on Earth. "Are they really necessary?" he asked. "My vision is fine, and all of those flat surfaces will probably create distortions."

"The Farlings have multi-faceted eyes and it's pointless to view their art without making an adjustment to your own vision. Just don't put the goggles on before you're standing right in front of the painting or you'll get dizzy."

"Thank you," Larry said. He entered the display area with the goggles dangling from one hand on the elastic cord and the Dollnick trailing at a polite distance. All of the paintings on the first set of partitions were photorealistic depictions of children playing or studying, and when he tried raising the goggles to his eyes, everything became blurred and confused.

"What are you doing?" the Dollnick demanded, grabbing Larry's shoulders before he could stumble into artwork. "These aren't the Farling paintings."

"Aren't they all from my shipment?"

"Yes, but the classroom scenes were done by Flower. A little saccharine for my taste, but she does have a way of capturing the kinetics of the scene."

"I didn't know Flower painted. She doesn't even have a body."

"Artificial intelligence can inhabit all of the robots it requires to do a task, and Dollnick colony ship bots are some of the finest multi-purpose platforms in existence. The Farling's paintings are around here," the alien continued, keeping an upper hand on Larry's shoulder while guiding him around the partition to the other half of the booth. "Compelling, aren't they?"

"Not the first word that came to my mind," Larry said. He tried to make sense of the abstract images that reminded him a little of cargo deck stains he'd seen over the years. "Are you sure these weren't damaged in transport?"

"The goggles," the Dollnick reminded him. "It may reduce blurring if you close your eyes while putting them on."

Larry followed the instructions, and when he opened his eyes again, the painting in front of him had morphed into something completely different. He felt drawn in by the endless whorls that seemed to be branching and building on themselves before his eyes, though he knew that must be impossible. Then he noticed a series of nearly invisible dots that conveyed a sense of significance despite his not having a clue what it could be. He removed the goggles and found that the stain had returned.

"Was that my imagination or was the painting really in motion?" he asked.

"It's like the old test for artificial intelligence," the Dollnick said. "If you can't tell whether or not you're talking with a sentient being, what difference does it make?"

Something beeped in Larry's ear, and he heard his own voice say, "Fiona," a reminder he had set to get back and relieve her at the booth. "Sorry, I have to run, but I'll try to come back tomorrow and look at these some more." He held out the goggles for the Dollnick to take.

"Keep them," the alien said. "It's good to know that they work on Humans, but the sterilizer unit hasn't been approved for your species so I can't offer them to another visitor."

Larry hurried back to the human section of the festival, breaking into a jog where space allowed, and arrived at his booth to see Fiona sitting on the table and reading on her smartphone. There wasn't a bead in sight.

"You even sold the six sacks I brought you after lunch?" he asked her in disbelief. "That's four hundred pounds. I don't have any handmade beads left."

"It's just as well," the girl said. "I promised Semmi that I would handle the press at her award ceremony and it starts in a half-hour. You guys are coming, right?"

"Of course, Georgia should be back any minute." Larry accepted the heavy cashbox from the girl and gave it a shake. "Wow. Didn't get many programmable creds, I take it."

"I'm not that fast with the mini-register, and the voice verification thing adds even more time because they have to come inside the booth," Fiona explained. "I started by offering a cash discount to keep the line moving, and ended by only accepting programmable creds for half sacks. I would have sold a full sack but I couldn't even lift it. Marco came by and helped me divvy up what you brought into the empties."

"You did as much business in a day as I did all week!"

"A few of the aliens commented on how I looked shorter than they remembered, so they must have been returning customers who bought samples from you and came back to stock up. Ellen told me that the weirder a species looks to us, the more we all look alike to them."

"That's pretty much the rule," Larry said. "If you can hold on a few minutes, I'll combine the cash and register receipts and figure out your commission."

"Semmi's waiting for me so we can settle up later," Fiona told him as she slipped back into her shoes. "Retail is tough on the feet. See you at the ceremony."

Larry spent the next fifteen minutes sitting in front of the mini-register and checking for counterfeits since Fiona had all but admitted that she hadn't bothered. All of the coins checked out as genuine.

"You look just like John in Semmi's prize-winning portrait," Georgia said as she entered the booth. Then she noticed the empty display cases. "I thought you were going to stop back at lunch and bring Fiona replacement stock. Were you having such a good time wandering around the fair that you forgot?"

"I came back, twice. She sold every last handmade bead I brought with me, and we started two weeks ago with a half-ton. Fiona must have a way with resellers because she sold eleven half sacks to different buyers. Maybe they were mom-n-pop businesses who bought samples from me earlier in the week and returned for commercial quantities after stringing some beads and making some sales, but still."

"Fiona is a closer. She sold all of John's reproductions in just a couple of days, except for a few that none of the aliens would even look at." Georgia passed the squirming baby to her husband. "I finished two interviews today, and James was perfectly quiet through both of them. It's like he knows when I'm working."

"Given the number of hours he sleeps, it's probably random," Larry said.

After a quick visit to their ship to change, they returned to the fair and went straight to Winner's Row, where the reception was just getting into swing.

"Look at Semmi," Georgia whispered to Larry. "Not a feather out of place, and she's loving all of the attention."

"John is pretty steamed about being the subject of her prize-winning painting," Larry said, turning a little to the side to shelter the baby in the carrier on his chest from a pair of large Verlocks plowing slowly through the crowd. "I've been enjoying the festival myself. If we hadn't already sold out the handmade beads, I would have been happy to stay a few more weeks."

"We'll have to visit more festivals in the future. I'm sure the Galactic Free Press will buy my interviews and food articles. I don't think Ellen had much fun, though. She's sure that something is going on with the alien interest in Earth's art but she can't nail it down."

An honor guard of space marines accompanied a high-caste Vergallian wearing the dress version of a Fleet uniform into the exhibition area and all conversation came to a halt. She walked directly up to Semmi and whispered in the gryphon's ear, receiving a quiet "Scraw" in return. Then the Vergallian tapped the spaceship emblem on her collar and began to speak in an amplified voice.

"As you all know, this is the first Aarden Arts Festival at which the Humans qualified for their own section. We've all been pleasantly surprised by the quality of the works displayed. This year's award for the Best Human portrait goes to Semmi of the Royal House of Tyrell for her painting *An Abundance*. Her work will be displayed on Winner's Row for the rest of the festival, and I'm sure you'll be disappointed to learn that all of her pieces have been sold."

"Did she say Royal House of Tyrell?" John asked Myort as the crowd surged forward to congratulate the gryphon and inquire about future works. "As in the whole species is named after her family?"

"It's not an exact translation," the Huktra said absentmindedly, squinting up at the night sky. "There's Flower coming out of the tunnel right on schedule."

"I can't see anything."

"Trust me," Myort said, handing John his drink. "I've got to run and get the ship out of the lot before midnight so the Vergallians don't start charging me a snout and a tail. Do me a favor and look in on Kyor if I get held up in orbit."

Ellen stepped up a moment later to take the vacant spot at John's side. "Where was Myort going in such a hurry?" she asked.

"To move that ship with M793qK's coat of arms painted on it up to Flower before the Vergallians start fining him," John said. "Did you know about Semmi being some sort of gryphon royalty?"

"Now that I see the way she's carrying herself with all of the reporters and wealthy patrons it seems obvious. I'd ask her to sit for an interview the next time we're in the tunnel but I'm not any good at reading the picture language she shares with Marco. I don't think I could take a whole interview's worth of telepathy. Look, she has Fiona acting as her secretary."

"With any luck, some of those aliens will offer to take Semmi to lunch and save us a fortune in food."

Ellen sighed and shook her head. "Why do you say things like that when you don't really mean them? Do you want every painting she does from here on out to be you worrying about money? Besides, you must have doubled your stake on those reproductions this week. I can't get over how well they sold."

"I'm going to pay Fiona a twenty percent commission on the net profit," John said. "I don't know whether I can keep the rest because I paid for all those reproductions with the programmable cred Blythe gave me for EarthCent Intelligence expenses." He took a sip from his drink and then spit it out, grabbed Ellen's drink, gargled, and spit that out as well.

"Classy," Larry said, offering John his beer. "Want to go for three?"

John accepted the plastic cup without hesitation and gargled a mouthful, but as he was about to spit it out, he noticed that some of the well-dressed aliens nearby were looking down at spots on their footwear. Changing course at the last second, he forced himself to swallow the foam, some of which came out his nose. The journalists in attendance had all noticed the disruption by this point, and the Grenouthian cameramen recording the event for their network captured the scene for holographic posterity.

"Have you been poisoned again?" Ellen asked in a panic. "Let me see your eyes. Speak to me."

"Myort," John croaked, his sinuses smarting from the beer bath. "He handed me his drink when he ran off and I forgot it was in my hand. I took a sip without thinking. Who knows what could have been in it?"

"Beer," Larry told him. "I bought it for him to catch up with the other night. Couldn't you tell from the taste?"

"If you wait until you can taste an alien drink it's already too late." John looked down at the sodden mess his best shirt had become. "I better go back to the ship and change."

"It's just beer with a little of my iced tea," Ellen said. "A bit of baking soda will have it as white as ever. And you can't leave before Marco plays."

"I didn't know he was part of the show."

"Fiona told me that Semmi asked him. He's been practicing a Tyrellian piece."

As if he had been waiting for Ellen to announce him, Marco chose that moment to begin playing. Everybody in attendance searched for the source of the sound, and all eyes went to the top of the scaffolding the Vergallians had erected for the open-air display.

"Look at Semmi," Georgia whispered a minute later, pointing towards the gryphon whose large eyes were glistening. "Do you think she misses home?"

"That's the most alien-sounding music I've heard in almost two decades of meeting informants in tunnel network bars," John said. "But it's also familiar somehow. Maybe I heard Marco practicing and it didn't register."

"He practiced in her crate, and you know it's soundproof," Ellen said. "Fiona told me that the Tyrellian composer was evoking the sound of wind blowing through their traditional nesting grounds in the mountains. I wonder how Marco can play it so well without ever having been there."

"Semmi probably had a recording for her crate to help her sleep, like some people play rain sounds or waves. When Myort first dumped her on me, I thought it was one of those deals where she was only comfortable closing her eyes in an enclosed place so she wouldn't have to worry about anything sneaking up on her. Now I'm beginning to suspect that her crate is the Tyrellian version of an immersive entertainment system."

"I hope when James gets to be Marco's age he has half of that kid's talent," Larry said. "Where does he find the time to practice the flute, create his upcycled artworks, and keep up with his regular schooling?"

A towering Dollnick placed his finger over Larry's lips while the other aliens in the immediate vicinity looked on in approval. After that, the two couples kept their comments to themselves through the rest of Marco's performance, which was immediately followed by a giant firework bursting overhead.

"Oh, that's too bright," Ellen said. "If I had been looking up, I would have gotten flash burn."

"I didn't hear any explosion, not even a rumble," John said a few seconds later. "And all of the fireworks I've seen fade slowly. That was more like a real explosion."

The Vergallian reporter Ellen had invited for a drink after the press conference passed in front of them, hurrying for the exit. He caught sight of John out of the corner of his eye and spun around, pulling out a reporter's tab at the same time. The Frunge journalist who had been at the same meeting arrived a moment later, extending her elbows to guard the valuable real estate. The slow-footed

Verlock reporter approached at a shuffle that amounted to a dead run for her species.

"What can you tell us about the death of the Huktra spymaster?" the Vergallian asked. "I saw Myort talking with you right before he left."

"Did anybody give you a package for him?" the Frunge asked, spreading her hands to encompass something the size of a watermelon. "It would have been this size and might have had a label with something like, 'Warning. Fusion implosion device.'"

"Antimatter," the Verlock opined.

"Did he say anything about recent threats?" the Vergallian added.

"What are you talking about?" John demanded, and then the meaning of their questions dawned on him and he looked up at the night sky. "Was that…?"

"The ship he was piloting disintegrated as soon as it left the atmosphere. Professional job, timed not to interfere with any of the local satellite traffic, though I suspect that some of the more delicate species who happened to be looking up will be seeing an afterimage for a few days. Were you both here on a mission to show the flag for M793qK?"

"Get that thing out of my face," John said, batting away the tab that was extended like a microphone. "You tell Fiona, Ellen. I'll find Marco. We better get back to the ship and—"

"Thank you all for coming, but I must request that you all leave now, except for the Humans and the guest of honor," an amplified voice interrupted.

At the same time, the space marines who had attended as an honor guard for the elegantly dressed upper-caste Vergallian suddenly appeared at the sides of John, Ellen,

Larry, and Georgia. The alien journalists backed away, clearly unhappy about losing their chance for a scoop, but they were smart enough not to interfere in an active investigation. The Frunge pointed at her own ear and mouthed something that was likely "Ping me," but lip-reading alien languages wasn't in Ellen's repertoire.

"Marco, come here," John called to the boy, who was climbing down from the scaffolding into the rapidly emptying space, but the upper-caste Vergallian shook her head.

"Keep them all separate," she instructed her guards, and then addressed the humans. "I'm not involved with fair security and the proper authorities will be here momentarily. I've been asked to relay that you aren't suspects, but it will be necessary to keep you separated until questioning so you don't unintentionally color each other's memories of the events leading up to this tragedy." Then she nodded to the guards, each of whom led the person in their charge a distance away.

More security arrived on the run, and by the time the Vergallian Intelligence officer and the truthsayer appeared, everyone had been provided with chairs. Marco quietly played his flute, and it occurred to John that the boy must have intuited what was going on. Then a temporary curtain was rigged and the interrogations began.

# Nineteen

"Why is the warning light on the centrifuge blinking?" Georgia asked Larry. "We haven't even used it since coming out of the tunnel at Aarden."

"Did you check the message display?"

"It's not showing anything."

"You have to turn it on separately when the centrifuge isn't running," he told her. "Great timing if it's broken. We can ping Flower's shipyard and have somebody come look at it."

"Pretty suspicious timing, if you ask me," Georgia said. "We just got here." She enabled the display and found a whole queue of pending messages, most of them helpful reminders for new parents, but the most recent one turned out to be for an automatically scheduled doctor's appointment. "M793qK wants us to bring James in for a checkup. I guess Flower reports to him when any of the two-man traders with the nursery package come in."

"Thick as thieves," Larry grumbled. "Is there a time? If it's walk-in, let's get it out of the way before lunch. I want to go around to the alien distributors later and see if I can put together some decent trading stock. We're cash-rich, but other than some children's shoes and clothes, I've got nothing in the hold."

"You should stop at Human Empire headquarters first and see if Samuel needs you to go anywhere as the Minister of Trade. It could make a difference in what you want to buy."

"Fair enough." He followed Georgia down the ladder to the cargo deck, removed the elastic strap that held the baby carriage to the bulkhead, and tucked James in. "You can tell he's got trader genes," Larry said proudly, clicking his heels to enable the magnetic cleats and wheeling the carriage down the ramp onto Flower's docking deck. "He sleeps through all the departures and arrivals."

"Isn't that opposite of what a trader should do?" Georgia asked.

"Not when he's flying supercargo. The first thing you learn on a small ship is that there can only be one person in charge at a time. By sleeping through the critical transitions he's expressing confidence in my leadership."

"He's three months old," Georgia said skeptically as they entered a lift tube. "He doesn't know he's on a little spaceship inside a really big spaceship. He thinks that you're a giant with non-functional nipples."

"Library," Larry instructed the capsule, and then added, "Is M793qK in his clinic, Flower?"

"And waiting for you," the Dollnick AI responded. "How did my nursery module perform during the tunnel passages to Earth and Aarden?"

"James loved it," Georgia said. "He usually falls asleep as soon as it starts spinning, but later he wakes up and wiggles around a little like he's getting exercise."

"And have you given up writing?"

"What? Why do you ask that? I didn't publish anything while we were on Earth because I was doing research to support Ellen, but I've submitted two interviews from food ship owners at the Aarden Arts Festival, and one of them has already run in the Galactic Free Press. And I wrote about—you weren't talking about my reporting."

"When you purchased the nursery module you agreed to fill out weekly feedback forms and respond to all moderate requests for information," Flower said. "I received a half-completed form when you arrived at Earth, and a mere scribble when you emerged from the tunnel at Aarden."

"But we weren't using the centrifuge when we were on Earth or Aarden, and nothing changed from the first trip to the second trip," Georgia protested.

"So you thought that writing 'Same as above' would be useful to my ongoing safety and quality program."

"Sorry. I guess I just don't like filling out forms. I promise I'll do better."

The lift tube doors slid open and they emerged in the corridor that led to the library. Georgia stumbled because she had been focused on the conversation with Flower and forgot to switch off her magnetic cleats.

"You should have told me you weren't filling out the forms," Larry said. "I like giving manufacturers feedback on products. It's the best way to get the improvements you want."

"But the centrifuge is perfect," Georgia said, coming to a halt just outside the door to M793qK's clinic. She lowered her voice. "Do you think he's going to ask about Myort?"

"Everybody knows that they were involved in some scheme together, but we weren't part of it. I don't imagine he would bring it up unless he's interested in the questions we were asked after the fact."

The door slid open as Larry pushed the baby carriage forward. They passed through the bank of medical scanners that the Farling had built around the entrance without setting off any alarms.

"Scale," M793qK rubbed out on his speaking legs, pointing at what looked like an old-fashioned spring scale from a fruit market.

"You can't tell the baby's weight from all of those fancy scanners?" Georgia asked.

"I can guess a baby's weight just by looking at it, and I've earned good money at carnivals doing just that. The scale is to convince you that I'm accurate."

Georgia paused with James in her arms and said, "Then you have to tell us your guess first."

"Six point four two kilograms," M793qK said. "But with the dry diaper and the jumper, you can add eighty-seven grams."

"I never learned alien units," Georgia said, placing her son on the scale. "Six point five."

"Six point five zero seven. You haven't been filling out the forms you agreed to submit when you purchased the centrifuge."

"Flower already warned us," Larry said. "Is that it? I want to get to Human Empire headquarters and find out if I'm on the hook for anything."

"Sit," M793qK said, pointing at the all-purpose examining and operating table that was the only piece of furniture in the room. "I understand you were interrogated by the Vergallians on account of the art I shipped with you, and a second time after that old wreck that Myort got out of a junkyard imploded."

"So it wasn't your ship after all," Larry said. "The Vergallians never believed him, but it did have your coat of arms painted on the side."

"As if I would travel in an obsolete Sharf cabin cruiser. What questions did they ask?"

"The first time it was how I came to be carrying your cargo and how well I knew you. I explained that you're our family doctor, and eventually, they let me go."

"And they didn't try to turn you?"

"I'm not sure what that means. They did ask that I tell John to check in with them if I saw him first."

"Interesting," M793qK said. "And the second interrogation?"

"Last night, after Flower arrived and, you know. They separated us and asked a bunch of questions about John and Myort, and the truthsayer told the officer in charge that we weren't hiding anything. They let us leave after twenty minutes or so."

"I saw Fiona this morning before we lifted off and she said the Vergallians let them all go soon afterward," Georgia said.

"And Semmi?" the Farling asked.

Larry shook his head. "She just scrawed at the truthsayer and took off before they started. I guess being from the Royal House of Tyrell is worth something."

"The Fleet Vergallians wouldn't consider an old Sharf cabin cruiser worth a diplomatic incident." M793qK twiddled his speaking legs for a moment, a rare hesitation on his part, and then asked, "What did you think of my paintings?"

"How do you know I went to see them?"

"The medical scanner picked up the lenses in your belt pouch."

"I forgot I had them," Larry said, pulling out the multi-faceted goggles. "It seemed to me that the paint, or whatever you used on those canvases, was in constant motion. And there was an overlaid pattern of dots that seemed to mean something, but I couldn't work it out. Maybe my brain just isn't suited for processing that sort of imagery."

"It's not," M793qK said, and he gestured with several limbs at a painting on the wall that showed well-dressed people mingling near the water in what might have been a park. "I picked up that Seurat when Flower stopped at Earth. What do you think?"

"Is it original?" Georgia asked.

"A one-third scale reproduction, though it was still relatively expensive. Pointillism is my favorite of the post-impressionist styles as it reminds me of an early Farling form. The sheer number of brush strokes involved make it one of the more expensive canvases sold by ReproMan. The colors can be appreciated by many different species since the blending is done in the eye of the beholder rather than on the painter's palette."

"I didn't know you had an interest in Earth's art."

"That and a surfeit of eBucks from my various ventures in placeboes and pharmaceuticals. I promised EarthCent I wouldn't trade into Stryx creds and crash the exchange rate so I've been putting money into art reproductions."

"I don't think that's really an investment," Larry said. "They can always make more."

"I'm the one making more, or rather, my ReproMan business is," M793qK rubbed out on his speaking legs. He took the reproduction of *A Sunday Afternoon on the Island of La Grande Jatte* off the wall and held it at an angle to the overhead light. "Look at it through your goggles," he said.

Larry obediently donned the multi-faceted goggles and the painting dissolved into a colorful smear with a grid of different size dots standing out as if they had been applied on an overlay. "What am I seeing?"

"Name, rank, and serial number," the Farling said. "In this case, my name, my rank, and the serial number of the painting. Every member of the Hierarchy who sees one of these reproductions will be left gnashing his mandibles in frustration that I'm still alive and well."

"You mean that all of the paintings John displayed at the arts festival carry the same hidden message?"

"Have they done well for him? When I saw all of the portraits based on Semmi that had been added to the catalog I knew that John must have visited my facility in Manhattan. I try not to micromanage, so I didn't ask what he'd purchased."

"He came to Aarden with at least two hundred canvases and Fiona sold practically everything for him," Georgia said. "I wonder if he's still trying to sell what's left or if Ellen convinced him to take the day off. John was much harder hit by Myort's accident than the rest of us."

Back at the art festival, John was staring at the remaining paintings in his booth without really seeing them.

"Forget about the leftover reproductions," Ellen urged him. "You can give them away or leave them with one of the art dealers in Flower's bazaar to sell on consignment. I'll bet this has already been the most profitable week you've ever had as a trader."

"You're forgetting about the decades of radio recordings picked up by the Huktra listening station on the moon that Myort gave me a cut of, or the prize money for the Verlock ship we took together."

"That's exactly my point. Myort was your friend and you need to take time to mourn. Semmi didn't even eat breakfast before she took off flying because she didn't want to be pestered by reporters all day. Fiona told me that some Vergallian gigolo was waiting to make a pass at her when she went to the farmers market and he pumped her for information about you."

"Where is he?" John demanded, balling up his fists. "Is Fiona okay?"

"She let him buy her some organic lettuce, flirted a little, and then told him she doesn't date aliens," Ellen said. "I'm not worried about her, I'm worried about you."

"You know that I was a mercenary before I got into trading and started working for EarthCent Intelligence. I've lost friends to violence, and none of them understood the risks they were taking better than Myort." John straightened the reproduction *The Minotaur* by Watts and stepped back. "Ugly. No wonder the aliens don't even want to look at it."

"I can't tell you what to do," Ellen said, taking her Galactic Free Press ID out of her purse and hanging it around her neck. "I have to get to a meeting with the alien arts reporters where they'll no doubt pester me for information about you, but I want to establish relationships for the future. Fiona is going to bring Marco by to keep you company and I'll see you all at dinner. As far as I'm concerned, we should head up to Flower and spend the week onboard while she's stopped here. EarthCent Intelligence owes you a vacation and we're not going to accomplish anything else."

"I'll think about it," John said, busying himself rehanging Botticelli's *Pallas and the Centaur*. The only other remaining painting was Draper's *Ulysses and the Sirens,* and he snorted on recalling Larry's comment about walking through the Drazen section and having to use the noise cancellation on his implant to avoid being drawn in by a choir.

A low rumble brought John out of his reverie and he turned to see a Verlock clearing his throat. "Is – that – a – Brynsal?" the alien asked, pointing at the elongated sculpture next to the mini-register. "It's – different."

"I put it out today so people could see it, but it's not for sale," John said. The question brought to mind going to help the Huktra intelligence agent and Kyor set up their display in Brynsal's booth. "I'm sorry, but I just remembered I have to be somewhere."

The Verlock nodded, apparently accustomed to the other species not having the patience to engage in slow-speed conversations. He started shuffling off as Fiona and Marco arrived.

"Fiona," John said. "I hate to do this to you on our last day, but can you take over the booth for a while? I have to go check on Kyor."

"Forget the booth," Fiona told him flatly. "No alien is going to buy those reproductions, and the humans shopping the festival are only interested in original art. Why don't you take Marco with you and I'll bring these back to the ship. Before she left this morning, Georgia told me to check out the fashion outlets and that's where I'm going to spend my afternoon. Marco hates shopping."

"All right," John said. "Ellen wants to head up to Flower after her meeting so try not to run too late. Can you grab the mini-register, Marco?"

The thirteen-year-old proudly took possession of the mini-register, one of the core pieces of technology that the Stryx licensed the more advanced species to build for use throughout the tunnel network. John took a last look around the booth and picked up the elongated sculpture gifted to him by the Verlock artist. They left Fiona creating a bundle from the last three canvases and navigated their way to the Verlock section where Myort had sublet a booth from Brynsal. Kyor was stacking crates on a rented floater cart when they arrived.

"Have the reporters and Vergallian Intelligence been giving you such a hard time that you're packing it in?" John asked the young Huktra. "The last thing Myort said to me was that I should look in on you if he was, uh, delayed."

"Is that a Human euphemism for being disintegrated into a mist of atoms?" Kyor asked. "My implant translated it in the sense of running late."

"The Vergallians told me that they're officially registering the ship's destruction as a fuel pack implosion because it was a known failing with those obsolete Sharf cabin cruisers if they weren't maintained. I don't believe it for a minute, and I'm going to—"

"Myort had more enemies than you have friends," the young Huktra interrupted. "I told him that painting M793qK's coat of arms on a ship and bringing it here was just looking for trouble, but he doesn't listen to hatchlings."

"The point is, if you're ready to get moving, we're leaving in a few hours."

"Are you offering me a ride?" Kyor asked, brightening up considerably. "If you're stopping at Flower, it's a deal. I hate space elevators and traveling commercial liners."

"Then we can take all of the crates back on my ship, though I don't know how you'll get them to your homeworld. I'm sure Flower will help arrange something. I'm pretty sure she liked Myort."

"Why would I want to take a bunch of old crates home? These are all going to recycling."

John gestured at the empty tables. "Did somebody loot the booth in the confusion after the ship disintegrated? I thought the Fleet Vergallians had much better security than that."

"What looting?" Kyor asked. "I sold out in the first hour after opening this morning, it was a madhouse. Everything got bid up way over the asking price, and they even bought my pieces just because I'm related to Myort. There's something seriously wrong with the collectors being willing to pay more for art when the artist's ship vaporizes. I'd call that a perverse incentive to murder, and I want to get out of here before one of those buyers gets impatient to make a profit on my art."

Marco nodded in agreement, and setting down the mini-register, began to pull the empty crates out from under the tables. John put down the sculpture he'd been gifted by Brynsal and pitched in. He was stomping down the dried grass Kyor had used for packing statues when he saw Marco's face go pale. John turned to see a large Farling accompanied by a pair of bodyguards from a shark-like species had entered the booth.

"Get out," Kyor hissed at the newcomer, and a short burst of flame escaped her nostrils. "I told you all I had to say last night, and if I see you again, I'll go to fair security and tell them everything I know."

"I'm just here to shop," the Farling rubbed out on his speaking legs. "Surely you wouldn't deny me the opportunity to buy a memorial of an old adversary, something to remember him by. I thought Myort rather talented for a Huktra."

"The lady said to leave," John said, pushing in between Kyor and the bodyguards. It occurred to him as he did so that he was just getting in the young Huktra's way should it come to a fight, but he couldn't stand by and watch.

"Ah, the Human is here too," the giant beetle said. "You'll have to forgive me for confusing you with the fair's maintenance staff, though on reflection, it would make more sense to apologize to them for my error. Have you finished distributing that seditious propaganda your species is passing off as art?"

"I don't know what you're talking about, and more to the point, I don't care. If I see you sniffing around my ship or my family, I'm going to shoot first and ask questions later."

"A threat," the Farling rubbed out, sounding highly amused, and the two shark-like bodyguards showed their scimitar teeth in appreciation. "We have a saying in the Hierarchy that those who can, do, and those who can't get their atoms spread across the universe in fuel pack implosions."

Something inside John snapped and he tried to step between the two bodyguards to get at the Farling. His foot caught on the corner of a crate, and as he fell against one of the sleek aliens, he tried to spin the opposite way to recover his balance. He ended up on his back with a stabbing pain in his side, and then he saw the elongated arm of his Brynsal protruding from his chest.

"I didn't touch him," the Farling rubbed out on his speaking legs, and even through the shock and pain, John picked up on the sudden anxiety that his implant attributed to the alien's words. "I'm contacting festival security, and all of you are witnesses that he tripped and fell."

As John's vision began to fade, he thought he heard a boy shouting in a voice that was cracking, "We need a stasis pod here."

# Twenty

"Stop playing dead, already," M793qK said, shaking his patient awake. "It was a simple impalement by a Brynsal sculpture—I used to see these all the time when I did a medical tour through Verlock space. The outstretched arm didn't even puncture your heart or your liver."

"Where am I?" John groaned, rubbing tentatively at his side without opening his eyes.

"I'll give you three guesses, and if you don't get it on the first one, I'm going to crack open your skull to see if your brain is shrinking."

"Stop teasing him," Ellen said, pushing in front of the Farling. "You're back on Flower, John. The emergency medical response team at the arts festival got you into a stasis pod before you died this time. Thanks to interrogating us last night, their security knew who we all were and contacted me right away. I told them I would bring you up to Flower rather than gambling on a Vergallian surgeon, though I didn't put it that way."

"Did you return the stasis pod?" John asked, sitting up on the operating table. "I can't imagine what those rent for on an emergency basis."

"Flower sent it back on her next shuttle."

"Where are the kids? Did you find Fiona and Semmi in time to bring them up on our ship? And Kyor, I offered her a ride."

"They're all here, John. Everybody is waiting at your recovery party except for Myort. He feels like it's his fault you almost died again since he's the one who got the Farlings all riled up. You never would have ended up impaled on a sculpture if he hadn't introduced you to Brynsal."

"Myort's dead," John said, and his joy at finding himself alive and whole began to slip. He turned to M793qK and demanded, "Why did you stick him with delivering your junky old ship? You had to know that showing your coat of arms at such a public event was like sticking a thumb in the eye of the Farling Hierarchy. I thought you were laying low."

"Some gratitude I get for repairing a punctured lung and a kidney without damaging the sculpture," the doctor rubbed out on his speaking legs. He picked up the Brynsal and brandished it at John as if he was considering putting it back where he'd found it. "I even washed off the gore for you."

"Myort is fine," Ellen told John, getting between the two again. "You remember that he was parked next to us? Myort rigged the fuel pack of his ship to implode above the atmosphere and then snuck onto our ship and did the rest by remote control. Marco found him sleeping in Semmi's crate when we reached orbit."

It took John a minute to digest the news, and then he asked, "But why? The Fleet Vergallians aren't going to be happy with Myort for making a scene at their festival and putting them in the middle of some sort of spy game with the Farling Hierarchy."

"I invited him here to explain himself as soon as you regained consciousness, so if you can hold onto this without killing yourself—" M793qK offered John the elongated sculpture, "—you'll find out in another minute."

"I'll take that," Ellen said, intercepting the Brynsal and leaving John feeling like a clumsy child who couldn't be trusted with a pointy work of art. "I don't want to hear anything that will create an ethical dilemma for my write-up of the festival so I'll see you at the party. Sometimes I think you all forget that I'm working press."

The clinic door slid open to admit Myort before Ellen came in range of the sensor, forcing her to wait for a few seconds because there wasn't enough clearance space between the medical scanners for her to get past the bulky alien. The Huktra stopped to examine the sculpture she held and nodded to himself. "Sintered pumice and six-part epoxy. I'll have to keep that in mind if I ever get back into the art game."

"You've got a lot of explaining to do," John growled, getting to his feet. "Next time you pull a stunt like that you better tell me first."

"Can you fly?" Myort asked innocently.

"What does that have to do with it? I never thought you were one of those aliens who looked down on us for not having wings, but I guess I'm learning the hard way."

"Is his brain alright?" the Huktra asked M793qK. "You know how poorly they do with oxygen deprivation."

"Don't try to tell me my job," the Farling rubbed out in irritation. "And if I don't hear a good explanation for using my coat of arms without permission, you're the one who's going to be suffering from oxygen deprivation."

"Is twenty percent of the take a good enough explanation for you?" Myort asked, offering the doctor a programmable cred. "That's what a top agent would make, and you didn't have to lift a limb."

"Galleries get fifty percent," the Farling said.

"Twenty-five percent, and I'll put the word out that you weren't involved. I've been thinking that it might be useful if the two of us were seen to have a falling out."

"Twenty-five percent, and you owe me one," M793qK countered, snatching the programmable cred before the Huktra could refuse. He turned it over and read the amount. "At least you executed it well. How much was Kyor in for?"

"Will the two of you stop talking in code and tell me what's going on?" John demanded. "I get that you both have wings and I don't, and with Semmi that makes three, but..." he trailed off as the meaning of Myort's rhetorical question finally penetrated. "Maybe there is something wrong with my brain. It was okay for Semmi to know you were faking your death because you knew she could fool the Vergallian truthsayer and skip out on the interrogation. You didn't tell the rest of us because the truthsayer would have known we were lying."

"And?" Myort asked like a patient teacher trying to extract the full answer from a pupil.

"And if your goal in painting M793qK's coat of arms on a junky spaceship and then publicly blowing it up wasn't to provoke the Farling Hierarchy, it must mean one of the other intelligence agencies put a price on your head and you needed to disappear."

"Why do you insist on turning everything into spy versus spy?" Myort asked. "Yes, there were plenty of intelligence operatives at the festival, but that's not why I went. I thought I explained the economics of the art world when we were shopping together on Earth."

John stared at the Huktra in disbelief, and then turned to the Farling, who nodded as much as his anatomy allowed. "You faked your death to drive up the prices for your old unsold sculptures?"

"Mixed media, and Kyor was able to sell all of the inventory for several times what I was getting at the height of my career."

"Those buyers aren't going to be happy when they find out you're alive."

"I want you to analyze your last sentence and then tell me why I should care," Myort said. "I'm not the one who told them I was dead, and Kyor wisely refused to entertain any questions on the topic."

"Art speculators are the lowest of the low," M793qK concurred. "The young Dollnick who Flower hired for our joint exhibit was instructed not to sell to anybody who couldn't demonstrate a deep understanding of our work."

John stared at the Farling, searching for twitches of humor. "You're pulling my leg, right?"

"I guess your brain isn't completely useless after all."

"But why start showing your art all of a sudden, and what's the significance of sharing a booth with Flower? Even if Myort hadn't blown up a ship with your coat of arms, I'll assume that Farling agent sniffing around the arts festival was good enough to spot your work."

"He'd better be, I trained him," M793qK said. "It's time that the Hierarchy is reminded of my existence, and Myort pulling off a Gb873JJ will ensure that word spreads to the ends of Farling space."

"A Gb—what?"

"A famous Farling artist who staged a public suicide around thirty thousand years ago to sell some unsold works he had cluttering up the studio. He's still alive and enjoying the profits."

"Artists are always trying to fake their deaths to move inventory, and not a few have been helped to their eternal rest by impatient investors," Myort explained. "In this case, I used a double misdirection to sell the act. That model of Sharf cabin cruiser did have an issue with imploding fuel packs if the owner failed to maintain the seals, and my use of M793qK's coat of arms to draw the ire of the Farling Hierarchy gave speculators a second motive to accept my apparent demise."

"What about the other intelligence agents we met up with who were working for him?" John asked, pointing at M793qK. "Were they all in on it?"

"After the fact," Myort said. "Giving them all busy work helped sell the Farling revenge angle to Vergallian Intelligence. I'll have to pay for the drinks the next time we get together."

"I'm still pissed that you tricked me," John said. As he turned to leave, he caught sight of the Seurat hanging on the wall. "Where did you get that painting? I sold both of mine last week."

"I picked it up at Earth while visiting my latest business acquisition," M793qK said. "I also ordered a portrait of Semmi while I was there, but Flower wasn't in orbit long enough for the artist to finish it. I suspect my managers at ReproMan underpriced the job given all of those feathers."

"Didn't hear, don't want to know." John kept his hands over his ears on his way to the door, but once he was out in the corridor, he pulled up his shirt and checked for a scar. There was the barest pink patch where he remembered the outstretched hand of the sculpture protruding.

"I saw that," Flower said over his implant. "Your family and friends are waiting for you at the *Blue Tea Café*. Myort and the doctor will be along when they finish arguing over which one should pick up the cost of your stasis pod rental."

"Oh, that's nice of them," John said. "You'll have to guide me to the café because I've forgotten where it is."

When he arrived five minutes later, his first thought was that he had somehow taken a wrong turn and ended up in Harry's cafeteria where the spies sponsored by EarthCent Intelligence congregated. Half a dozen aliens he knew by sight were gathered around the projection from a holographic entertainment system watching a news show with the English closed caption – "Death at the Aarden Arts Festival?"

"I don't believe this," John muttered as the Grenouthian announcer began showcasing each of Myort's mixed media pieces that had been sold at the art fair, chuckling over the price differentials from earlier, nearly identical works.

"Over here," Ellen called from where several tables had been pushed together to seat the large party.

John slipped around the knot of aliens and slumped into a chair across from Ellen. "How long was I unconscious?" he asked, suddenly realizing that he might have been in stasis longer than he thought. "That looked like a weekly news magazine show everybody is watching."

"Five days, give or take a few hours. The doctor insisted on growing you a replacement kidney, and it was easier for the nanobots to repair your lung while you were in stasis."

"I'm pretty sure we only need one kidney."

"M793qK questioned your ability to maintain your balance if he removed the old one and left a hole, though I think he was kidding," Ellen said. "If you're wondering why it looks like an intelligence convention, I needed to talk with some knowledgeable aliens who wouldn't pull punches, and Myort made the introductions. After all their help, I thought it would be appropriate to pay for a treat."

"Wouldn't pull what punches?" John asked as he signaled the waitress. "Did you want their opinions about Earth's art?"

Ellen shook her head. "It was after we went over Fiona's notes on her sales for the week. Why don't you explain it to him since you did most of the work," she said to the teenager.

"Let him order first," Fiona said.

"I'll just have the special of the day and a black coffee," John told the waitress, and then corrected himself when he saw Ellen wince. "I mean, and a blue tea."

"You're not starving?" Larry asked him.

"I guess the doctor must have topped me up with something before waking me," John said. "I can't wait to see the bill."

"M793qK said that he feels in part responsible for your accident since it wouldn't have happened if you weren't a known associate of his," Ellen said. "He's not charging."

"And you agreed to that? Now I'll owe him another favor." John looked down at the smartphone that Fiona pushed across the table to him and saw a photograph of *The Minotaur*. "Did you sell it in the end?"

"It's still wrapped up with the other two in our hold," Fiona said. "Now that we figured it out, I didn't think Flower would want us displaying them on the ship. Scroll down. Do you see it now?"

John thumbed past the Botticelli to the Draper before it hit him. "As the sirens climb onto the ship to seduce Ulysses, you can see that the one in the water is a mermaid." He thumbed back a picture and continued, "A centaur is part horse and the minotaur is part bull. All three paintings feature humans merged with another species."

"It turns out that buyers at the Aarden Arts Festival register their purchases over five hundred creds because they can get validated spaceship parking or discounted hotel rooms," Fiona continued. "Flower persuaded Avisia, the Vergallian spy who runs a finishing school on board, to ask an associate on Aarden to check the paintings we sold against their records. She came up with a list of alien names, and the other intelligence agents on board did background checks for us. The big buyers of our reproductions were all representing facilities managers for alien businesses that hire human contract workers."

"I know the aliens take responsibility for feeding and housing the human contract workers they bring in, but I can't imagine that they're taking on interior decoration," John said.

"That Grenouthian documentary gave the aliens the idea of setting up museums and cultural centers for human workers, and art reproductions are only part of the deal," Georgia told him. "We found out that they're arranging for touring companies from Earth to put on plays and for bands to perform. Isn't it ironic? Our bosses were worried about alien art and culture invading Earth, and it turns out that the aliens are worried about the exact opposite."

"You've lost me again."

"It's the whole going-native problem that Ellen told me EarthCent worries about so much," Fiona said. "I guess human contract workers can't help imitating their hosts, but when it goes beyond that, the aliens start freaking out."

"As soon as the show is over, I'll bring—" the rest of Ellen's sentence was drowned out by the approving roar of the aliens as they watched the hologram of Myort's ship imploding like a new star. "Jorb," she called out as the group who had been watching the news magazine started to break up. "Can you come here a minute?"

The part-time Drazen intelligence agent who ran the local dojo as a cover job approached, accompanied by Lume, the Dollnick station chief who owned a lunch counter in the food court.

"What a great story," Jorb said, obviously referring to the segment about Myort's faked death. "Nobody's pulled that off in centuries."

"We were just explaining to John about the run on Earth art reproductions by facilities managers responsible for human contract workers," Ellen told him. "Can you explain to him how the different species were making their choices?"

"Let's start with the process of elimination," the Drazen said to John. "Did you figure out why nobody bought the reproductions that didn't sell?"

"They all depicted mythical creatures—humans merged with animals," John replied.

"Exactly. Did you ever see Vivian with her prosthetic tentacle and thumbs?"

"Clive and Blythe's daughter? Yeah, now that I think of it. When she was a co-op student working at Drazen Intelligence."

"Samuel was still working to wean her off those extra thumbs months after they got married," Jorb said. "I think in the end he had to hide them. Playing alien dress-up is all in good fun for people in our line of work, but some second and third generation Human contract workers on

Drazen worlds have started seeking medical interventions."

"You mean they're having surgeries to attach real tentacles and thumbs?" John asked. "I hadn't heard of that."

"And Lume could tell you horror stories about botched black-market surgeries where Humans get another set of arms attached. There's no way to make that work on your torsos."

"The Council of Princes has announced rules that any alien attempting surgical alterations to pass as Dollnick will be ejected from our space," Lume told them. "But our strong preference would be to prevent our human guest workers from falling into the trap of advanced-species worship."

"Did Fiona show you the list of which reproductions were purchased by the different species?" Jorb continued. "You'll see that the Frunge are buying up art showing women with luxurious hair to provide alternative role models for contract workers who wish they had hair vines. And the Drazen buyers were especially interested in portraits showing hands with five fingers or views from the back with no tentacle in evidence."

"The Fillinducks have been acquiring artworks that include couples or pairs, anything but a threesome," Lume said with an amused whistle. "And buyers for Dollnick princes have been concentrating on paintings with bare chests—no chance of an extra pair of arms hidden under a shirt or dress. Facilities managers for contract workers have always invited restaurateurs from Earth with ethnic cuisines and the like, but that wasn't enough to keep your people in touch with their roots."

"Do you really think that reproduction art can have that kind of impact on people?" John asked skeptically.

"Art doesn't have a great track record for starting social movements, but it does a good job of positive reinforcement and creating a feedback loop," Georgia said. "Taken by themselves, a few dozen paintings in a town for guest workers wouldn't accomplish much, but we understand that the aliens are going to require that Earth's arts receive a more prominent role in the educational curriculum for the children of contract workers, with frequent visits to the new 'Museums of Humanity.'"

"Who bought up all of those religious works from the Renaissance?" John asked.

"Hortens," Jorb said. "Even though their evangelicals welcome all comers, they're finding it difficult to worship Gortunda while surrounded by a sea of Humans who don't tithe."

"Or bathe as frequently as the Hortens would like," Lume added.

"I hope that EarthCent Intelligence is willing to accept your article as a report because I'm not looking forward to writing this up," John muttered to Ellen.

"I already heard back from Roland and the paper isn't going to run the story," she told him. "We'll do a piece about the museums, of course, but contract workers will have to work out the reasons for themselves, just like we did."

"And how about our people living in sovereign human communities on open worlds?" John asked. "Some of them go native as well."

"Not to the extent of contract workers," Ellen said, "and the Human Empire is taking the lead on dealing with it. That's where Proxy Shoppers fits in. You tell him, Fiona."

"Ellen and Georgia took me to Human Empire headquarters to talk with Samuel and Vivian about what we learned, and it turned out that they're the ones funding Proxy Shoppers," Fiona said. "The merchandise all ended up on Flower, and when she stops at the sovereign human communities on her circuit, Vivian will visit a local high school and pass out presents. The idea is to keep young people in those communities in Earth's fashion loop so they don't turn to the aliens for a substitute."

"I've heard dumber ideas," John admitted. "Where are Marco and Semmi? You know, I would swear I heard him shout for a stasis pod back on Aarden."

"If he did, it was a one-off," Ellen said. "And he's at the back bar, modeling with Semmi."

"I was hoping that painting twenty-four hours a day was just another one of her phases," John said, standing up and looking towards the back of the café. He couldn't see over the small crowd of patrons, and after a moment's hesitation, climbed up on the high wrought-iron stool.

Semmi was standing on her hind legs behind the bar, her paws on the counter, and Marco was sitting on a stool in front of her to the right, posed with his flute, but not playing it. To his left, a four-armed maintenance bot was floating in front of a canvas, employing three brushes at the same time to paint the scene.

"Come down from there before you hurt yourself," Ellen told John. "You're making everybody nervous."

"Why does that setup look so familiar?" John asked as the waitress returned and placed an omelet and a pot of blue tea on the table. Larry waved off his friend's attempt to pay, and added a generous tip for the server with the green-dyed hair.

"Flower has been helping us all week with database research and she took such a liking to Manet's *A Bar at the Folies-Bergère* that she wanted to paint her own version,"

Ellen said, fighting to suppress a laugh. "Got everything straight now?"

"Everything except for what I got in return for the money I spent on that non-fungible token I bought back on Earth," John said. "I don't even understand where it went."

"On here," Fiona said, shaking her smartphone. "But it doesn't exist unless we're on Earth because the blockchain doesn't work over the Stryxnet. Got it?"

"So as long as you don't go running off on your own, my money's safe," John said. "Can we count on you to stick around for a while?"

"I guess somebody needs to keep an eye on Marco and Semmi," the girl said. "It's nice to be needed."

## From the Author

If you've read the four EarthCent Auxiliaries books starting with **Freelance on the Galactic Tunnel Network** without reading the original EarthCent Ambassador series, I recommend starting with **Destiny: Union Station.** You can sign up for e-mail notification of my new releases on the **IfItBreaks.com**.

## About the Author

E. M. Foner lives in Northampton, MA with an imaginary German Shepherd who's been trained to bite central bankers. The author welcomes reader comments at e_foner@yahoo.com. He's also online at:

facebook/E.M.Foner/

Also by the author in reading order:

Destiny: Union Station

Date Night on Union Siation

Alien Night on Union Station

High Priest on Union Station

Spy Night on Union Station

Carnival on Union Station

Wanderers on Union Station

Vacation on Union Station

Guest Night on Union Station

Word Night on Union Station

Party Night on Union Station

Review Night on Union Station

Family Night on Union Station

Book Night on Union Station

LARP Night on Union Station

Career Night on Union Station

Last Night on Union Station

Independent Living

Soup Night on Union Station

Assisted Living

Freelance on the Galactic Tunnel Network

Con Living

Empire Night on Union Station

Space Living

Traders on the Galactic Tunnel Network

Orphans on the Galactic Tunnel Network

Swap Night on Union Station

Made in United States
North Haven, CT
07 April 2022

18005262R00143